Miss Frost Braves the Blizzard

A Nocturne Falls Mystery
Jayne Frost, book five

KRISTEN PAINTER

MISS FROST BRAVES THE BLIZZARD
A Nocturne Falls Mystery
Jayne Frost, Book Five

Copyright © 2018 Kristen Painter

ISBN: 978-1-941695-35-7

Published in the United States of America.

For my dad: thanks for all your love and support.
Someday I'll get you that boat.

Welcome to Nocturne Falls – the town that celebrates Halloween 365 days a year.

Jayne Frost is a lot of things. Winter elf, Jack Frost's daughter, Santa Claus's niece, heir to the Winter Throne and now…private investigator. Sort of.

Christmas is over, the new year has begun, and life is thankfully slowing down for Jayne, giving her more time to chill with her new guy. That is, until Myra Grimshaw's death reveals the elderly fae had a strange obsession with Jayne's royal family and an unauthorized collection of exclusive winter elf objects. Including one very questionable snow globe.

Then a whiteout of magical proportions snows the town in and unraveling the mystery of Myra and the objects becomes job number one. Especially when Jayne suspects one of those objects is behind the dangerous creatures now roaming the town's streets.

Things take a chilling turn when one of Jayne's dearest friends is kidnapped and rescuing her means cracking the secrets of Myra's past. But when Jayne discovers blood really is thicker than water, her own life is suddenly on thin ice. Can she save the town *and* her crown?

January 2nd

Just the sound of that date filled me with a sense of peace unlike any other day. For winter elves, the second of January was a magical day. The holidays were over, taking the madness of preparations with them, and a week of rest had begun. The air was fresher on January 2nd. There was a sense of possibility, of achievement, of new beginnings. And I'm not just talking New Year's resolutions. Mostly because I hadn't come up with any yet.

What I meant was that anything was possible in the year ahead, but we had a whole week off before we even had to think about plans for the New Year.

Well, winter elves in the North Pole had a whole week off.

In Nocturne Falls, we were still at work. Santa's Workshop couldn't just close down for a week. Sure, we weren't on holiday hours anymore and store traffic trickled to a bare minimum, but we were open all the same, and the place had to be managed. (Mostly by me, Jayne Frost.) And restocked.

The crazy pace of the holidays was definitely behind us, though, and we indulged in that even further by taking our time with the tasks to be done. Two days to inventory, restock and rebuild the doll section instead of an afternoon, that sort of thing.

I kept the mood lifted by using company funds to buy lunch each day that week—pre-approved by my dad and uncle, of course. We had pizza from Salvatore's, BBQ from Big Daddy Bones, bacon cheeseburgers from Howler's, the blue plate special from Mummy's (turkey pot pie!) and then pizza again from Salvatore's, because that wasn't something we were about to get tired of any time soon.

Sinclair Crowe, owner of Zombie Donuts, and the new hotness in my life, sent us a large box of assorted doughnuts every morning. I'd ordered them and told him to bill me, but he hadn't yet. Sweet of him to do, but I wasn't asking for a handout because we were dating.

I'd specifically placed an order through official channels (by which I meant I'd gone in when he wasn't there so one of his employees could write it up). It was generous of him, for sure, but I didn't want him to think I was expecting that kind of treatment just because we were a thing.

I wanted to support his business. Something I'd proved right after Halloween by getting my dad, Jack Frost, to send a baker from the North Pole kitchens to help Sinclair out when he'd taken a bullet for me and had to have his arm in a sling. That baker, Archie Tingle, had returned to the NP about a week before Christmas. Sin had healed up very nicely and had been ready to take over as main doughnut maker again.

But more than just wanting to support his business, I needed it to do well. Partially because I wanted him to be successful—he deserved it, his doughnuts were ridiculously good and he was a hard worker. But also because as long as he was doing well, he wasn't going anywhere. Not that I thought he was on the verge of leaving or anything.

But maybe I was a little gun-shy. Who could blame me after losing my last two beaus in rapid succession?

See, I liked Sinclair. A lot. Truthfully, it was more than like. It was the other L word, but we hadn't quite gotten to that part of the relationship yet. But all of those feelings translated into me wanting to keep him around. We were good together. Really good. He understood what it meant to run a business, and having that in common really brought us together.

Then there was his overwhelming handsomeness and sex appeal. He was breathtakingly hot. Sometimes, I'd catch myself staring at him without even realizing how long I'd been focused on the thickness of his silver streaked hair. Or the broadness of his shoulders. Or the kissableness of his—you get the idea. I secretly wondered if he thought I was a little touched with all that staring, but he hadn't said anything so maybe I was getting away with it.

He also had a beautiful white cat named Sugar. She and my cat, Spider, had gotten to know each other on a couple of play dates and were surprisingly cordial with one another. The massive amounts of catnip we gave them might have helped. Whatever the reason, they were cute together, all stoned from the nip, stalking each other and running through our respective apartments with the occasional wrestling match thrown in. They were especially adorable when they curled up together to nap. Very yin and yang.

There would be no adorable tuxedo kittens, however, as both Spider and Sugar had been fixed. Sinclair and I weren't sure the two cats had romantic intentions anyway. Those were probably best left to their human caretakers.

As far as the other men in my life went, there weren't any. And I was okay with that. Cooper, my college ex, was still at his parents'. About three months back, his mom had suffered heatstroke that had put her in a coma. Heatstroke was to summer elves what heart attacks were to humans. She'd pulled through the coma at last, but the recovery was going to be long. I knew Cooper's being there was a huge motivator for her and a big help to his dad and I didn't begrudge him not returning to Nocturne Falls. I would have absolutely done the same for my parents.

But I did miss him. Thankfully, our friendship rose up out of the ashes of our relationship in a way that was sweet and surprising. We texted now and then, which was good. Sent the occasional email. He even called me on Christmas Day. It kind of felt like we'd graduated from our romantic relationship into something new and very adult. It was nice. We were better friends now than we ever had been.

On the other hand, things with Greyson, my broody Irish vampire ex, weren't so merry. He still resented me dating Sinclair, not because I'd brought another guy into the picture, but because Sinclair was a necromancer, a kind of supernatural that Greyson felt posed a real threat to vampires. Which he did, in a theoretical kind of way, but Sinclair wasn't that kind of guy. He was truly a lover, not a fighter.

Greyson refused to be convinced, however, and as a result, we'd grown further apart. I understood that he had some basis for his cautious attitude since his sire had been killed by a necromancer, but Sinclair had been in town for a while now without a single aggressive act toward a vampire. (Not to mention, he'd signed a pact with the Ellinghams stating he'd never do harm to any citizen of Nocturne Falls.) In my mind, it was time for Greyson to move past his grumpiness about Sinclair.

Not that I'd said that to him. I hadn't spoken to him since the day he'd given me the "me or him" ultimatum and walked out of my office. I wished him well. He was a good guy.

Which was why I missed him, too, sort of. I mean, I guess what I missed was how things had been between us. The romantic dinners, the affection, the banter, the entertaining company. But with Sinclair in my life, I wasn't *really* missing those things. Sinclair took care of all of that and then some.

Truthfully, the man was spoiling me. And not just with doughnuts.

Like right now, he was spoiling me with time. His. Even when I knew he had to be up super early to get things ready at the shop, he was sprawled on the couch next to me in all his lanky, muscled adorableness, petting Spider and watching old movies with me.

And while you might not think that hanging out

on the couch and watching movies was some fascinating date night, I loved it. Sinclair seemed to as well. At least I think he did.

I looked over at him and the bowl of salted caramel popcorn sitting between us. "Are you having a good time?"

He took his eyes off the screen to look at me and smile. "I'm having a great time." His smile suddenly vanished. "Why? Are you bored? You want to do something else?"

"No, I love this. It's just probably not the most exciting night you've ever had."

"Considering some of the nights that have gone down in this town, I'll take one like this any time." He picked up my hand and kissed my knuckles. "You and me, a movie, popcorn, could there be a better way to kick off the New Year?"

"Doughnuts?"

He laughed. "I love you." His eyes widened suddenly. "I mean, I love your love of doughnuts. I didn't mean to say, that is, I know we've only been going out for—"

"I know what you mean." I was laughing, but on the inside, there were fireworks going off in my head. Just hearing those words coming out of Sinclair had been pretty thrilling. "I adore you, Sinclair. I hope you know that."

He squeezed my hand and the panic left his face. "I do."

We went back to watching the movie, basking quietly in our mutual awesomeness and affection for each other until the credits rolled.

He picked up the bowl of popcorn (now just kernels and a few stragglers) and carried it to the kitchen. "Thanks for dinner. And dessert."

"Thanks for being impressed with my attempt at chicken alfredo." It was my mom's recipe, and I'd followed it to the letter, but it still didn't taste like hers. Good, but not Mom's homemade good. And my kitchen looked like ground zero for the zombie apocalypse. Minus any actual zombies.

"It was very good." He dumped the popcorn remnants in the trash, then took the bowl to the sink. "And I was extra impressed that you cooked for me."

"Good, because that's what I was going for. Plus, you cook for me all the time." I fiddled with the bracelet at my wrist. The strand of rainbow obsidian had been a gift from Sinclair. "I thought you deserved a home-cooked meal in return. I just hope you don't get botulism."

He snorted as he started filling the sink with hot water. "Pretty sure it would take more than that to do a necromancer in."

I got up and walked over to lean against the island. "What do you think you're doing?"

He glanced over his shoulder at me. "Cleaning up. You cooked, I clean."

"Yeah, no. That's sweet, but I've got this. I don't have to get up at four tomorrow morning."

He cranked the water off. "Babe, I can't leave you with all this. You used every dish in your kitchen."

"Joke's on you. I have paper plates." I laughed. "No, really, you have work so early. And I have a dishwasher. I'll load everything up and be done in five minutes."

He left the sink behind to slide his hands around my waist. "Are you trying to get rid of me?"

I shook my head slowly. "Not even for a second. But I don't want you groggy and falling asleep in the doughnuts, either. Hey, speaking of which, I owe you for the week's shipments. And do not say they're on you. They were for my employees and my shop has an account for that kind of thing. So bill me, okay?"

He smiled in that indulgent way he had when I was putting my foot down about something. "As you wish, Your Highness."

Before I could protest, he leaned in and kissed me.

And I forgot all about doughnuts for a minute.
Or five.

The next morning I was up bright and early. Not as early as Sin, but early for me. In fact, I wasn't just awake, I was ready for the day. Today's outfit was the gorgeous galaxy-blue leather jacket Sinclair had gotten me for Christmas with a silky black dress tee underneath, a pair of black trousers, and black suede ankle boots. Some diamond studs and my rainbow obsidian bracelet, which I pretty much wore all the time now. I felt like a million bucks.

Feeling that way helped me forget just how early it was. But the other reason I was up at such a rare hour *and* in a good mood was because I was having breakfast with Birdie Caruthers. We hadn't had a chance to get together since I'd just gotten back from visiting the North Pole a few days ago.

The trip had partly been to see my dad and uncle, since I hadn't seen them in a long time, while my mom and aunt had been down over Halloween for the Black and Orange Ball, but there'd been a big working component to the trip too. I'd sat with my dad and uncle and dug into the sales over the past year and, in finer detail, the sales for the Christmas season. Even allowing for returns, it was easy to see that this year had been our best ever.

I was getting a nice bonus for that, as were all my employees. I hadn't told them yet, because I wanted to take them all out to dinner and hand them their checks in person. They were going to be so excited. I'd decided the private room at the Poisoned Apple, the pub that had fast become a favorite with Sinclair and myself, would be the perfect place.

But this breakfast with Birdie would be a real bright spot in my day. I loved hanging out with her, and she'd done me the huge favor of watching Spider (and my apartment) while I'd been away. This breakfast, and the gorgeous piece of North Pole crystal that I was bringing her, was my way of saying thanks.

I strolled into Mummy's at seven thirty. Like I said, *early*, but Birdie had to be at the reception desk at the sheriff's department by nine and I had the store to open, so the earlier we got to breakfast, the more time we'd have to catch up. With not seeing each other since before I'd left, I had no doubt we had tons to talk about. Birdie still had the key to my place too. Not that I was worried about that. She'd had a key to my place off and on for a while. I was actually thinking about letting her keep it. For emergencies and such.

Arty, my new favorite waitperson, gave me a wave. His sleeves were rolled up to reveal his tattoos: a pinup girl on one forearm and a heart bearing the word Mother on the other. "Morning, sunshine. What brings you out before the sun?"

It wasn't *that* early. "Breakfast with the mayor." I winked as I used his nickname for Birdie.

He gasped. "The Lady Caruthers?"

"The one and only."

"Well, now, y'all come right back on here to this reserved booth."

I followed him. "Who's it reserved for?" The diner was busy but not so swamped there weren't other tables. I didn't want to take someone's seat.

"Hot dames and royalty. So you're in luck."

I snorted. Arty was never boring.

He slapped two menus down. "Coffee?"

"Actually, I think I'm going to do a hot chocolate today."

His brows went up almost to his slicked-back pompadour. "Can I make a suggestion?"

"Sure." His suggestions were always worth listening to.

"Small coffee, small hot chocolate in one large cup with a large swirl of whip."

"Huh." I thought about that for a second. "Any chance of sprinkles?"

"Every chance. Yes?"

"Yes."

"Be right back." He disappeared as Birdie stepped through the doors.

I waved at her, and she broke into a big smile and came on back.

"Hi, Princess." She hugged me as I got up.

"Hi, Birdie. Your hair is still blue." She released me and I sat back down.

She slid into the booth and shrugged. "Jack likes it, so I'm keeping it for a while."

Now my brows went up. "Jack? As in Jack Van Zant? I know he was one of your dates at the Black and Orange Ball, but when did you start to care what he thinks about your 'do?"

Birdie's cheeks took on a pink gleam. She toyed with the edge of her menu. "Since you were away."

Arty came back with one coffee and one tall mug topped with a mountain of whipped cream and chocolate sprinkles. "Hello, gorgeousnesses. Can I tell you about the specials?"

Birdie pointed at my drink. "You can tell me what that is first."

He grinned. "Coffee *and* hot chocolate."

"I need that," Birdie said.

"Whip and sprinkles?"

"Whip and sprinkles."

He nodded. "Coming right up." He took off again.

Birdie made a face. "Sorry. I should have let him tell us the specials first."

"No worries. They're usually in the menu too." I opened mine. "Yep, look. Ooo…apple pie waffles with caramel sauce and vanilla ice cream."

"Finally," Birdie said. "A dessert that qualifies as breakfast. I'm in. With a side of bacon, of course."

I laughed. "A girl needs her protein."

"That's right." She pushed her menu to the edge of the table.

I did the same, then sat forward and laced my fingers together over my placemat. "So. Back to Jack. Spill it. What's going on?"

"Well…to really do that, I have to go back to when I was babysitting Spider."

"Cool. We haven't talked about that yet either. Two birds with one stone." Then I winced. Jack was a familiar, and that particular kind of supernatural could shift into a raven. At least in his case, he could. Not sure every familiar was a bird shifter. "Sorry. I didn't mean—"

"Phfft. Forget it. Jack would." She paused as Arty returned with her java mocha whip thing.

"Here you go. Want to hear the specials, or are you ladies ready to order? Have any questions? What can I do for you?"

Arty was definitely a morning person. I looked at Birdie. "I think we're good to order, right?"

She nodded. "Two of those apple pie waffle specials."

He took our menus. "With two sides of bacon, am I right?"

I grinned.

Birdie did too. "I love a man who listens."

"I'll get this in for you ASAP." Arty tucked the menus under his arm and headed to the kitchen.

We got back to talking.

"So what happened while I was gone? You two, obviously. But how? I want details." I sipped my coffee drink. It was delicious. No surprise there.

"Telling you this means I have to tell you something I'm not too proud of, Princess, but one of my New Year's resolutions is to be more forthcoming. Did you make any resolutions?"

I stilled. "No, and don't change the subject. What happened?"

She grimaced. "I opened the window for Spider, just like your note said to do, and…he got out."

I sucked in a breath.

"But," she continued. "It was fine. He was fine. We don't even know if he really got out."

"Okay, back up. Start at the beginning." I drank some more of my coffee hot chocolate. The sugar was very soothing.

"All right, here's what happened…" A few minutes later, she finished with a big smile. "And that's how Kaley got Kizmet! Isn't that great?"

"It is. Wow, what an adventure."

"And Jack made you a whole new replacement screen. He's very handy like that." Her brows suddenly knitted together. "Are you mad?"

"No, why would I be?" I was impressed with how far she'd gone to make things right. "You were just doing what I said to do. I have no doubt Spider saw something that interested him on the street below, leaned into the screen and popped it right out. He probably scared himself silly falling through. In fact, I bet he hid under the bed or the couch or someplace the rest of the day."

"Well, that would explain why we couldn't find him."

"And you didn't need to buy him a new collar. I want to pay you for that."

"Oh no, I don't want your money." She made another of those motherly *phfft* noises. "Poor thing was so worried you were going to be mad at him. I just wanted him to feel better, you know?"

A weird vibe trickled through me. I leaned farther forward and spoke slowly. "How did you know he was worried?"

"Because he—oh! That's the other thing." She leaned in. We must have looked like two spies trying to pass state secrets. She whispered at me, "Did you know Spider can talk?"

I sat back. "Um, yeah, but he's never done it

around anyone but me. Otherwise, I would have given you a heads-up."

Birdie leaned back and shrugged. "Must have been the blue hair." She sipped her drink.

"Must have been." I thought about that for a second. Spider was a strange little dude, but he must have really taken to Birdie to speak in front of her. "So listen, about that collar, what do I owe you? Ten bucks cover it?"

"Princess, you stop that right now. Let's just say it's Aunt Birdie's Christmas present to Spider and leave it at that, okay?"

"Well, okay. But since you mentioned presents..." I reached into my purse. "I have something for you. My way of saying thanks for looking after Spider."

I slid the small silver and cobalt-blue wrapped gift toward her, loving the way her eyes lit up when she saw it.

"Oh my," she whispered. Then she looked at me. "Did you bring this back from the North Pole?"

I nodded. "I did."

"And is that the royal Winter Court seal?"

"It is." I knew she'd like that little detail.

She clasped her hands in front of her and sucked in a breath that got hitched up on a sniffle. "I think I'm going to cry."

"Don't cry, you'll make me cry. And no one wants tears in their waffles." I blinked hard and grinned. I was a sympathetic crier *and* an ugly crier. Not a great combo. The last thing I wanted was to be out at breakfast with a bright red nose.

My uncle always said I got that from Rudolph. That's my uncle, funny guy. Bet you didn't know Santa Claus was such a crack up.

Birdie laughed. "Just happy tears because this was so unexpected and sweet!"

I shrugged. "You took care of my cat for me. Go ahead, open it."

"I hate to ruin the wrapping. It's so pretty. And that seal, I definitely want to save that." She pried the tape loose on the back and carefully unwrapped the foiled paper to reveal the snowy-white square box underneath.

She took the top off of that, rustled aside the

tissue paper and gasped again. "Oh my stars, that is the most beautiful thing I've ever seen."

"Well, I don't know about that. But it was custom-made for you." I couldn't help but smile knowing what the box held.

"Custom-made for me. Are you serious?"

"For real."

She lifted the delicate hand-cut crystal snowflake pendant out of the tissue by the silver chain attached to it. The light caught it, sending a shower of rainbow sparks over the table. "It's just so pretty. And sparkly."

"I'm glad you like it."

"Oh!" She sat back like she'd been slapped. But in a good way. "That's the same snowflake from the Winter Court crest, isn't it?"

"It is. Made just for you by my father's jewelers. That's winter elf crystal. If you move the snowflake in the light, you can see a flash of blue inside." I lifted one shoulder. "Winter elf jeweler magic."

My father's jewelers had a technique for making crystal that caused it to hold strands of luminescent blue light inside, like a moonstone, but clear. It was very pretty, and very rare for a piece to leave the NP. If it did, it was usually because it had been given as a gift.

"Well, it's just gorgeous. I'm putting it on right now." She reached back and attached the clasp, then adjusted the snowflake in the hollow of her throat. "How does it look?"

"Lovely. Really picks up the blue in your hair."

She laughed. "Thank you so much."

"You're welcome. Thank you for minding Spider."

She rolled her eyes. "Yes, well, *that*."

"Ooo, nice sparkler there, Ms. Caruthers." Arty showed up with a tray of food. "I hope you're ready to eat."

"We are," I said. I was starving.

He dished the plates out and we dug in, only chatting briefly for the first few minutes and then mostly about how amazing the apple pie waffles were, because they were everything I'd ever wanted in a waffle without realizing that's what I'd wanted in a waffle.

After a few more minutes, the edge was off our hunger and we returned to a more civilized demeanor. I sipped the glass of water Arty had brought me. "So, tell me more about Jack."

Birdie was all smiles. "I don't know what there is to tell."

"Oh, please. Look at you being coy. Who are you, Birdie Caruthers? Spill it. How many times have you been out?"

"Just twice since you were away. It hasn't been that long." Her smile remained even as she stabbed a warm apple chunk and just held it on her fork.

"But he's making me dinner this weekend."

"Wow. Nice." I stabbed an apple chunk of my own, which I promptly ate. "I love when Sinclair cooks for me. He's so good at it. And between us, a man that can cook is really sexy."

Her brows shot up. "Isn't it? My lands." She fanned herself before eating the piece of apple.

"You know what? We should double-date. The four of us. Go out to Guillermo's for a nice pasta dinner."

"Oh, come on. You and Sin don't want to double-date with old people."

I frowned at her. "Not with old people, no. But we'd happily go with you two."

She laughed and shook her head. "You're sweet. And that would be fun. I'll ask Jack. I'm sure he'll be up for it."

"Good. I'll mention it to Sinclair."

We weren't two minutes back into the remains of our waffles when Birdie's phone buzzed.

She glanced at it. "I better get this, it's Hank."

"Hey, if the sheriff calls, you gotta answer." I ate my last strip of bacon. I wasn't intentionally eavesdropping, but I wasn't trying not to listen either.

"Hi, honey, what's up? Having breakfast with—who?" Her brows knit together. "Oh, that's so sad. But she was getting up there. Okay. Will do. See you in a bit."

She hung up.

"Everything okay?"

"Myra Grimshaw passed away. You wouldn't know her, I don't think. Unless maybe she'd ever come into your store, but I don't know why she'd be shopping for toys. She was part fae, I believe. Nice woman. Quiet. Had to be well into her hundreds. Or older. You know how the fae age."

I did. Pretty much the same as elves. Very slowly and with little sign of time's passage.

"Anyway, her neighbor found the body, and Hank was just calling to tell me he wouldn't be in straightaway because he has to stay until the ME, that's the medical examiner, shows up to collect her. He's on his way over there now to stay with the body. Poor thing."

I wasn't sure if she meant Hank or Myra. "I'm sorry to hear that. Did you know her well?"

"Not too well. Enough to say hi if I saw her at the Shop-n-Save, that sort of thing. Her great-nephew and Titus were in school together, if memory serves. I think he's moved away, though. I think to California. Pretty sure that's where her people are from. Anyway, it was sad when he left. She was so active in that boy's life."

"Why didn't she go with him?"

"I suppose he wanted his own life. Might have been weird for his great-aunt to follow him out there."

"I suppose."

Her phone buzzed again. She glanced at it. "It's Hank. By text this time." She picked the phone up and read, then looked over the edge of the screen at me. "He wants to know if I can find you and bring you to Myra's."

Odd. "Why?"

She shook her head. "He didn't say. You want me to ask him? He's not always a fount of information over text."

"No, it's okay. I have time. We can head over." Wasn't much left on our plates anyway.

"You sure you're okay with it?"

"Sure. Why? Is there something you're not telling me?" I put more than enough cash on the table to cover our breakfast and Arty's tip.

"Well, have you even seen a dead body before?"

I let that sink in a moment. "Only at a funeral. But I guess that's about to change."

Birdie drove, naturally, since I didn't have a car. Myra Grimshaw's place was in one of the older residential areas of town. It was nice and the homes were neatly kept, but they weren't showplaces. Cute enough, though. Some of the mostly one-story cottages (like hers) had actual white picket fences outlining the yards. Seemed like a nice area to live in, but then, Nocturne Falls didn't have any bad spots that I knew of.

We parked on the street and walked through the

gate and up the stone path to the front porch. Hank's police car was in the driveway, along with an older gray sedan. The house was white with black trim and a blue door. There were yellow window boxes on the two front windows, but the plants in them were plastic.

Maybe Myra had a brown thumb. Or maybe that was her way of keeping things bright during the winter months. Either way, I wasn't judging. Plastic flowers were more cheerful than bare dirt.

Birdie knocked. "Hank, we're here."

He opened the door a second later. "That was fast."

"We were having breakfast," I offered.

"Thank you for coming."

"Sure thing." I peered past him, not sure what I'd see. There was no body in the immediate viewing area.

He cleared his throat. "She's in the bedroom. Which is not where I need you."

I looked at him again. That meant no dead-body sighting. I was okay with that, but also strangely disappointed. "Okay."

Birdie put her hand on my arm as if to keep me from going anywhere. "What's this about, Hank? The princess has a right to know."

"Easier just to show her." He tipped his head, and just like that we knew to follow, so we did.

My curiosity was piqued, but Myra's house

wasn't giving anything away. It was about as normal inside as you might imagine an old lady's house to be. Doilies on the chairs, flowered upholstery, an upright piano covered in family photos—mostly of one particular young man who I assumed to be her great-nephew—and a dish of hard candies on the coffee table. It smelled a little of peppermints and chicken soup. Maybe she'd been sick recently.

I said as much to Birdie. "Had she been ill?"

"I don't know. Hank, had she been sick? The place does have that sort of smell about it."

"Not that I know of. The coroner will make that determination."

"Will there be an autopsy?" I asked.

He nodded as he took us through to the kitchen. "In a case like this, where there's no obvious cause of death, yes."

"How old was she?" The place was tidy, I'd say that much. Not a speck of dust anywhere.

"Hundred and seventeen."

"Probably natural causes, then, right?"

Hank shrugged. "Maybe. But she was fae. That tends to extend a person's years."

"It does." I looked around the kitchen since we'd come to a stop. "Is what you wanted to show me in here?"

"No." He moved toward a door on the sidewall. "In the basement."

I cringed. Basements and I weren't the best of friends. "Is it creepy?"

"No." He opened the door and headed down. The lights were already on.

Birdie looked at me and shrugged.

With no other choice, we followed.

The basement was mostly finished off, which took away a lot of the creepiness I'd expected. Florescent lights and drywall were much friendlier than concrete block walls and bare bulbs. The floor was just plain cement, but the basement was just as clean as the rest of the house, which was nice. Not a cobweb in sight.

Other than an old armoire against the far wall, the rest of the walls were lined with shelves filled with jar after jar of homemade preserves, jams, and jellies. One bottom shelf had a thick stack of old Tombstone newspapers, but all the rest held the little jars. The glass glistened in the light, showing off their juicy colors like rare jewels. Miss Grimshaw had apparently had a hobby. I approved.

There was a deputy standing by the armoire, notebook in hand. "Sheriff." He nodded at Birdie. "Ms. Caruthers."

Hank introduced me. "Deputy Jansen, this is Jayne Frost. Miss Frost, this is Dave Jansen."

I shook his hand, since he offered. "Nice to meet you, Deputy."

"You too." He seemed a little nervous. Eager to please maybe. I'd never met him before, which didn't mean anything really, but he gave off a very new-to-the-job vibe.

Hank nodded at the armoire behind the deputy. It was a beast of a thing, but the dark wood was well-polished, making it seem cared for. So why keep it in the basement? "Open it up."

Jansen tucked his notebook under his arm, turned and pulled the double doors wide.

My mouth fell open. "Son of a nutcracker. Are you kidding me?"

"That's why I asked Birdie to bring you over."

The inside of the cabinet was shelves from the middle down. Those shelves were filled with all sorts of knickknacks, trinkets, boxes, packages and whatnots. There was even a commemorative cup from one of my father's coronation celebrations. But from the middle up, the cabinet was open space.

And every inch was covered with newspaper clippings. Almost all about my family. Most with pictures.

"That's my dad. And my aunt. Me. My mom. My uncle. Christmas on a cracker, we're all up there."

"Did you know Myra Grimshaw?"

"Not in the slightest." I took a step toward the cabinet so I could read one of the articles, but it was hard to focus on just one. The armoire was like a shrine to the Winter Court. I reached to smooth the paper of one clipping.

"Don't touch anything. Please."

My hand stopped midair.

"Hank," Birdie chided. "It's not a crime scene."

"We don't know cause of death yet."

I held my hands up. "Sorry. Hands off." Then I went back to checking out the articles. I scanned a few of them. They were mostly things like store openings, parade scenes, official functions that weren't all that serious. I finally turned to the sheriff. "These articles are all about my family from what I can tell, and all from one newspaper, the Christmas Star. That's the local North Pole paper. The fact that she has clippings from that paper — and some recent ones at that..." I shook my head as I checked a few more dates. Maybe not that recent. The most current one I could find was just under a year old.

"What?" Hank asked.

"It's weird. The Christmas Star is a local paper. Like the Tombstone in Nocturne Falls. Except, it's not delivered outside of the NP. And especially not to someone who isn't a winter elf."

His eyes narrowed and he nodded. "Someone was sending it to her."

I stared at the wall of articles, but then my gaze drifted down to the shelves. "Hold on just a hot Christmas minute."

I bent down to get a better look at something I never thought I'd see anywhere outside of my office or apartment. A snow globe. It was almost exactly like mine, like the ones I used to communicate with my family back in the North Pole. The only difference was the slim, red velvet ribbon tied in a bow around where the globe met the base. "How is that possible?" I whispered.

The magical snow globes were what we used instead of cell phones. Electronics and the weird electrical stuff at the North Pole didn't mix, making standard methods of communication basically unusable. But to my knowledge, no one outside of my family had one.

"How is what possible?" the sheriff asked.

I looked over my shoulder at him. I wasn't ready to spill court secrets just yet. At least not with Deputy Jansen listening in. "This woman has things she shouldn't have."

"Such as?"

I stood. I could only imagine what else I might find in this cabinet. And considering the personal nature of what it held, I ought to be allowed to look through it. Which meant I was going to have to share the significance of the snow globe if I wanted the sheriff's go-ahead. But I still didn't want to discuss the snow globe in front of a deputy I didn't know. Hank and Birdie, I could trust, but Deputy Jansen? I mean, I was sure he was a nice guy, but this was proprietary elf magic here.

As if understanding my hesitation, the sheriff gave the deputy a look. "Jansen, run up to the car and call the ME. See what's taking so long."

"You got it, Sheriff."

As Jansen's footsteps faded away, the sheriff's brows went up. "Better?"

"Yes, thank you." I pointed toward the snow globe. "That's top-level elf magic. Nobody has one of those but members of my family. That I'm aware of. I'll call my dad and ask as soon as I get into the office."

The sheriff made a face. "The snow globe? How is that magic?"

I had to tell him. "It's how we communicate. Electronics are completely unreliable in the North Pole due to all the extra magnetic interference, so we use the globes. It's all elf magic, and I don't begin to understand it, but I know enough to know the fae Myra Grimshaw shouldn't have one."

He was silent a moment. "See anything else that doesn't belong?"

I turned back to the cabinet, skimming over the shelves.

"I do," Birdie said.

I glanced at her in time to see her pull a pen from her purse.

She used it to nudge a piece of paper out of the way, revealing a small glass paperweight. Except it wasn't glass, it was winter elf crystal. The exact same kind that made up the snowflake pendant I'd just given her. Birdie looked at me. "Should she have that? You said it was rare and not usually seen outside of the North Pole."

"Wow, no. I mean, maybe it was a gift. She clearly knows someone in the North Pole, but—"

"Knew." Birdie shrugged.

"Right. Knew."

"What is it?" the sheriff asked.

I explained about the crystal.

He sighed. "None of this means her death was anything besides natural causes, but it certainly raises some questions."

Birdie put her hands on her hips. "Who's the next of kin?"

"Her great-nephew is coming out to claim the body. Should be here tomorrow."

"Nate?"

Hank nodded.

Birdie patted my arm. "That's the boy who went to school with Titus that I was telling you about."

My attention was on the armoire, but I managed a response. "I guess Titus will be excited that he's coming to town. Always nice to see an old friend."

Hank snorted. "I wouldn't say Nate and Titus were old friends. Rivals more like it. Friendly enough, but still."

Birdie nodded, a knowing look on her face. "They were both after the same girl."

"Charlene Paris Monroe." Hank's gaze had gone somewhere far away. "She was a pretty little thing."

"Who'd she pick?"

"Neither one of them." He came back to the present. "Her head was turned by a boy a year older. Brett Gonzales. He had two things Nate and Titus didn't." He broke into a rare grin. "A license and the keys to his daddy's car."

"Sheriff?" the deputy called out as he came down a few steps. "The ME just pulled in."

"All right, I'll be up." Hank looked at me. "I can't stop Nate from taking possession of these things. As far as I know, this house and everything in it goes to her kin."

"I understand that. But I might be able to stop him. Well, my father might be able to. Royal court order."

32

"But she was fae," the sheriff countered. "If her people want to, they can tie the whole thing up with a supernatural magistrate."

He was right. Inter-species supernatural judicial matters could take forever. Within a species, however, things usually went quickly. "Except I don't think she was fae," I said. "I think that's just what she told people."

The sheriff's eyes narrowed. "You think she was winter elf?"

"That's what my gut is saying. And if you let me see the body, I might be able to tell." I didn't really want to see Myra Grimshaw's corpse, but if it meant protecting my kingdom's secrets, I'd do what I had to do.

The sheriff pondered that for a moment, then tipped his head. "Follow me."

Okay, I've seen dead people before. It's not like I've never been to a funeral. But those people have already been fixed up by the mortician. What I've never *ever* seen is a dead person right where they died. In what might technically be a crime scene. (Call me paranoid, but I wasn't ruling anything out.)

So in that regard, this was a completely new and sort of uncomfortable situation.

Also, we were in Myra's bedroom, which added another layer of strange. Or maybe it was just me, but being in someone's bedroom was like entering their inner sanctum. And we most definitely hadn't been invited.

Probably why we were all so quiet.

Myra didn't look that dead. Really, she looked like she was sleeping. She was a short, roundish woman with wispy hair so white it was faintly blue. That might have been from a rinse like Birdie's, or it might have been because of the winter elf blood formerly pumping through her veins. (Yes, I was sticking with that.) She was also pretty pale, but it was winter, and in Nocturne Falls, pale wasn't that unusual. Hello, vampires, I'm looking at you.

Regardless, I thought I would have been able to tell if she was a winter elf just by looking at her. I couldn't. I mean, sure, she looked like one, but in retrospect so did a lot of other people in town. Having blue hair wasn't just an elf thing anymore. And just because she had pointed ears didn't mean she was an elf. She could have been fae like she claimed.

I sighed, finally breaking the silence. "Snowballs. I can't tell if she's a winter elf or not." So much for helping the situation.

Birdie looked at me. "What now?"

"What now," Hank said, "is the ME takes the body."

"But we still don't know how she got all this winter elf stuff," I said.

"I understand that," he said. "And I know you're concerned about it, but verifying the ownership of those things isn't my immediate job here. Seeing that Myra is properly looked after is. Unless you can provide proof they were stolen. Which would actually be a new case."

"I can't give you that. Yet." The sheriff was using a tone that made me think he was trying extra hard to be patient with me, so I did my best not to get frustrated. I understood that he had a job to do, but Myra had things that didn't really belong to her. Mostly the snow globe, but that crystal was questionable. And who knew what else was in that armoire? I couldn't see letting those things go to her next of kin, either. Unfortunately, I wasn't quite sure how to argue with his point, so I settled for a displeased expression instead.

He stuck his thumbs in his belt. "I know you're concerned about those things getting out into the world, but unless I have a royal court order, there's nothing I can do."

I tried to look sweet and innocent and like a person who should get her way. "Couldn't I just take the snow globe and the crystal and—"

"Miss Frost." He crossed his arms. "You're not suggesting I allow you to steal Myra Grimshaw's property, are you?"

That was exactly what I was doing. "No."

His expression softened, and he dropped his arms back to his sides. "Talk to your father. Get me some official paperwork and I'll do what I can. Right now, however, I need to go speak to the ME and let him take Myra out of here."

"Or!" I stuck my finger in the air. "I do have another idea…"

He and Birdie looked at me.

I wasn't sure I should even suggest this, but I was dying to know how Myra was connected to my family, because I felt like that might help me figure out how she'd gotten those NP trinkets. I had so many questions. Was she linked to the North Pole in a lineage kind of way? Or just a royal-family stalker? It happened. People got obsessed with us. And how on earth had she gotten that snow globe?

"Tell us your idea, Princess," Birdie said.

I took a breath. "We could call Sinclair."

Hank's eyes narrowed. "Are you suggesting…"

Birdie spoke up. "That's a great idea, Princess."

Hank glared at his aunt. "No, it's not."

"Why?" I asked. "That's his skill set. That's what he does. Why not let him do his thing? This is exactly the kind of situation where he can be useful. And I bet he'd want to."

Hank seemed to be thinking about it. "Kind of a violation of the dead person. Don't you think?"

Birdie snorted. "Hank, she's dead. What does she care?"

"That's what I was thinking," I said as I pulled out my phone. "I can text him. See if he can run over here."

Hank grunted a firm, "No."

The inflexibility of that word made me put my phone away. It didn't, however, stop me from sighing loudly and with great frustration.

He clearly got my mood but didn't care. He wasn't budging. "Talk to your father first. Let's not bring anyone back from the dead just yet because of a *snow globe*."

I frowned. Obviously, the sheriff didn't get the seriousness of keeping that snow globe from falling into the wrong hands. "It would just be temporary. Long enough to ask her a few questions."

He repeated his earlier statement. "Talk to your father first. Now I'm going outside to meet the ME."

He left Birdie and me alone in the room with Myra. Which was weird, I couldn't lie. Like, super weird. Myra might have been dead, but her presence felt very much alive. I don't mean that her ghost was there or anything like that, just that it was impossible to pretend I wasn't in the same room as a dead woman.

I nudged Birdie's arm while keeping my eyes on Myra. "Maybe we should wait in the other room?"

Birdie nodded. She'd been clutching her purse to her chest like a shield and seemed pretty happy about leaving Myra to rest in peace.

When we were in the living room, she finally spoke. "How do you think Myra got all those articles about your family? Why would she have them? And all those mementos? Do you think she was in love with your dad, or obsessed with your family, or something else I haven't thought of?"

"Beats me." Through the front windows, I could see the sheriff on the lawn talking to the ME. "I guess my dad is the most likely target. She could have had some kind of crush on him or something. Which is odd if she's not a winter elf, but maybe not that odd. Most supernaturals know who he is."

Birdie nodded vigorously. "Jack Frost is kind of a celebrity in the supernatural world. So is your uncle. And he was in a few of the articles."

"Sure, but given the whole 'belly like a bowl full of jelly,' I don't think most women find Santa Claus quite as sexy as Jack Frost. Unless they're into dad bod." I wrinkled my nose. "I can't believe I'm talking about how comparatively sexy my dad and uncle are. This is not at all the conversation I thought I'd be having this morning."

"I'm sure." Birdie was trying not to smile, I could tell. It was funny. In a bizarre sort of way.

I twirled a strand of hair around one finger as I thought. "But for anyone to be that obsessed with the Winter Court of the North Pole to collect all those clippings and keepsakes...yeah, that's not completely standard behavior."

"Is it more, or less, weird if she's actually a winter elf?"

"I don't know. Less, maybe, because if she was a winter elf and had lived at the North Pole at some point in her life, at least she'd probably had contact with my dad. Or if not contact exactly, she would have been around him. More so than if she was fae. So she'd have had a more reasonable opportunity to fall in love with him. Or get obsessed with us. I guess. But being a winter elf would also explain how she was getting the Christmas Star sent to her, because she would probably still have family in the NP. But you said you thought her people were in California."

Birdie shrugged. "That's what I thought, yes. But I can do some research into that. See what I can find out."

Birdie was awesome at that kind of stuff. "That would be great. In the meantime, do you think I could have a picture of her to show my dad?"

"You want to take a picture of her?"

I looked around. All the framed photos were of friends and family. I assumed that's who they were, the ones who'd lived on the West Coast. There were a few pointed ears visible, but nothing that screamed winter elf to me. Too bad physically taking one of her framed photos was probably something the sheriff would classify as stealing. "Unless you see one lying around that your nephew wouldn't mind me borrowing, I guess I have to. Is that weird?"

Birdie looked back toward the bedroom. "Not any weirder than anything else that's happened today."

I ended up taking pictures of Myra *and* her cabinet to show my dad, who I called on my snow globe the second I walked into my office.

He answered right away with a big smile. "Morning, Jay. How are you?"

"Good." Everything else was weird, but I was good. "How are you?"

"Better now that my darling daughter has called me."

I laughed. "You say that now, but you don't know why I called."

"True. What's up?"

"Does the name Myra Grimshaw mean anything to you?"

He was silent a few seconds while he thought. "Can't say that it does. Who is she?"

"She's a resident here in town. Or was. She passed away recently. But the reason I'm calling is she has quite a collection of North Pole goods. Including a snow globe and a piece of winter elf crystal."

"A snow globe? You mean the kind we use for communication?"

"That's what it looks like. Just like the ones we use, except—"

"That shouldn't be." He frowned, his mind working hard on explanations, if the lines in his forehead were any indication.

"That's why I'm calling you. And there's more."

The smile on his face was completely gone now. "What else?"

"She had pictures of you, Mom, Uncle Kris, the whole family. All in clippings from the Christmas Star. Any article that talked about us, basically."

He stared at me through the globe. "Like in a scrapbook?"

I pulled up the photo on my phone. "Like in a cabinet that was basically a Winter Court/North Pole shrine." I held the phone up so he could see.

A long, quiet moment passed.

"You have got to be kidding me."

I took the phone away. "I wish I was. It was pretty strange. You sure you don't know her?"

He shook his head. "The name isn't ringing any bells, but I'm going to ask Elf Resources if they have any record of her. Do you have a photo of her?"

"I do, but be warned, if it looks a little strange, it's because she's not alive in the picture."

His brows lifted. "You took a picture of a dead woman?"

"What else was I supposed to do?"

"Did she have a driver's license? You could have snapped that."

"Huh. I never thought of that." That would have been much less icky. "Do you want to see her or not?"

"I do."

42

I showed him the photo.

"Nothing familiar about that face either." He sighed. "As for the bulk of what's in that armoire, it would be nice if you could go through it and see what else is in there, if that's at all possible."

"I don't know if it is."

His eyes narrowed slightly. "This isn't something I would normally tell you to do, but if you can't legally gain access to the house again, feel free to use other means."

"Dad!"

"Winter magic is very strong, Jay. If she has other powerful artifacts from the NP and the wrong people get ahold of them, it could be disastrous. Which is why you *must* get that snow globe. For it just to be out there where anyone could lay their hands on it…that can't happen."

"I agree, but I think we should try the legal route first. Because if anything goes missing, the sheriff is absolutely going to come knocking on my door."

"True. And we don't need that."

"He said if you can supply him with a royal court order, that should be enough for him to protect those items for us."

My dad nodded. "I'll have legal draw one up today. I'll send it through the Santa's Bag as soon as it's ready. It's early there, right?"

"Right." I checked my phone. "Not quite nine yet."

"Okay, I'll have it to you by lunch."

"Thanks, Dad."

"You're welcome. And send me anything else you can on this Myra Grimshank, will you?"

"Grimshaw. And yes, I will."

"Love you, Jay."

"Love you, too, Dad."

We hung up. Out in the warehouse, the apartment elevator doors pinged.

I got up to see if it was Juniper coming down to work. It was. I smiled at her. "Morning."

"Hey, good morning. How's it going?"

I smiled weakly and leaned against the door of my office. "I'm not sure where to start. Actually, I am. And it requires doughnuts. Hold down the fort until I get back?"

"For doughnuts?" She grinned. "I would build you a new fort."

I walked into Zombie Donuts just after nine a.m. The smell of sugar and fried dough zipped through me like the best side-effects-free high in the world. I inhaled, smiling. If ever there was such a thing as my happy place, this was it. For a couple of seconds, I didn't even care that some little old dead lady had possibly been stalking my dad.

The shop was still plenty busy, but I knew the real morning insanity had already passed. That happened much earlier, when people with more get-up-and-go than I had came in to fuel themselves for the day with coffee and their pastry of choice. Which, in this shop, generally meant a doughnut or something doughnut-adjacent, like a bear claw, an éclair, or a fruity turnover. The possibilities were nearly endless and, in this shop, ever changing.

But I wasn't here for the pastries. I was here for

the owner, the equally delicious and infinitely appealing Sinclair Crowe. Okay, I was sort of here for pastries, because how could I be here and not indulge? But Sin was my main reason. I wanted to see my guy. And bounce today's craziness off him.

He was coming out of the back with a tray of maple-glazed, bacon-studded doughnuts when he saw me. "Hey, beautiful. How did I get so lucky that you're in my shop and not your own?"

I grinned and lifted one shoulder. "Clean living, I guess."

"Yeah," he said, amusement lighting his eyes. "That must be it." He lifted the tray. "Sweets for my sweet?"

"Sure. But…" I glanced past the tray to point at the display case. "I'd rather have one of those lemon creams."

He slid the tray into its spot and blinked in surprise. "That is not your usual by a long shot." He grabbed a square of waxed paper, picked up the doughnut I'd requested and handed it to me.

"It's been a strange morning." I took a bite, and the tart, lemony burst of flavor was exactly what I needed. The tang seemed to cut through some of the noise in my head.

"You want to talk?"

"I'd love to."

He tipped his head toward the small office he kept in the back. "C'mon."

As I started around the counter, he pointed at one of his employees. "Johnny, call me if you need me, I'm taking five."

"You got it, boss." Johnny gave me a wave. "Hey, Jayne."

"Hi, Johnny." I returned the wave on my way by.

In Sin's office, he shut the door and pulled out his desk chair for me, choosing to sit on the edge of his desk himself. "What's going on, babe?"

I took the seat, trying to figure out where to start.

"You look phenomenal this morning, by the way. Not that you don't always look great, but I love you in that jacket."

"You have great taste."

He wiggled his eyebrows. "Clearly. Look who I'm dating."

I laughed. The man was so, so good for me. I licked a smudge of lemon icing off one finger. "I knew coming here was the right move."

"Yeah? Why's that?"

"Because you make me feel better. And I was in a weird place earlier. Still am, kind of."

"And again, why is that?"

"Saw a dead body this morning."

His eyes widened a bit. "Do tell."

So I did, spilling the whole story about Myra and the armoire and the snow globe. I trusted Sin, and he'd met my mom and aunt and earned their approval, so I was cool with him knowing how that particular magic item worked. Also, he'd saved my life. So there was that.

He let out a long, low whistle. "That is quite a story."

"Right? Anyway, my dad is supposed to send me a court order by lunch today, and the sheriff said that would be good enough for him to seize the items under supernatural law. But I'm still dying to know why she had all those pictures of us. And how she got the snow globe in the first place."

"I bet. I'd be dying to know too."

Not quite the answer I'd hoped for. "I was wondering...do you think maybe you could use your skills to find out?"

He ran a hand through his hair and shifted back on the desk. "I don't want to tell you no, but I actually try to use those skills as little as possible. I really only do it in matters of life and death. No pun intended."

"I see." I was disappointed and I'm sure it showed.

"Hey." He gave my arm a quick squeeze. "If you really want me to, I will. It's just..."

He kind of grimaced and didn't say anything else.

"It's just what?"

"Using my power costs me."

"What do you mean? How?"

He sighed and stared at the floor. "For every minute that I return a soul to life, I pay."

"In what way?" All kinds of awful things popped up in my head.

"That time...is deducted off mine."

That was worse than what I'd imagined. "Snowballs. Nope, never mind. Forget I even brought it up."

"Listen, I will if you really want me to. It's just something we need to be prepared for so that it can be done as quickly as possible."

"Good to know. But I can't imagine I'll be asking again after that bit of news."

He smiled a little. "I just thought you should know."

"I appreciate you telling me. Anything else I should know about your gifts?"

"Lemme think." He squinted. "Bringing someone back is a one-time, one-shot deal."

"What do you mean?"

"I can only bring someone back once, and it only lasts for as long as I'm touching them. I let go and they're permanently back to being dead." He squinted. "Unless you have another necromancer around. Then, in theory, they could bring that person back again. Not sure about that. It's never come up."

"Interesting. And while I still really want to know what was going on with Myra and my family,

I think I'll let Birdie do her digging and see what she turns up. One more question, though. For curiosity's sake. It's a little…icky."

"I can handle it."

"Okay then. Can you still work your magic if a person has been embalmed?"

"You mean at the funeral? Yes. And the other nice bit is the person has to tell the truth. Dead people, really dead people now, I'm not talking about vampires, are incapable of lying."

"Get out. Is that where that saying dead men tell no tales comes from?"

He nodded. "Sometimes those weird sayings are true."

"How about that." I ate the last bit of my doughnut, wadded up the waxed paper and tossed it in the bin under his desk. "You're pretty awesome, you know that? Doughnuts and death magic. That is quite a combo."

"That was almost the name of my band in high school."

I snorted as I pushed to my feet. "You're crazy."

"About you." He grabbed the edges of my jacket and pulled me close. "You still think I'm awesome even after I turned down your request for help?"

"Yes. I totally get you being reluctant to use your gifts when they come with so high a price. Don't give it another thought." I really did not want to be the reason his life-span shortened.

If anything, I wanted him around more, not less.

"I don't want you to be upset with me."

"I'm not, I promise." I wasn't, and I had no reason to be. Sin was too good a guy for me to get upset over something like that.

"Good." He kissed me, and I leaned in, wrapping my arms around his neck and enjoying every second of his mouth on mine.

When we finally came up for air, I was in a nice little blissed-out state. "I guess I should let you get back to work."

"Likewise. Thanks for stopping by. Always a nice surprise to see you."

Neither of us had let go of the other yet. "Thanks for the doughnut."

"Hey, you want to take your order with you? I don't think your delivery went out yet."

"That reminds me. That's why I came in." I gave him my most serious look. "But you have to let me pay for it."

"Sure. The cost is dinner."

I poked my finger into his chest. His hard, muscle-y chest. "I'm serious. I'm giving you actual money, and I don't want you turning it down. But I'm glad you brought up dinner, because I want to go on a double date with Birdie and her new man. To Guillermo's, that nice Italian place."

"Set it up, I'm there."

I kissed him again. Because *girlfriend privileges*.

Then I finally let him go. "All right, let me buy a box of doughnuts off you, and then I'm going back to the store."

It took a few empty threats, but I managed to get him to take my money for the doughnuts. That made me happy. But not as happy as Kip and Juniper were when I returned with that box in my hands. I put it in the employee break room and let them dig in.

Kip took a chocolate peanut butter cream and ate it standing in the doorway between the shop and the warehouse so he could keep an eye on things. "I'm really glad you started dating this guy."

"Me too," Juniper added. She'd selected a blackberry basil jam.

"Well, that's really all I wanted." I was eating a Dr Prepper, the Dr Pepper doughnut that seemed custom-made for me. "Store-wide approval of my love life."

They laughed.

I swallowed the bite I'd just taken. "Any news while I was out? Calls? Santa Bag shipments?"

Juni shook her head. "I haven't checked the Santa's Bag. Kip?"

"Haven't looked either, but I can run back there."

"No," I said. "I'll go do it. You guys enjoy the fruits of my relationship." I headed back to the Santa's Bag to see if my dad's court order had come through yet, but the bag was empty. It was early yet, so I wasn't worried.

I hung out in the shop for a bit, letting Kip and Juniper enjoy another doughnut without worrying about having to help a customer. Only one person came in, a man looking for a gift for his daughter's birthday.

I helped him, enjoying the leisurely pace of non-Christmas shopping. He settled on a chemistry set and I rang him up.

As he left, Kip came back to the register. He hooked his thumb toward the warehouse. "I checked the Santa's Bag before I came up here. There was an envelope in it. I put it on your desk."

I made sure the court order was in the envelope, then I threw my jacket on, grabbed my purse and hightailed it down to the sheriff's department.

Birdie was so focused on her computer she didn't look up when I came in. I smiled. I loved her dedication. "Find anything good yet?"

"Hmm? Oh, hi, Princess. No, nothing yet, but I've only begun. We had a few things I had to take care of this morning before I could really get going."

"Well, I have faith in you." I had to. Asking Sin to work his magic was off the table now that I knew the cost. Birdie would have to come through, but I didn't want to put that pressure on her. Not yet anyway. I lifted the envelope. "My dad sent the court order."

"Excellent, let me buzz Hank." She picked up the phone, punched a button and spoke. "Hank, honey, Princess Jayne is here with that CO."

She hung up and he came out of his office a minute later. He glanced at the envelope. "The North Pole legal department moves fast."

"My dad can be very motivating." I handed the envelope over.

"I'm sure." He pulled out the paperwork and scanned it, then nodded. "All right, this will do it."

"So I can go to the house and take all that stuff?"

"Not exactly. All this entails is the snow globe. And it doesn't mean you can have it, just that I have to write up a writ of possession order and serve it to her great-nephew when he arrives notifying him that the globe has been seized. Which I can't do until he's been served. If you can prove Ms. Grimshaw was a winter elf, then it's a different story. But as she's listed as fae, the globe's fate will have to be decided by a supernatural magistrate."

"Oh." I frowned at the anti-climactic-ness of it all. Why did the court order only cover the globe? I could only guess that getting a court order for one thing was faster than having an order drawn up for everything that *might* be in that armoire. I trusted my dad and the elves from legal to know what was best in this situation. I just wished I was taking possession of the thing immediately.

"Also, you may be entitled to the snow globe, but it's in the house that now belongs to Myra's family. Her kin have to be made aware of what's going on."

"I see." I didn't, but supernatural law wasn't something I'd ever studied beyond the basics required for most royals. Not to sound all fancy, but that's why my family *had* a legal department. (Not to mention the people who try to sue Santa Claus. As if that's not going to get you on the naughty list.)

"Don't worry. I'll get Jansen to go over and cordon the house off with police tape. Hopefully, that will be enough for Myra's great-nephew to come here first."

Hopefully? I wasn't crazy about the sound of that. "What if he doesn't? What if he ignores the tape and goes into the house and helps himself to whatever he wants?" That sounded a little panicked even to my ears. I cleared my throat and made myself calm down. "I mean, I'm sure that's not what's going to happen. Just throwing it out there, though."

"Even if he does," the sheriff started, "your father's royal court order takes precedence. Nate can always file for a countermand, but I don't see that happening over a snow globe. I doubt that item is even on his radar. Most relatives are on the lookout for obvious valuables. Jewelry, collectibles, coins, cash, that sort of thing."

Which made perfect sense. I laughed at how silly I'd been. "Of course. Why would he think that snow globe was worth anything? He'll probably take one look at that armoire's contents and think his great-auntie was harboring some silly crush."

"Exactly. And Nate was always a decent fellow when he lived here. Can't imagine he's changed much."

I nodded. I was feeling better about the whole thing. "I'm sure you're right."

Hank gave the papers a little shake. "If you'll excuse me, I want to get Jansen over there."

"Of course, thanks."

He went back into his office as he pulled the radio off his shoulder and called the deputy. He closed the door and I leaned on the reception desk. I think I was still a little freaked out about what Sin had told me earlier. But there was no reason to be. Things were being handled. Birdie was typing away at her computer. The sheriff was taking care of the house situation.

And I had a shop to run.

"Call me if you find anything, Birdie."

She nodded, eyes still on the screen. "Will do, Princess."

I headed for the door. I was about to push it open when Birdie let out a huge gasp.

"How about that!"

I turned around. "What?"

She looked at me, eyes wide and shaking her head. "I think Myra Grimshaw might have been adopted."

"What do you mean 'might have been'?"

"Well, I can't find any records on her earlier than when she was twelve."

I did some quick math. "That would have been 1913, right? What kind of records do you think they kept on kids back then?"

"Good point. But there should be something. Humans aren't the only ones who do genealogies, you know."

"Still, I don't think that necessarily means she was adopted." And even if she was, it wasn't quite the earth-shattering news I'd expected based on Birdie's gasp. Unless…she was actually related to the royal family? Was that even possible? I couldn't imagine it was. "But I guess that could mean she might be a winter elf. Adoptions outside the NP are pretty rare. Any idea who her birth parents were?"

"Not yet. I'll keep digging, though."

"Okay, call me if you find any names. I can have my dad run them through ER and see what comes up."

Birdie's eyes narrowed. "ER?"

"Elf Resources."

"Oh, right. Okay, will do. Have a good day at work."

"You too." I walked back to the shop, a little dejected at how things had gone. I'd expected to come home, snow globe in hand and the matter behind me. Well, as behind me as it could be without knowing why Myra had been obsessed with my family.

As it stood, the matter was at the forefront of my mind. Good thing I had my shift at the store. Since there wasn't much paperwork to do this week, I'd be in the shop with Kip and Juniper, and that would be fun. It would be more like hanging out than work. That would be good.

And it was. The day went by faster than I'd thought possible. We laughed and talked and took care of the few customers who came in, all while slipping back to polish off the doughnuts I'd brought from Sinclair's. Kip went to Howler's to pick up lunch (pulled pork sandwiches with coleslaw and fries), and by the end of the day shift when Buttercup and Holly came in, I'd almost forgotten about Myra and the snow globe.

Almost.

Birdie hadn't called, so I had nothing new to report to my dad. I was pretty aware of that. But there wasn't much I could do about it either.

Juniper was going out with Pete, and Sinclair and I hadn't made any plans, so I spent the evening binge-watching a season of British murder mysteries, snacking on candy corn (I buy out the after-Halloween sales) and playing with Spider.

I probably should have gone for a walk to see the Christmas lights one more time before they were taken down this week, but it got dark so early in the winter that I couldn't muster the energy. The weather had been reasonably nice too. So nice that, before I went to bed, I opened the window a crack for Spider. "Here you go, baby."

He trotted over and hopped up.

"No pushing the screen out," I said to him, giving him my best stern-mother face. I modeled it after the one my mother had always used on me. "Aunt Birdie told me what happened while I was away."

Spider stared up at me with big, round Puss-In-Boots eyes. It was the look he gave me when he knew he was in trouble. Like the time I'd foolishly left a six-pack of toilet paper on the bathroom counter and come home to what looked like a blizzard in my apartment thanks to his shredding abilities.

He blinked up at me. "Spider got new collar."

Classic distraction ploy. "Yes, I know all about that too. And I'm very glad you didn't get hurt or lost or worse. Just be careful when you sit on the windowsill, okay?"

"'Kay. Spider loves Mama."

"I love you too." I bent and kissed his head. "You rascal."

I made sure his food bowls were full, then I went off to bed to read. At some point, I fell asleep with my tablet in my hands. I know this because I woke up to Spider sitting on the tablet, which was on my chest.

"Oof, Spider, you're crushing me." He'd put on a little weight lately. Not surprising, considering how he ate. "And why is it so dark in here? And so cold?"

"Winter has come, Mama."

"I'd say so." I'd also say Spider was picking up too much of what I watched on television. I blinked, trying to see him better, but it was so dang dark. I kept an LED night-light in the bathroom that normally spilled a little soothing blue light into the hall, but I must have forgotten to turn it on.

I climbed out of bed, pulled on my robe and hustled into the living room to shut the window I'd left open. About a yard from the window, my bare feet slipped out from under me.

"Whoa!" I grabbed the edge of the couch to catch myself and realized what I was standing on.

Ice.

I skated to the window and tried to shut it, but it was frozen in place. Just like my feet were about to be if I stood here much longer. There was no ambient light coming from the street, and no light coming from the microwave clock or cable box, meaning my apartment was pitch black. I went to the kitchen to flip a light on, but nothing happened when I hit the switch. This was crazy. What kind of snowmageddon had hit us that the power was out? I didn't even remember the forecast calling for snow.

Putting my hands on the window frame, I used my magic to absorb all of the cold, freezing it in place into myself. I shivered as it passed through me, an incredibly powerful cold unlike anything I could remember feeling in a long time. After a few moments, the window budged.

Absorbing cold was one of my least-used skills, but at the moment, I was glad to have it. I got the window shut and went into the kitchen, feeling my way along the counter until I came to the junk drawer.

I dug around in there for a flashlight. I knew I had one. Kip had given us all one for Christmas. It was some tactical thing that supposedly worked under water or frozen and had some megawatt powerful beam and about three or four settings that were supposed to be useful in emergency situations.

Pretty sure this qualified.

I pushed the button to turn it on and nearly blinded myself. I blinked a few times to get the spots out of my eyes and still couldn't believe what I was seeing. Ice and snow had spilled through the couple inches of open window and halfway into my living room.

No wonder I'd nearly busted my butt. "Snowballs."

Spider sat at the edge of the frozen puddle, batting at it with one paw. The flashlight beam cast his shadow on the living room wall, making him about ten feet tall. "Winter is here, Mama."

"You can say that again."

"Winter is here, Mama."

I snorted, even though there was nothing remotely funny about the mess. At least I had the skills to clean it up. I got my new jar candle lit, this one a Christmas gift from Juniper. It was appropriately scented Sugar Cookie. The smell was incredible.

Then, flashlight in hand, I jogged back to the bedroom and put on sweat pants and a sweat shirt and my new thick wool socks. You guessed it, another Christmas present. They were from my aunt Martha and had been part of a larger package that had included a scarf and hat. Which I might also be putting on if the power didn't return and kick the heat back on soon.

Sure, I was a winter elf, but even we got cold in the right circumstances. And this was one of those, because this chill was more than just your standard winter. It was ice age cold.

"Spider, are you warm enough?" Because Aunt Martha had sent a matching sweater, scarf and hat for Spider as well. No socks, though. Apparently a sweater, scarf and hat were just fine, but socks for a cat were a bridge too far. My family. Adorable. "Do you want to put on the sweater Aunt Martha made you?"

"Mama, Spider already has fur."

"Yes, you do. I just want to make sure you're not getting cold, even with that fur. There's no heat on right now, baby. You tell me if you get chilly, okay?"

"'Kay."

With the flashlight on, I could see my breath, which was a strange thing for a winter elf. My phone buzzed, reminding me that not everything was dead. At least it wasn't for as long as the battery lasted.

I checked the screen. A text from Sinclair.

You're probably still sleeping, but I just got up to find the power out. Looks like we got hit with a major storm. Text me when you're up. I want to know you're okay.

I smiled. That guy. *I'm okay. Up because Spider woke me. No power here either. I think the whole town's out. You okay?*

All good here. Guess I won't be opening today unless power comes back on.

Us either, I texted back. *You think they'll open some shelters? It's really cold.*

Weirdly cold. Yes to the shelters. Humans will need a place to stay warm.

So will the rest of us if the sun doesn't add a few degrees. Maybe not the vampires. They were technically already dead, and that was about as cold as you could get. Sin hadn't suffered too much when Lark had frozen us all at the Black and Orange Ball, so that made me think his necromancer abilities offered him some protection from the cold too.

True. I'm going to the sheriff's department when it's light out.

I'll meet you there.

Good. Save your battery until then. And be safe.

You too. I went to stick the phone in my pocket,

but my sweat pants didn't have any. I carried it back out to the living room and set it on the counter next to the jar candle.

Then, flashlight in hand, I went to the window for a look outside. The window was almost entirely covered with frost.

Not just any frost. Fancy, swirling, feathery lines of it. I stopped in my tracks. That frost looked familiar. But how was that possible? It wasn't. Not here. I laughed it off. Frost was frost. Except I wasn't sure that was true. But I'd never seen a big storm like this anywhere but in the North Pole. It was very possible that big storms just naturally formed that kind of distinct pattern of frost.

I stood on my tiptoes to try to see out above the iced-over part of the window, but I couldn't get high enough. I pulled a dining chair over, got it positioned on a non-icy spot and climbed up on it. I shone the light down to the street one floor below.

Everything the flashlight beam hit glittered white. Everything. The street, the streetlamps, the walls of the buildings. The snow and ice went on as far as I could see in every direction. And the snow flurries were still coming down. The town looked like it had been iced in dazzling, blue-white buttercream. It was beautiful.

And horrifying.

Nocturne Falls was frozen in. And without

power. A shiver ran through me that had nothing to do with the cold.

I tried to be calm. The sun would come up and melt some of this. I hoped. In the meantime, I needed to deal with the small glacier that ran from the window into my living room.

A couple long seconds of thought and I'd formulated a plan. I could absorb the cold from the snow and ice, but that wouldn't do anything about the water that would be left behind, which meant I'd have a small pond in my apartment. That could create more issues, like leaking through the ceiling into the warehouse below. I didn't want my floor ruined or any of the merchandise downstairs to get damaged.

That meant removing the snow and ice while it was still snow and ice. I could do that. I opened the window again. Wide this time. The gust of cold that came in sank through to my bones and put me into overdrive.

I turned toward the mess, held my hands out and focused on levitating it up and out. It creaked as the force of my magic worked to detach it from the floor. It was an eerie, wintery sound that reminded me of the snow cyclones that occasionally came through the NP, but the ice refused to budge.

I dropped my hands for a second and rolled my shoulders. I could do this. I thrust my hands forward again, demanding the ice and snow obey me.

With more unnatural groans of protest, it lifted like a giant shelf of ice. I moved my hands, floating it out the window. With no light to see by, it was impossible to tell how far down to the street it was, but I couldn't just drop the ice for fear of damaging whatever might be in its path. At least there had been no one around, so I felt certain I wasn't about to drop it on anyone's head. I held on to my magical grip and kept lowering it slowly until I heard the crunch of it connecting with something. The sidewalk? I had no idea, but only then did I let go.

The sounds of ice shattering and metal bending filled the unnerving quiet. Nope, not the sidewalk. I cringed, hoping I hadn't demolished someone's car.

This kind of frozen nightmare reminded me of the Black and Orange Ball and the deep freeze my old frenemy Lark had put everyone in so she could mastermind a jewel heist, but this couldn't be Lark's doing. She was in a deep freeze of a different kind. The North Pole Women's Correctional Facility.

This was winter magic all right, but not Lark's, and not the good kind.

Fortunately, my phone wasn't the only thing that didn't need electricity to run. I used the flashlight to find the end table next to my couch. I picked up the snow globe.

If anyone would know what to do in a situation like this, it was my father. As the Winter King, he was technically in charge of winter. And like Spider had pointed out, winter had most definitely arrived.

He answered quicker than I expected. "Hi, honey. You're up late. Or early. What's going on?"

"Daddy!" Apparently being snowed in and powerless made me a little needy. "Something really weird is going on."

He nodded. "Is that why you're talking to me in the dark?"

"Yes! The power is out. There's been a horrible winter storm. The town is completely frozen over."

"The power isn't out in the building, is it?"

"Yes, but hang on. You haven't had any kind of magical malfunction, have you?"

"Are you asking me if I caused the storm?"

"Maybe."

He snorted. "My magic is just fine, thank you."

So much for that.

"Now listen, the building shouldn't be without power. We installed a generator system. It should have kicked on, but if you don't have electricity, then something's wrong. The number for the company who did the work should be in your office files. Maybe they can send someone out to fix it."

"I'm sure they could if we weren't completely

snowed in. I mean completely, Dad. Everything is covered."

He sighed. "Let me think." After a few seconds, he spoke again. "Okay, take me downstairs and let me see if I can figure this out."

"All right, just give me a sec to get everything together." I gathered my flashlight, slipped some shoes on, and grabbed my phone. I held my flashlight and my phone in one hand, and in the other I held the snow globe. Then I remembered something. "Oh man."

"What now?"

I frowned. "I'm going to have to take the stairs. You know, because no electricity means no elevator."

My dad laughed. "A little exercise will be good for you."

"Right," I said. "Spoken like a true parent."

"Don't forget your office key. I can't remember if there's a lock on the generator or not, but if there is, the key for it will either be in your office or it'll be the same as your office key."

"In that case, I'm going to need my purse. I only have two hands." I threw my purse strap over my head and across my body, then stuck my phone and keys into it.

Armed with the flashlight and the snow globe, I left my apartment. The hall was a little spooky. Very quiet and pitch black. Except of course, for my flashlight. But it was casting weird shadows everywhere, and I was already slightly creeped out to begin with.

I made my way to the stairs and pushed through the door. The staircase was worse than the hall. Here the shadows went long and angular, and every sound echoed, making me feel like I wasn't alone in the stairwell. Snow globe clutched against my side, I jogged down to the warehouse, anxious to get off the stairs. I wasn't the kind who ever went to haunted houses, so this was sort of pushing the limits of scary for me.

With great relief, I walked into the warehouse. But the light from my torch turned the racks of inventory into all kinds of strange, monstrous shapes. Why had I never realized what a perfect setting this place was for a slasher movie?

"Hey," my dad said.

I jumped. "Oh, I forgot you were there."

"Sorry, but you looked a little freaked out."

"I am. I don't like being in this much dark. This is not fun."

"Don't worry," my dad said. "We're about to have the lights back on any second now."

"Okay, good." I wondered if he could hear my heart pounding. I was such a wimp. "Where's the generator?"

"It should be in the back corner with the fuse box."

I gave my dad a look. "You seem to think that I know where the fuse box is."

"It's in the utility room."

"Ah, that I know." I walked to the rear corner of the warehouse through the creepy racks of inventory and further into the darkness. If the batteries in this flashlight gave out now, I was going to strangle Kip. Not really. But the thought gave me a sort of morbid comfort.

The utility room was a space that I had never gone into. I passed it briefly, but it was in the far back corner of the warehouse and not one I visited much. I tried the knob. "Locked. Good thing you told me to bring my key. Let's hope it works."

Outside, a low howl rattled against the building as wind funneled down the street. I swallowed and took a breath as I jammed the key in the lock and turned. Thankfully, it opened.

I pushed the door wide and shone my flashlight in. "Ew."

"What's wrong?" my dad asked.

"You didn't tell me it was going to be cobweb central in here."

"This room doesn't get used much, but a few cobwebs aren't going to hurt you."

"It's not the cobwebs that bother me." I gave my dad the side-eye, which I wasn't sure he could see given that he was looking at me through his snow globe back in the North Pole. "It's the venomous spiders that inhabit them I'm worried about."

"I don't think Nocturne Falls has any venomous spiders. You'll be fine." He was trying not to laugh. I could hear it in his voice. And I knew for a fact that there were poisonous spiders in Georgia, but I didn't want to dwell on that. He cleared his throat. "Do you see the generator? Should be in a big green metal box on the floor."

"Yes, I see it. It's about all that's in here except for all the electrical panels on the walls and an old broom." I was thinking about brandishing that broom as a defense against the spiders, but I didn't have enough hands.

"Open it up and let me have a look inside."

"Okay, hang on. I have to put the globe down for a second." I set it on the floor, then unlatched the generator's lid and lifted it with both hands. Weighed a ton. "Wow, that was heavy. Even for me."

I picked the globe back up and aimed it so my dad could see in. I moved the beam of the flashlight as I moved the globe, giving him a good view.

"Hmm. Connections on the battery don't look corroded. All of the wiring looks intact."

"Has this thing ever been tested?"

"It should have been, but I don't know for sure. I wasn't here for the installation. I would assume that the manager at the time wouldn't have signed off on it if they hadn't seen it run."

"Doesn't it need gas? Maybe it's out."

"It's connected to the town's natural gas lines. So there's nothing to fill—lower the globe so I can see where it's connected to the gas line."

"Hang on, it's going to take me a sec to figure out which one the gas line is."

"Should be marked with yellow."

He was right. "Yep, found it." I moved the globe and the flashlight so he could see it.

"There's the problem," he announced. "The gas line is turned off. Twist that knob and open the line and you should have power as soon as it kicks on. But brace yourself, it's going to be loud."

"I can live with loud if it means we have heat and light." I twisted the knob like he told me to, and sure enough, a few seconds later the generator kicked to life.

Loud was an understatement. "I feel like I'm standing in a jet engine," I yelled.

Okay, that was an exaggeration, but after the dead silence of the last half an hour, the sudden noise was a shock to the system. I shut the generator lid, got out of the utility room and closed that door as well. I could hear myself think again.

"You see why we keep it in the utility room?"

"I do. And I can see more than that. Look." I moved the globe around so he could tell that the nighttime lights had kicked on. It was just enough to take away the creepiness.

"Excellent."

"Thanks, Dad." I gave him a big smile and blew him a kiss.

"You're welcome, honey. Let me know how things go, okay? And feel free to close the store until this weather situation is resolved."

"Thanks. Love you and I'll be in touch."

"Love you too. Oh, one more thing." His nose scrunched up. I knew that look. It usually preceded bad news. "The generator will keep your heat and lights on, but it won't power the elevator. Those big hydraulics take too much juice. You'll have to tell the employees that they probably won't be able to run a lot of appliances at once, either."

"We can live without too many extras for a while, but no elevator?" I playfully rolled my eyes and sighed. "I'm going to have to eat more sugar to compensate for all those extra calories burned."

"Do try to hold up." He winked at me, then the snow in the globe settled as his face disappeared.

I double-checked that the utility room door was locked, then tucked the globe in my purse, turned my flashlight off and headed back upstairs. This time the stairs weren't so scary with the emergency lights on. Neither was the hall with the normal low hum of things in the background. Funny, but I'd never really noticed that sound until it was gone.

Spider ran toward me as I walked into my apartment. The kitchen light was on, making the place bright. Spider's tail was up, a sure sign he was happy. "Mama, lights."

"I know, baby. Your grandfather helped me fix that." I laughed. What would my dad think if he knew I was calling him that to my cat?

I turned the kitchen light off, plunging myself into semidarkness again. But with the ambient light that came off the cable box, the coffeemaker, and the light under the microwave, it wasn't that dark at all. It was the evening glow I was used to.

I headed back to my bedroom, happy to see the

bathroom night-light casting its blue gleam into the hall. I went to the window and looked out. The rest of the town was still dark, as far as I could see. Frost edged the corners of the glass here, too, but not as bad as the living room window.

I stood there for a moment, staring into the darkness. There was a faint flicker of light in the distance. What was that? I wasn't sure. But it seemed like it was coming from the residential area. Maybe someone out there had a generator too.

There had to be more in town. Nocturne Falls might be in Georgia, but it was in the mountains and winter storms were definitely a possibility. I couldn't believe the Ellinghams hadn't thought of that when they'd taken over. They'd thought of just about everything else. They were the most prepared vampires I knew.

Vampires. The word swirled around in my head for a moment. There might have been vampires out when this storm had hit. Outside of the Ellinghams and my ex-boyfriend Greyson, the general undead population could go out only after dark.

How fast moving had this storm been? Maybe I was gun shy from the insta-freeze we'd all been subjected to at the Black and Orange Ball, but I couldn't shake the image of some poor, random vampire citizens of Nocturne Falls out there, possibly frozen in place.

If they were still there when the sun came up, they'd die.

I couldn't let that happen. "Snowballs." So much for going back to bed.

With a much beleaguered sigh, I pulled on my boots and my winter coat and buttoned it up. I slung my purse across me again, minus the snow globe, which I returned to its spot on the end table. "Spider, Mama has to go out for a bit. You be a good boy, okay?"

"'Kay, Mama." He curled up on the bed, tucked his tail over his nose and closed his eyes like returning to sleep was the easiest thing in the world.

"Show-off," I muttered as I left.

I was plenty warm after two flights of stairs for the third time, so I was ready to get outside in the cold. But getting the warehouse door open proved a bigger task than I'd expected. Much like my window, it was frozen shut. Where was my favorite summer elf when I needed him? Taking care of his mom, so I really couldn't begrudge him that, but right now, Cooper Sullivan would have come in extra handy. I wouldn't even have given him any grief for breaking up with me, in exchange for him using his heat magic to melt the door open.

But Cooper wasn't here, and this was another job that I was going to have to figure out on my own.

I put my shoulder against the door and pushed. I was stronger than the average human, after all. Not vampire strong, like Greyson, but I could open all my own jars.

There was straining and creaking, but no budging. Apparently, anything that could be frozen shut, was. I planted my hands on the metal and concentrated on absorbing some of the cold so that the ice would melt away.

I shivered as the cold seeped into me. This cold was *really* cold. Almost supernaturally so. When I'd had as much as I could take, I backed up, then rammed my shoulder into the door again. It popped open, tossing me into a large drift that had blown against the building.

All this and I had yet to have any sugar. I lay there for a moment, wondering why I hadn't grabbed a Dr Pepper. I blamed that on lack of sleep.

I got up, brushed myself off and assessed the world around me. Fortunately, I'd had the forethought to tuck the flashlight into my purse and zip it closed, so I hadn't lost it or my phone in the tumble.

Flashlight on, I turned in a slow circle. The sheen of ice coated everything, just like I'd seen from the window, but down here, seeing it up close and personal was something else. Snowdrifts, some reaching as high as the second story, were everywhere. And that big hunk of ice I'd dropped out the window? It had bent the streetlamp.

I frowned, thinking about what that was going to cost. I sighed, sending a puff of frosty breath into the darkness. There'd be time to deal with the damages later. Right now, I needed to make sure no vampires were about to be turned into flame-cicles when the sun came up.

I headed to Main Street, sort of skidding-walking-skating along the sidewalk. It was more of the same—ice and snow and darkness. I stood there and shone the flashlight in both directions. No vampires. No anyone. Didn't mean there wouldn't be someone out here somewhere.

I picked a direction and started walking. I should have asked Sinclair to come with me. I still could, I guess, but I was meeting him at the sheriff's department at dawn. No need for both of us to be out in this cold. Except that I'd rather be with him than by myself. I pulled out my phone. *Headed to the police station early.*

Because I was. I'd just decided that was the place to go. If there were citizens in trouble, they'd know about it. The place never closed. And even if they didn't have power, there would be someone there.

His text came back quickly. *Meet you there. Be safe.*

I smiled. Five words and I already felt less creeped out.

The department did have power, something I realized as I approached. Maybe not full power, but there were lights on in the building. They must have a generator too. Made sense. You'd think places like the sheriff's department, fire station, and hospital would all be equipped with that kind of backup.

Suddenly, the street and store lights around me came to life. Well, not all of them. Only every other street light and none of the little fairy lights that outlined the shops, but they were lit up down both sides of Main. I guessed that only the alternating ones had been turned on because there was only so much power to go around. After my dad telling me our generator couldn't run the elevator, it made sense.

I tried the door of the sheriff's department, but it was locked. I knocked. "Hello? Anyone in there?"

I rubbed away a circle of frost and peered in. There was no one visible.

And then there was. I jerked back as a deputy instantly appeared on the other side of the glass. I knew he hadn't just "appeared"—his speed was a vampire thing. I just hadn't been prepared for it.

He unlocked the door and held it open. "Come on in out of the cold. I'm Deputy Remy Lafitte. Call me Remy. What can I help you with?"

I was happy to go inside. "I'm Jayne Frost, I manage the Santa's Workshop toy store?"

"Sure, I know it. I don't think we've met, but I've seen you around."

He had a nice accent. Southern. Kind of. "Any idea what's going on? How did the lights just come back on?"

"No idea what's going on with this crazy storm, but the lights are back on because the crew working on the main generators must have fixed things."

"Doesn't surprise me the town has generators."

He nodded. "Banks of them."

"In the Basement?"

"Some of them are, yes." Curiosity lit his eyes. "How do you know about that?"

"There's a town employees-only elevator in my warehouse that goes down there. And let's just say I'm the relentlessly inquisitive type."

He laughed. "Is that what brings you to the sheriff's department on this bitter morning, Miss Frost?"

"Not exactly."

"Then what has brought you out?"

"Vampires," I said. That earned me another look. Maybe because he was one. I kept going. "It occurred to me that if this storm came on as suddenly as I think it did, there could be some citizens frozen to the streets out there. And if they're vampires and the sun comes up—"

"Right." His eyes went wide. "If you can stay here and answer the phone, I can check the streets."

My mouth came open in disbelief. "There's no way you can check the whole town by yourself."

"Sure I can. I have the speed and the stamina. And I have Nick Hardwin and Ivan Tsvetkov on speed dial."

Nick was a gargoyle and Ivan was a dragon shifter. Both men, in their other forms, could fly. "You're going to have them check things out from overhead?"

"Yes."

"Brilliant. I'll be happy to answer the phone for you."

Which was how I came to be sitting behind Birdie's desk when she and Sinclair walked in together.

"Hey, you two." I'd been at the station a little over three hours. Thanks to the vending machines and all the loose change in my purse, I'd had three Dr Peppers, a bag of M&M's, two boxes of Junior Mints, and a honey bun. (Which was a sad thing compared to the pastries I was used to from Sinclair's.) Oh, and a granola bar I'd found in the break room, the eating of which proved what I'd always thought about myself. I was not a granola person.

I was, however, still starving. The large Zombie Donuts box in Sinclair's hands was the most beautiful thing I'd seen in a long time. Outside of Sinclair himself, of course.

"Hey, babe." He slid the box onto the counter. "Thought these might be appreciated."

"Does a yeti love fish?"

His brows pulled together. "I'm going to say yes."

I laughed. "They do. They love fish." I wished he'd been able to come sooner, but he'd texted not long after Deputy Lafitte had left to say two of his employees were trapped in their houses due to the ice. Sin had gone to help them. Then, after a text from Birdie, he'd gone to help her with the same problem. Which I supposed was why the two of them were here now, about twenty minutes ahead of sunrise. "How did you get everyone unfrozen?"

"Crow bar. I pried the ice loose from their doors. Then applied some brute strength."

"Nicely done."

"He was a great help," Birdie added as she looked around. "Princess Jayne, are you manning the fort all by yourself?"

"I am, because all the deputies are out helping people. So I'm actually doing your job. And not that well, I'm ashamed to add. The phone's been ringing off the—" It rang as if to prove my point. I groaned. I already had a pile of messages, and my handwriting had gotten progressively worse with each one.

"I'll get it." Birdie hustled around the counter and grabbed the receiver. "Sheriff's department, Birdie Caruthers speaking."

I got out of her way, sliding past her to stand with Sin. He caught me in his arms and hugged me. "You okay?"

I nodded. "Yes, you? You must be exhausted from digging everyone out."

"Nothing more than a good morning workout." He kissed me, short and sweet, but nice all the same. "How's Spider?"

How could I not be crazy about a man who asked after my cat? "He's good. Although you know how I leave the window open a little for him sometimes? I did that last night. You wouldn't believe the mess I woke up to. Ice and snow everywhere."

"You want help cleaning it up?"

I wiggled my fingers at him. "No, I took care of it." I left out the part about the bent streetlamp. "Sugar okay?"

"She got fed. That's all that mattered."

"I hear that."

The radio behind the desk squawked. That had to be Deputy Lafitte. He'd been checking in every so often. Birdie was still on the phone and in the middle of taking a message, so I picked it up. "This is Jayne, go ahead."

"Jayne, this is Remy. I'm off duty and back at my house. Daybreak is just a few minutes away. But I wanted to say it was nice meeting you. And thanks for your help. I found a handful of people who owe you one."

"Just being a good citizen. I'm glad you were able to rescue them."

"Me too. Also, Van got the go-ahead from the

Ellinghams to clear Main Street, so be on the lookout."

"Clear it? How?"

There was laughter in his voice when he answered. "The way only a dragon can."

Just then, a whooshing sound filled the air, and through the windows, we could see a slanted column of bright, focused fire making its way up the street. Clouds of steam billowed up behind, making for a pretty spectacular show. Good thing this was the slowest time of the year and there weren't many tourists in town. "I see him. Nicely done. Enjoy your daysleep."

"Will do. Over and out."

I put the radio back in its holder, then ran to the windows with Sin to watch the rest of Van's flyover. It was incredibly impressive. I'd seen him close-up in his dragon form before. He'd been having some issues shifting due to an injury, but he was healed and that was all behind him now. Of course, a dragon of any size would have been something to see, but Van's dragon was the size of a bus. A big bus.

"Look at that." Sin pointed to where Van had just been. The ice he'd evaporated was now falling back to the ground as snow along with the rest of the snow that was still coming down.

"Yeti poop. That's not good. It's undoing all of his work."

"Not totally. It'll be easier for the plows to clear snow instead of ice."

"I suppose that's true."

Hank Merrow, the sheriff, came in through the back door. Nick Hardwin was right behind him. They stood there for a bit, stomping snow off their boots. The sheriff gave Sin and me a nod, but spoke to me. "Miss Frost. Thanks for helping out. Remy told me."

"No problem, I was happy to do it. Hi, Nick."

Nick nodded in response.

I spoke to the sheriff again. "How's it going out there?"

The sheriff shook his head. "The roads in and out of town are impassible, but we've decided to let them stay that way for a bit. No need for any more tourists to get stuck here until this weather quits."

"Good thing it's a slow time of year. What about businesses that need restocking?"

"We're hoping that can wait a few days."

Sin shrugged. "If I'm not open, I don't need supplies."

"True. And we don't rely on trucks, so my shop is good. Anything else happening?"

The sheriff grunted and looked at Nick.

I wasn't sure what that meant, but I wasn't one to stay ignorant if I could help it. "What does that mean?"

Nick glanced at the sheriff. The sheriff's mouth

firmed into a hard line. "Let's go into the conference room and talk."

Sin squeezed my hand. "I'll wait out here."

"No," I said, tugging him toward the room with me. "Come along."

The sheriff cleared his throat like I should rethink that.

"It's okay," I said. "I'm sure it's nothing Sinclair can't hear."

"All right then."

We headed into the conference room and sat. Sheriff Merrow came in last and was about to shut the door when Birdie came in.

He looked at her. "Don't you need to answer the phones?"

"The service can pick them up."

"Birdie, we're in the middle of a crisis here. The phone needs to be answered. I promise to fill you in when we're through, but I need someone with your capabilities out there making sure things are handled properly."

I tried not to take that as a comment on my *lack* of capabilities, but I wasn't too proud to admit when I sucked at something.

"And there are doughnuts out there," Sinclair added.

Birdie gave that a few seconds of thought. "You're right, Hank. I'm on it. But you'd better tell me what's going on when you're done."

"I will. Also, Cruz and Blythe are on duty, and we've got Titus and the fire department out there, but call some of the regular volunteers and see who else is available. We need all the help we can get."

"Okay." She left.

My stomach rumbled. "I wish I'd grabbed a doughnut."

Sinclair got up. "I'll get you one. Anyone else?"

"I'll take one, thanks," Nick said.

"I will too." The sheriff rubbed his forehead. "Left the house before I could eat."

"Be right back." Sinclair left.

I turned to the sheriff. "So what's going on?"

He sat back. "It's Nick's story to tell."

Nick rested his hands on the table. "I was doing the flyover, looking for anyone trapped by the weather, and I went over a house that looked very different than the rest. It was hard to tell exactly what I was seeing in the dark. I can see just about as well as any supernatural at night, but with the snow swirling around, visibility was tough and I was focused on finding people, not patterns in the snow. I went lower for a better look."

He took a moment. "The house below me was almost completely devoid of snow and ice, unlike every other house I'd flown over. And more than that, the snow around it looked like it had cratered."

I frowned. "What do you mean, cratered?"

He flattened his hand on the table. "Like the house had been dropped into the snow and blown the loose, top layer away. It was all pushed out from the house in sort of a regular pattern."

I had no idea what that meant. "How odd."

"Very," Nick said.

Sinclair came in carrying the box of doughnuts. He opened the lid and put the box in the center of the table, then took the seat next to me. "What did I miss?"

The smell of sugar instantly made me happier.

Sheriff Merrow took a doughnut. "Nick found a house during his flyover that had very little ice or snow on it and has a weird pattern in the snow around it. Only one like it he saw."

"Strange," Sin said.

"Totally." I grabbed my favorite, the Dr Pepper doughnut, knowing Sin had put it in the box especially for me. "Maybe it's just a side effect of how quickly things froze over."

Half of the sheriff's glazed doughnut was already gone. "Have you ever seen anything like that in the North Pole?"

"No. Not that I can think of."

Nick took a doughnut. "Could you create something like that with your kind of magic?"

"Sure, I suppose I could. It wouldn't be that hard, really. It's just a pattern in the snow, right?

91

But who would have done it to that house? Because I didn't."

"We know you didn't," the sheriff said. "But someone, or something, did, and because of the house it's at, it raises some questions."

A weird feeling filled my stomach. "It's Myra's house, isn't it?"

He nodded. "And we'd like you to come with us when we go back inside."

They were right about the pattern. It looked exactly as if the house had been picked up and dropped, causing the snow to fluff out around it in a kind of flower petal effect. It was pretty, actually. But the strangeness of it, and the strangeness of Myra's house being the only building in town that wasn't plastered with snow and ice, made it hard to admire.

The furls of snow extended out almost to the sidewalk, which was where Sheriff Merrow, Sinclair, and I stood. Nick had gone back to work helping free people and businesses from the grip of this weather.

And even though the sun was up, the day remained gray and windy, and the flurries showed no signs of letting up. The plows were working overtime and still falling behind. I pulled my scarf a little tighter and was thankful that both the sheriff and Sin had put snow chains on their tires.

I stared at the lines of swirled snow extending from the house. I imagined they'd been sharper before they'd been covered with a fresh layer of powder. "I almost hate to walk through it."

The sheriff opened the gate in the picket fence and strolled through, his boots destroying the pattern. "That help?"

I snorted. "Yes." I trailed after him, then Sin after me.

We stomped our feet off on the porch. I looked around. "I thought you sent Deputy Jansen over here to put police tape up. So Myra's great-nephew wouldn't go into the house."

The sheriff grunted. "Must have come down with the snow." He glanced over the porch railing. "Don't see it, though."

I didn't either. "It could be under the snow." It had covered everything. "Wait, there's a piece of it."

I bent and fished out a small section of yellow police tape. It looked like it had been chewed through. "I wonder what happened to the rest of it."

"Maybe it blew away." The sheriff unlocked the door and grunted again as he went in. "The great-nephew, or someone, has been here."

I walked in behind him. The house was as cold

inside as it was out. "Wow. I'd say. If not him, then maybe looters."

The place, which had been neat as a pin yesterday, looked like a whirlwind had blown through. Cabinets and drawers were open, papers strewn about, and knickknacks tumbled about. The kitchen was just the same. Even the fridge was open. Although there didn't appear to be anything edible inside other than condiments.

Sin let out a whistle. "What a mess."

The sheriff took a long look around. "But there's a method to this chaos. Whoever was here was looking for something."

"Then I need to go to the basement." I headed in that direction, practically galloping down the stairs. "Son of a nutcracker."

The cabinet was wide open. And the snow globe lay shattered on the concrete floor, its glass in a hundred pieces. The water that had been inside was now frozen in a puddle the size of a dinner plate.

The faint smell of marsh permeated the room. Like seafood on the verge of going bad. Weird. I let out a sigh as Sin and Sheriff Merrow joined me. "So much for that. At least I can return what's left to my dad. You think it was accidental?"

"Hmm." The sheriff sighed and clicked the radio on his shoulder. "Birdie, get me Jansen."

I glanced at him. "You think the deputy knows something?"

"He was acting squirrely when he returned from taping this place."

Birdie came back with a, "Ten-four."

The sheriff's attention shifted to the shelves around us. He picked up one of the jars of preserves. The jar was empty, but very messy with gobs of jam stuck to the outside. "Whoever was in here must have a sweet tooth."

I turned to look. Every single jar of preserves had been cleaned out. At least, the ones that remained were empty. I could have sworn there were jars missing. Some of the jars were broken. Most lay on their sides, sticky with the remains of the jam they'd held. "It could be Nate. Especially if he's related to Myra. Winter elves love sweets."

"*If* she's a winter elf," the sheriff added. "But he wouldn't be. He's her great-nephew, not her grandson."

"Even so, he'd been traveling and was tired. That jam might have seemed like the perfect pick-me-up." It was the only thing I could come up with.

One of the sheriff's brows went up as he gave me an odd look. "You ever eat jam straight out of the jar, Miss Frost?"

That felt like a terribly personal question. "Maybe."

He looked at the jar in his hand, then the stairs, then back at me. "You wouldn't go up to the kitchen and grab yourself a spoon? Maybe toast some bread and slather it on a few slices?"

I shrugged. "Maybe. Maybe not. A hungry winter elf can do a lot of strange things in the name of that hunger."

Sin chuckled under his breath.

The sheriff put the empty jar back on the shelf and let the winter elf comment go. "I'll take your word on that." He put his hands on his belt, then turned to look into the cabinet. "Anything else gone?"

I studied it a second. The little piece of crystal was still there. So was the commemorative cup. And the stacks of papers and the trinket boxes. "As far as I can tell, the snow globe is all that was moved."

"All right." He gave me a little nod. "You want those broken pieces, you can take them."

"Even though there's been no magistrate decision?"

"I'll handle it." His radio squawked with an incoming call.

"This is Deputy Jansen." He sounded nervous.

The sheriff answered. "Deputy, you know anything about the broken snow globe at Myra Grimshaw's?"

"Um, about that…" There was an audible gulp. "I'm real sorry, Sheriff. I only wanted to look at it and it just slipped. I didn't mean to drop it."

The sheriff's expression went stony. "My office. Later."

"Yes, Sheriff."

He sighed as he let go of the radio. "That answers that. I'm very sorry, Miss Frost. If you tell me what that globe was worth, the department can reimburse you."

"Getting the pieces back is plenty." I had a feeling that's all my dad would care about. "And don't worry about it being broken. Could have happened to any of us." I felt oddly happy about it. After all, a broken snow globe was an unusable snow globe. It seemed to me the threat of it falling into the wrong hands had been nullified by Deputy Jansen's fortuitous accident. Unless there were more snow globes in the wild that shouldn't be. I needed to check on that with my dad, too.

Sinclair glanced around the room. "Still no telling what caused that weird pattern around the house."

"Pretty sure Jansen isn't to blame for that," the sheriff said. "Best go look around upstairs a bit."

While they talked, I grabbed an old copy of the Tombstone, the local Nocturne Falls paper, from a stack on one of the shelves and crouched down to put the remains of the snow globe into it. I wasn't sure if returning it to my dad mattered anymore now that it was broken, but I figured it would at least wrap the issue up.

I gingerly pinched the first shard of glass and—nothing. It didn't budge. I gave it a wiggle. Still nothing. Not even a crack in the ice it was frozen to. "Huh."

"What's that?" Sin asked.

I stood up empty handed. "That snow globe puddle is *really* frozen to the floor. Maybe the cement is super cold because there's nothing beneath it but ground. I'm going to have to use a little magic to get this free."

I reached my hand out to melt the ice, throwing a burst of power at it. The magic bounced right back at me, sending a shock wave through me and knocking me off my feet.

Sin caught me as I tumbled backward. "Whoa there, you okay?"

"Yeah, thanks." I held on to him as I straightened. A small trickle of magical energy pulsed down my spine and made me shiver. Talk about weird. My ears were ringing. Like the sensation was still rattling around in my head.

"What happened?"

I shrugged as I studied the ice puddle. "I'm not sure. It's like my magic recoiled at me. Then went through me."

The sheriff came down two steps. "Has that ever happened before?"

"No." My knees buckled, but I still had hold of Sin. "Really took the stuffing out of me."

Sinclair's arms went a little tighter around me. "I've got you, babe."

"Something's going on here." Sheriff Merrow squeezed the radio on his shoulder. "Birdie, come in again."

"I'm here, Hank."

"Which deputy is closest to Myra Grimshaw's?"

She was quiet a second. "Besides Jansen?"

"Yes."

"Jenna."

"Send her over here."

"Roger that. Oh, also, Nate Grimshaw just called. He's stuck outside of town at the Pinehurst Inn until the roads are passable."

The sheriff spoke to us. "That means we won't be able to serve him until we can reach him." Then he squeezed the radio again to answer Birdie. "Call the proprietor. Find out what time he checked in and let me know."

"On it."

The sheriff looked at us. "Sinclair, get Miss Frost home, will you?"

"Absolutely." He looked at me. "You should probably get some rest."

"I'm fine." Maybe not fine, but I wasn't about to keel over dead or anything.

"Even so," the sheriff said. "I'd feel better if you took it easy today. I'm going to stay here until my deputy comes, then she and I are going to secure this house. It's officially off-limits until we know what in blazes is going on here. Then I plan on having a talk with Mr. Grimshaw."

"Well, I'm going to have another talk with my dad when I get home."

"Good." The sheriff hooked a thumb on his utility belt. "I think that's an excellent idea."

A short while later, Sin pulled his SUV to the curb outside the warehouse. I was really glad my dad had okayed keeping the shop closed. I was beat from running on so little sleep. And maybe also from the weird, magical whiplash.

"Look at that," Sin said. "The weight of the snow and ice bent that lamp pole."

"Yeah, about that...that's not storm damage. Not the way you might think."

He looked at me. "What then?"

I told him about levitating the mini-glacier out of my apartment and accidentally crunching the pole.

He shrugged. "It can be fixed. C'mon, let's get you upstairs and into bed."

My brows shot up. "Shouldn't you at least buy me dinner first?"

He laughed. "To sleep."

I grinned. "I know." We'd agreed to take things slow, and I was happy about that. Getting involved too fast could end up with my heart in as many pieces as that snow globe. And yes, I was a little hesitant after Cooper and Greyson, but then, who wouldn't be?

"All right, let's get you settled, make sure everything is okay, and then I'm going to run home. I need to check on my shop and Sugar."

"Is your store on the grid that got emergency power from the town generators?"

"Yes, and that emergency power is great, but it's not enough to do much more than keep the walk-ins going and some heat on."

"Our generator does a little more than that, but it's not enough to power the elevators. I'm thankful I don't live on the third floor."

He snorted, and I remembered he lived on the second and didn't have an elevator at all. I turned toward him. "Hey, my couch pulls out to a sleeper. Why don't you pack a bag and bring Sugar over here? At least until they get the main power back on. Which will probably be tomorrow. What do you think?"

His eyes narrowed like he was considering it. "You really think you're ready to shack up with me?"

I laughed. "It's not shacking up. It's conserving energy. Pooling resources. Making the best of a bad situation with neighborly kindness."

He was trying not to laugh. "Neighborly kindness, eh? Why do I get the feeling you're going to expect me to cook?"

I pursed my lips. "Um, maybe because you're so much better at it? So yeah, bring food."

"Oh, my sweet Jayne. Never change." He hopped out of the car and came around to open my door and help me out.

We went inside and trudged up the steps slower than I'd hoped, but as it turned out, that magical blow had definitely weakened me. So much so that he insisted on carrying me up the last flight and into my apartment.

He put me on the couch, fixed me a cup of hot chocolate, then kissed me on the forehead. "I'll be back as soon as I can. If you need anything, call me, okay?"

"Okay."

"And try to get some rest."

"I will, but I have some texts to send and calls to make."

"After that then."

I felt very well looked after. "Take that key by the door. The one with the Christmas tree keychain. It's for the warehouse door. Then you can come and go as you please."

"Thanks. See you in a bit." He grabbed the key, blew me a kiss and slipped out.

I would have loved to nap until he got back, but I really did need to take care of a few things. First, I texted my employees that the store would be closed until the weather improved.

That also meant that dinner at the Poisoned Apple this evening was canceled. That was a bummer, but we could do it another time. I'd still make sure everyone got their bonus check.

Second, I had to call my dad. I leaned over, picked up the snow globe from the end table and gave it a shake.

My mom answered. "Hi, honey. Oh, Jaynie, you look tired. What's wrong?"

I explained to her what was going on and how long I'd been up.

"No wonder you look beat."

"Don't worry, Dad said I could keep the shop closed until this power outage is over, so I'll be napping as soon as I talk to him. Where is he, by the way?"

"Just coming in from the stables. He and Uncle Kris were meeting with the stable master about new tack for the reindeer." She glanced off screen. "Honey, it's Jayne."

My dad leaned in and kissed my mom, then took over the chair as she vacated it. She waved over his shoulder. "Talk to you soon, honey. Get some rest now."

"I will. Love you, Mom."

"Love you, Jaynie." I saw her shake her head at my father. "Jack, you smell like manure."

He rolled his lips in to keep from laughing. "I might have stepped in some."

"And you're still wearing your boots? Oh, for the love of—" She leaned back into view. "Don't be in a rush to get married, honey. It just means your house never stays clean."

My father slanted his eyes at her. "Now, Klara, I don't think I tracked anything in."

"This floor is definitely going to have to be mopped," I heard her say.

He looked at me again and shook his head. At least he had the good sense to look sheepish. "Your mother's a little mad at me because I ate half of the cupcakes she made for the book club." He shrugged. "I didn't know they were being saved."

"They had books on them," my mother yelled back. "Why would I make cupcakes with books on them for you?"

I chuckled. My parents' fights were rare and barely constituted fights, but I had my father's sweet tooth, so I understood how he'd gone wrong. "Well, I'm sure you didn't mean to eat the wrong cupcakes."

He sighed and small tendrils of ice vapor curled into the air. "I didn't. But enough about that. What's going on there?"

"Besides this ice age we're living through, there's a little something else to report. The snow globe that was in Myra Grimshaw's house? It got broken. Purely by accident. I don't know if you want the pieces back or you just want me to—"

"It's broken?" The sharpness of his voice made my brows go up.

"Yes, in about a hundred—"

"Did that globe have a red velvet ribbon tied around it?" His expression had gone from relaxed to serious in a split second.

"Yes, why? What's going on?"

He muttered a few choice words before answering my questions. "I was able to locate a globe that went missing. It's old news. Or should be. Forty-two years ago, we were working on a new version of the snow globe technology. Trying to combine communications with transportation. We couldn't get it right. Still haven't. Anyway, the globes were too buggy to put into daily use and eventually they were scrapped. They're all still in storage. All but the one that went missing."

Buggy magic might explain the shock I'd gotten, but I wasn't sure why my dad was so bothered by it. "So that's the one Myra had? Well, it's not missing anymore."

"Jayne, those globes were unstable. There's a reason they were shelved."

I nodded. "Right, I get that. But this one isn't an issue anymore. It's in about a hundred pieces. It's also frozen to the floor of Myra's basement, but as soon as this deep freeze is over, I should be able to collect them and send them back to you."

He rubbed the bridge of his nose. "This is...not good."

"Can you elaborate? How not good is it?"

"There's an excellent chance that breaking that globe opened a portal between the North Pole and Nocturne Falls. It's very likely why your weather turned so sharply. The North Pole is spilling through."

I thought about that. I wasn't sure when Jansen had broken the globe yesterday, but the timing seemed right. If he'd broken it in the late afternoon, which was what I was guessing, then the portal could have opened, and the North Pole weather would have started leaking in. It seemed reasonable that the ice and snow in town now could have built up that much overnight. Winter magic was a powerful thing.

With a nod, I answered, "I knew it felt like winter elf magic and not an ordinary storm." Maybe the opening of the portal had created that weird pattern in the snow around the house. Like a small sonic boom of magic. But that couldn't be. The snow had to have been there first. "But is it really that bad? I mean, it's just snow and ice. Once I get the portal closed, it should all go away. Right?"

The look on my dad's face didn't inspire confidence. "Yes, it should. However, I don't think closing that portal is going to be easy."

"Well, I can tell you I tried to absorb the cold out

of it so the ice around it would melt, and it shocked me pretty good. Kind of threw my magic back at me."

Concern filled his eyes. "Are you okay?"

"A little light-headed, but fine." I smiled to show just how fine I was. "But if magic won't work, I'll melt it the old-fashioned way. Heat." If only Cooper were here. He could use his magic to turn that ice puddle into slush in a heartbeat.

"I don't think it will respond to that. Think about when you create something with your power. Our ice is pretty impervious to heat."

He was right. The things I could make out of ice and snow weren't like normal ice and snow. They were much, much more durable.

"And complicating things is the magic of the North Pole has now mixed with the magic of Nocturne Falls. This is brand-new territory. I'll have R&D get to work on it, but in the meantime, keep people away from that basement and that portal. There's no telling what might come through."

I frowned. "Come through? Dad, it's a broken snow globe. That puddle isn't any bigger than a dinner plate. And how could anything come through a communications device?"

"It couldn't, if this was a standard snow globe."

"But it's one of those experimental ones. Right, you mentioned that. What does that mean, exactly, in terms of capabilities?"

He shook his head slowly. "I wish I knew. And that unknown was a big part of why we shelved those units. I can tell you this much, that red velvet ribbon that was around the base? That wasn't any red velvet ribbon. Those were cut from a Santa's Bag."

I sat back, a new chill creeping up my spine. "I thought…nothing living has ever successfully been sent through a Santa's Bag."

"Nothing has. That wasn't the case with these snow globes." His jaw set with resigned firmness. "Be careful, Jayne. That's all I'm saying."

After my dad and I hung up, I sat on the couch just staring into space and thinking. The North Pole was an amazing place. It was filled with more wonders than you could imagine. Ice caves that glittered like jewels. A sky that lit up with the most amazing aurora borealis. A town that looked like it was built from gingerbread. There was magic everywhere. But like all things, there were two sides. Even to the North Pole.

Mischief and mayhem existed in the North Pole, just like they did everywhere else. But the mischief and mayhem that live in the NP aren't like anything you'd find in the mortal world. The presence of darkness wasn't a subject winter elves spoke much about, except maybe to their children when parents wanted to get them to do their homework, or eat their vegetables, or go to sleep already.

Don't be fooled, though. All magic had a dark side. Some was darker than others. And in the land of snow and ice, there were some fearful things.

We have glacier goblins and frost giants. Ice serpents. Polar tempests, a sort of living winter tornado. The occasional wendigo, an absolutely terrifying creature that lived in the most secluded depths of the polar forests.

And there were some things that were less fearful and more just flat-out bothersome. Swarms of snow flies. Blizzard badgers, whose only purpose seemed to be to get into the trash. Krampers, a kind of burrowing worm that weakened ice sculptures and destroyed snowmen.

But then there were the yetis.

Yetis were a mix of fearful *and* bothersome, with a few other adjectives thrown in. And let me get one thing straight right now. They were not the abominable snowmen that the human world would have you believe. Oh, they're abominable all right. But not in the kind of way human mythology had painted them.

For one thing, they're not these lumbering, eight-foot creatures. They're fast. Very fast. And small. About the size of a four-year-old. And just as easy to reason with. Which was to say not at all.

In fact, they're a lot like four-year-olds in several ways. They abhorred discipline. They fought with each other constantly. They're always getting into things they weren't supposed to. Which was why they were usually covered in something sticky. And they were not house broken. They also had short attention spans and were easily distracted, except when they wanted something. Then they were mercilessly focused.

They also found farts and burps to be the height of comic genius.

But I would be remiss if I didn't mention the ways in which they differed from four-year-olds. They smelled bad. (That one maybe wasn't so different.) They had mites in their fur. They loved raw fish. And rolling in garbage. Or dead things. They also had pointed, needle-sharp teeth and dagger-like talons, which they were quick to use.

And they wielded winter magic.

The good news in all this was that they were also generally very shy. They tended to run in packs and stick to the deepest, darkest sections of the polar forests, hiding among the pines and making their snow forts far away from any possible elf interaction.

They would occasionally venture into the outskirts of town, but there had to be a strong lure. During the salmon runs, for example. Or when the sugar pines had been tapped and the juice was being boiled down for syrup. The smell of that even used to wake me up with a smile on my face.

Other than those rare moments, we didn't see

them much. Which was a good thing considering that they also had unbelievable appetites. Like a cross between a goat and piranha, my dad once said.

Oh, they don't eat people. Or pets, as far as I knew. But anything else that wasn't nailed down was fair game.

All of that just meant I still needed to make sure Myra's house was a no-go zone. I called the sheriff's department and filled Birdie in on what I'd found out from my dad and how the house now more than ever needed to be cordoned off. "I know Sheriff Merrow said he and Deputy Blythe would do it, but this is a dire situation."

"Don't worry about it one bit, Princess. I'll run out there on my way home tonight and make sure things are locked up tight."

"I hate for you to go out of your way, Birdie. This isn't the kind of weather anyone needs to be doing extra driving in."

"Myra's is only a couple blocks away from my place. It's no inconvenience."

"Well, I appreciate that." That gave me some peace of mind that things would be okay until my dad and his Research and Development department could figure out how to close the portal.

"Of course! Now you rest up. Hank told me you had a little trouble at the house with your magic."

"I'm resting, I promise." We said goodbye and hung up.

A second later, Spider crawled onto my lap and leaned his face in toward mine until our noses touched. "Mama sick?"

Amazing what he picked up on. "No, baby. Just need a little rest. And guess what? Sinclair is coming back to stay with us for a little bit and he's bringing Sugar."

Spider's tail went up. "Spider likes Sugar."

"I know you do. You two can have all kinds of fun together. It'll be like a kitty vacation." Although I didn't know what a cat would need a vacation from.

I was just nodding off when I heard a knock on the door that was followed by, "Hey, babe, it's me."

Sin was back.

I almost yelled for him to come in, then I realized he'd have his hands full. I put Spider on the cushion beside me and got up to get the door. My head was only faintly buzzy. The worst of the magical backlash was gone.

I opened the door. Sure enough, Sin's arms and hands were loaded. He had Sugar in her carrier in one hand, a duffel bag slung over his shoulder, and two fabric grocery bags brimming with food in the other hand. "My boyfriend, the supernatural pack mule."

He grinned as he came in. "I didn't want to make two trips."

"Stairs too much for you?" I teased.

He put the carrier down and let Sugar out, then set the rest of his bags on the kitchen counter. "No, I just didn't want to have to leave you again." He pulled me into his arms. "How are you feeling?"

"Almost normal. Which is about as normal as I get."

"Tell you what. You take a nap and I'll make us some brunch. What do you think?"

I think I was being spoiled, and I was okay with that. "Seems decadent to take a nap on a work day."

He kissed my forehead, then went into the kitchen to unpack his bags. "Extenuating circumstances."

"I guess." I went back to the couch. A nap sounded pretty awesome, actually. But so did food. That one doughnut and all that vending machine junk wasn't really holding me. "What's for brunch?"

"House special."

"Which is?"

"Whatever I can make up from the stuff I brought."

I laughed. "Okay, I'm not picky."

"Probably why we're dating." He winked at me. "Really, it's one of your best qualities."

"Sweet talker." I put an old movie on, covered myself with the throw off the back of the couch and snuggled in. "Don't let me sleep past brunch."

He twirled a frying pan by its handle. "I won't."

And he didn't. A while later, he woke me up

with the most beautiful plate of food. My apartment smelled amazing. I blinked at the plate in his hand as I sat up. "That came out of my kitchen?"

"It did." He set the plate down on the coffee table, then joined me on the couch with a plate of his own. He'd already set out silverware, napkins, and glasses of juice.

"I had no idea that space was capable of eggs Benedict and home fries." The man was incredible. There was even a little sprig of red grapes on the side.

A bell went off. He put his plate on the coffee table. "That would be the apple turnovers."

I pinched myself to make sure I wasn't still dreaming. I wasn't. I watched him take the pastries out of the oven and got a little glimpse into what a future with Sin might be like.

Looked pretty good, I had to say.

He came back and sat beside me. "They need to cool a bit. Shall we dig in?"

"Absolutely."

The food tasted better than it looked, which was hard to believe. At one point during brunch, Spider and Sugar tore through the living room, around the kitchen island, then back into the bedroom, leaving Sin and me in a fit of laughter. They were clearly enjoying their time together as much as we were.

When we were finished, I reached for his empty plate. The least I could do was clean up.

He stopped my hand. "What are you doing?"

"You cooked, so I'll clean. It's only fair."

"You need to rest after that jolt. I've got this. Plus, I'm the guest. I need to pull my weight."

"One, you already pulled your weight by cooking that meal. And two, that's sort of the opposite of how being a guest works. And three, I'm fine."

He took both plates into the kitchen. "You might feel fine, but I still think you should rest. A day of relaxing on the couch, watching movies, and taking it easy isn't going to hurt you."

I leaned back and kicked my feet up on the coffee table. I really did feel fine, but I knew that there was no point in arguing with him. And really, to what end? We couldn't go anywhere anyway, and my dad had told me to close the shop, so I decided to just enjoy the downtime. Still a weird feeling, but I was sure that weirdness would soon wear off. "Are those apple turnovers still in play?"

He laughed and shook his head. "They absolutely are. I just need to ice them. And not to ask a dumb question, but with or without cinnamon-bourbon ice cream?"

"Did you make ice cream while I was asleep?"

"No, it's from I Scream." He rinsed a bowl in the sink. "I had a pint of it in my freezer. I figured we might as well eat it before the power went out again and it melted."

"Sounds like a plan. Yes to the ice cream. And yes to you leaving those dishes for later and joining me over here. I have a dishwasher. No reason to hand wash all that stuff."

He put a pan in the sink, then lifted his hands in surrender. "Okay, let me get the turnovers and ice cream served up, and I'm on my way."

We spent the afternoon in the most wonderful and laziest way possible. Right there on the couch, snacking our way through two On Demand movies that we'd both missed in the theaters, then finding a channel that was running a *Twilight Zone* marathon.

When we weren't noshing, his arm was around me, or we were cuddled up close. We laughed and talked a little, but mostly we just enjoyed the rarity of a day off together. Even if it had been brought on by less than ideal circumstances.

Sugar and Spider joined us on the couch too. After all that playing, they'd worn themselves out. It was nice. I don't think it had anything to do with the jolt of magic I'd taken, but I felt so blissful it was like I was still light-headed, but in a good way. The day wound down with no sign of the snow letting up, but when I looked out the window that evening, more of the town was lit up than had been before. I took that as a good omen. The generators were doing their thing, and this would all be over soon.

Sin yawned before I did, but that was

understandable. The man got up early, so it made sense that he'd crash before me. Except I was ready for bed too. Despite having a day off, I was fine with turning in before my normal bedtime. All that lack of sleep had caught up with me.

I helped him pull out the bed from the couch and get it set up, then I got myself ready for bed. We kissed good night, and I went off to my bedroom.

I left the door open. There was no other option. Spider would have yowled his head off if he didn't have access to the bedroom, and his litter box was in the bathroom, so there was no shutting him in with me.

But it was no biggie. I was safe with Sin. The man had already saved my life once. If he turned out to secretly be a serial killer, he was better at hiding things than the Easter Bunny.

I read a little, but my eyes were soon drifting shut. I turned my tablet off, stuck it on my nightstand and rolled to my side to sleep.

And I did. At least until my phone rang at six a.m.

"Hmm, hello?" I was too bleary-eyed to look at the caller ID.

"Miss Frost, this is Sheriff Merrow. Sorry to wake you, but I believe that answers my question."

"Huh, what?" I rubbed at my face, trying to figure out what was going on.

119

"I'm looking for Birdie. She's not answering her cell or house phone, and there was no answer at her door this morning."

"Birdie?"

"Yes."

I was a little more awake now. "I haven't seen her. Maybe…" I wasn't sure it was my place to say what I was about to say, but I wasn't entirely alert and my judgment was iffy. "She might be at Jack's. What with the power out and all. Two is warmer than one."

He grunted. Which was when I grasped what I'd just said to the sheriff about his beloved aunt.

I was now completely awake. "I just mean, Sinclair stayed over here because his building didn't have as much power as mine does, but not in my—that is, he slept on the couch, and I thought maybe Birdie had stayed at Jack's or he stayed at her place, probably on the couch, too, and that's why—"

The sheriff cleared his throat. "She did mention something about going to see him. But she ought to answer her cell no matter where she was. Sorry to wake you."

The line went dead. But right before it had, I realized it was possible to hear embarrassment in a werewolf's voice.

I snickered as I put the phone down and stretched.

Mmm. The scent of coffee reached my nose. That put a smile on my face as I got out of bed, put on my robe and slippers and headed for the kitchen. Only as I was walking through the living room did I remember that I hadn't done a thing to my hair. Probably looked like I had a yeti clinging to my head, but well, it was high time Sin understood what he was getting into.

He was at the stove cooking. He was in pajama pants and T-shirt and looked way better than anyone had a right to at this hour. Sweet fancy Christmas, that was a sight to wake up to. I slid onto one of the stools at the island. "Morning."

He turned around, smiling at me. "Morning, beautiful."

I ran a hand through my hair. My fingers got tangled on a knot. I yanked them free. "I'm not sure I should enjoy how convincingly you lie."

With a soft chuckle, he held up a cup. "Coffee?"

"Yes, please."

He filled the mug and brought it to me. "You look adorable. Despite whatever that is on your head."

I laughed. Today was going to be a good day. Even if I had accidentally ratted out Birdie's extracurricular activities to her nephew.

Sin brought me a plate of French toast next. "Want to take a drive over to the shop with me after breakfast? I just want to check on it and

121

the apartment. Make sure everything's okay."

"I'd love to."

"Great." He brought over a second plate and sat next to me. His gaze went up to my hair one more time. "This is a brand-new side of you."

"Rethinking things, huh?"

His eyes lit with unbridled amusement. "Just wondering if I should have gotten you a brush for Christmas instead of that jacket."

As soon as breakfast was over, we were in Sinclair's doughnut-scented SUV (a side effect of his deliveries), crawling through the streets of Nocturne Falls. Any reasonable speed was impossible since the roads were thick with fresh snow and more was being added by the minute. I had a feeling the snowplows had given up. At this pace, the normally ten minute trip to his shop would take us forty-five minutes. I didn't really care, though. Spending all this time with him was a real treat.

Sin peered up through the windshield. "It has to stop snowing at some point."

I pointed my hands at the road. "You want me to see if I can do a little something about it?"

"That seems like it would require a lot of magic on your part, and I don't want you wearing yourself out. Besides, it's not coming down so hard

I can't see. Just wondering how much more of this we're in for."

"I wish I could tell you. Winters in the North Pole are much more controlled than this. Mostly because my dad's in charge of controlling them." I sat back. "At least we're in no rush. Take your time."

"I will."

My phone rang. I dug it out of my coat pocket and checked the caller ID. I didn't recognize the number, but I wasn't going to screen calls considering the current state of emergency in town. "Hello?"

"Princess Frost?" The male voice rumbled through the receiver. "It's Jack Van Zant."

"Hi, Jack. Please, just call me Jayne." That was Birdie's influence right there. "Everything all right in your end of town?"

"Not exactly. Have you seen Birdie?"

The little hairs on the back of my neck stood up. "No, I thought she was with you. I take it she's not?"

"No. She's not with Hank or Titus or Bridget either."

This wasn't good. Birdie might be a werewolf, but that didn't mean she was impervious to weather. And if she wasn't at her home or Jack's or with any of her family, then that was reason enough to worry. Especially because Hank had been looking for her earlier. "I'm out with Sinclair right now. We're in his SUV." I looked at Sin. "We can drive around and have a look for her, see if her car is anywhere."

Sin nodded at me, agreeing to what I'd just said we'd do without actually knowing what it was. He'd probably figured it out from what he'd overheard. Something his necromancer senses had undoubtedly helped with too.

"Her car is at her house," Jack said. "But that's where her trail stops. Any other help you could give us would be great. Her family is trying to track her, but this damned snow is making it impossible." He sounded so worried that my heart ached. "Sorry about the language. Thank you. Call if you find *anything*."

"I will. Right away. You too."

He hung up.

"Birdie's missing." I chewed on my lip.

"I gathered. You think she'd go out in this weather? Where do you want me to go?"

"I don't—actually, I have an idea. I asked her to make sure Myra's house was off-limits, and she said she was going to check on it herself on the way home. I'm guessing that was around six or seven last night since that's about when she gets off, I think. Anyway, let's start at Myra's. See if we can follow her tracks."

"Didn't Jack say something about her car?" He

raised his brows. "I wasn't eavesdropping. Necromancer hearing is pretty sharp."

"No worries. And yes, he said her car was at her house but that's where her trail ended."

"So she must have made it to Myra's, then home."

"Unless she walked to Myra's. She said she only lives a few blocks away. Maybe she had to run home first, then intended to go over to Myra's only to find out her car had conked out with the cold. Walking there from her house wouldn't be out of the question if they're really that close."

"Myra's it is, then."

I nodded. "My gut is still telling me Myra's is the place to start. Especially with that open portal." I pursed my lips. "I wonder if it's possible to fall through a portal like that."

"You think Birdie might be in the North Pole?"

"Anything's possible. Maybe we'll be able to tell when we get there."

"Let's hope." He took the next turn, and we headed in the direction of Myra Grimshaw's.

The house was pretty much as we'd last seen it, except the flowery pattern of snow around it was basically invisible now. The combination of continually falling snow and many sets of footprints had obliterated the original shape. It was hard to make much of anything out with the fresh cover of powder.

There was also bright yellow police tape across

the front door and going from railing to railing on either side of the steps up to the porch. I was guessing the sheriff had done the door, then Birdie had added the bit on the railing. When Birdie did something, she did it all the way. "I'd say Birdie was here."

"Looks that way." Sin parked, and we went up the sidewalk.

We had to duck under the police tape to climb the porch stairs, and when we got to the front door, it was locked. As it should have been.

I tried the handle one more time like it might magically open on the second try. "Well, it's supposed to be locked, so I can't complain about that."

Not that locked doors could keep me out. My inherited Santa Slide ability meant I could get into any space that wasn't airtight. I wasn't quite ready to pull that trick out of the bag in front of Sin, however. I had to think fast. "Hey, you want to check around back? See if there's an open window or back door?"

"Sure." He lightly pressed his hand to the small of my back as if to reassure me that he wouldn't leave me for long. It was sweet, and a gesture that was very him. "Give me a couple minutes."

"Thanks." As soon as he disappeared around the side of the house, I took a quick look around for nosy neighbors, then did my thing.

I materialized on the other side of the door on all fours. I rocked back on my heels and took a few seconds, leaning against the door to catch my breath and let my head stop spinning. It might have been a smidge worse than usual, but then again, I might have just been paranoid. Or still feeling some aftereffects of the magical whiplash I'd endured earlier.

I knew I'd sat there long enough when the knob on the kitchen door jiggled. Sin was on the back porch. I forced myself to my feet. That gave me a moment of light-headedness, but it passed pretty quickly. I started forward, wobbling a bit, but I was walking a straight line by the time I was in the kitchen. I unlocked the back door and smiled at Sin.

"How'd you get in?" He wiped his feet on the outside mat before entering.

"Magic." I didn't want to lie, so I hoped he didn't ask for more explanation than that. I changed the subject as quickly as I could. "Let's head downstairs and see if we can find any evidence of Birdie having been in the basement."

He was studying me a little too hard. "I'll go first. You look pale. Then if you fall, I'll be your safety net."

I made myself smile. "I'm fine. Just weird being in a dead lady's house." Which it was.

He snorted softly, but let it go. He went to the basement steps, flipped the light on and went down.

I followed, my view blocked by his broad back and shoulders. Which was why, when he let out a soft curse, I wasn't sure what it was all about.

The second my gaze hit the floor, I understood. "That ice puddle has gotten bigger."

"Yes, it has." He moved to the side so I could come down off the landing. "I'd say by another six inches. What does that mean?"

"I don't know. My dad didn't mention that was even a possibility." I crouched down by the ice puddle.

Sin took a step forward and put his hand on my shoulder. "What are you planning on doing?"

"I was going to touch the puddle. No magic. I just want to see if I can stick my hand through it and feel if the portal is...turned on or whatever. Then we'd know if it's a two-way deal or not."

"Here." He held out his hand to me. "Give me your other hand, so I can hold on to you in case it tries to suck you through or something."

I almost made a snarky comment about tying ourselves to the railing, too, but I didn't. Sin's main goal always seemed to be my protection. I wasn't going to give him grief about that.

"Okay." I took his hand. "Thanks. Just so you know, if I get another magical shock, you might feel it."

He shrugged and squeezed my hand. "I'll deal."

I smiled and turned back to the puddle. "Here goes."

I reached out and carefully touched my fingertips to the surface of the puddle. It was shockingly cold, which was saying something coming from me. A shimmer of blue light—magic—danced across the face of the ice. And just like that, my hand slipped in.

I swear I touched something...furry? But the surprise of it was so intense I jerked back, falling against Sin's legs.

"You okay? What happened?"

"My hand went through."

"I saw that."

"And then I touched something. Something that absolutely wasn't Birdie."

"You okay?"

I nodded and got to my feet. "The portal is definitely operating on both sides. But I don't see any sign that Birdie might have fallen through." I looked around. "I mean, she's a werewolf, right? If she realized she was getting pulled through a magical portal, or falling through one, she would have fought it."

"For sure." Sinclair bent down and ran his hand along the smooth concrete beside the ice. "There would be claw marks on this floor at least."

"I think so too." I sighed. "So where is she?"

He straightened. "I wish I knew. Let's go over to

her house. Can't hurt to check there too."

"No, it can't." And we had no other leads anyway.

We went out the front door, turning the latch to lock it behind us, and got back into the SUV. Sin cranked up the heat and pulled back onto the snowy road toward Birdie's. We got only a few blocks before a fallen tree blocked our path.

"There will be more trees down if this snow keeps up. They can't take the weight." He turned right. "This will add a few more minutes to our trip, but we should be able to get to Birdie's, no problem."

"I'm not that familiar with this part of town. And I've lived here longer. How do you know it so well?"

He smiled. "Deliveries."

"That makes sense."

"When I first opened, I did anything to make a sale. Including delivering doughnuts to whoever wanted them whenever they wanted them. Now I just do big orders. And I'm not always the one who does the delivering, as you know."

"Who ran the shop then?"

"Johnny."

"I didn't realize he'd worked for you that long."

"Yeah, he's a good kid. Works at the store, then leaves at two, heads home for a bit then goes to evening classes at the community college."

"Wow, that's dedication."

"For sure."

We took a left and up ahead one of the small parks that were scattered throughout the residential areas of town came into view. Except I'd never seen it look like this before.

Sin laughed and shook his head as he slowed down even more. "I guess that's what happens when you give supernatural kids a bunch of snow days."

I inched as far forward in my seat as the safety belt would let me. "Holy giant snowballs."

Sin peered through the windshield. "Is that…an ice castle?"

"Yeah, I think it is." The structure rose up out of the middle of the park, towering over the houses around it. There was a statue in the center of that park, but the kids must have built around it. The fortress had everything you'd want in an ice castle. Except for maybe a door, which must have been on the other side. Turrets, look-out slots, larger windows—a small, blue furry thing zipped past one of the windows.

"Stop the car!"

Sin hit the brakes. We skidded a few feet, but I didn't wait for the SUV to settle as I jumped out and ran to the fortress.

Sin came up behind me a few seconds later. "What happened?"

I stood in front of the ice wall and stared up at the frozen monstrosity in front of me. A familiar stench settled over me, telling me everything I needed to know. "This wasn't built by kids. This is way worse."

"Worse? How?"

"It was built by yetis."

"You're sure about that?" Sin looked skeptical. I didn't blame him. Most people hear *yeti* and conjure up images of an abominable snowman. Sometimes it's a scary one, sometimes it's a giant Muppet.

"Positive. I saw one go past the window. They don't look anything like what most people think. And now I know why this weather is so bad. In fact, everything is falling into place. The smell at Myra's. The preserves being eaten." I shook my head in disgust for not realizing it sooner. "They must have started coming through the moment the portal was formed."

"Wait, the yetis are causing the weather? They can do that?"

"Yes. They wield strong winter magic. It's a defense mechanism, mostly, but in this case, I think they're trying to re-create the North Pole here. Although they're overdoing it a little."

Then a shockingly familiar face peered over the top of the wall. "Princess? Is that you?"

"Birdie?" I almost fell over. "What are you doing up there? Come down here."

"I can't. These rotten little blue rodents kidnapped me. I was at Myra's, making sure everything was secure, when they ambushed me."

"Can't you just come down?"

"Nope. I tried to leave and one bit me. Didn't break the skin, thanks to my coat, but it hurt. Then I tried snarling at them, you know, all half-wolf, to get them to back off, and they practically attacked. I can't imagine what they'd do if I went full wolf."

"Are you okay otherwise? Are you warm enough? Do you need anything?" This was not good.

"I'm fine, all things considered. Could I be warmer? Sure. But that's not the worst of it. These things smell like a garbage truck had a baby with a dog food factory on a hot summer day."

I nodded. "They're known for their stench. We'll get you out of there." I wasn't sure how, though.

"Well, until you do…" She leaned over the wall a little more, and the light glinted off the crystal snowflake pendant at her throat. "Let Jack and the kids know what's going on, would you? One of these walking bath mats ate my cell phone."

I pulled my phone out. "I'll do it right now." I dialed Jack first, since I'd promised him I would.

Sinclair pointed toward the other side of the ice

castle. "Going to do a little recon. Be right back."

I nodded at Sin as Jack answered.

"Hello?"

"Hey, Jack. I found Birdie. She's basically fine. She's at Balfour Park. You need to come here."

"She's okay? What's she doing there?"

"Yes, she's okay. It's kind of a long story." I didn't want to tell him over the phone she'd been kidnapped by yetis. "You want to call Bridget and Titus while I call Sheriff Merrow? Then you can all come over here and see for yourself."

"You're sure she's okay?"

"Absolutely. She can tell you herself when you get here."

"Okay. On my way as soon as I call the kids. See you in a few."

"Great." We hung up and I dialed the sheriff.

It took him a lot longer to answer, but then I'm sure he was swamped. "Miss Frost?"

I'd had enough dealings with him to know how he liked his information straight up and to the point. "Birdie's at Balfour Park. Kidnapped by yetis that came through the portal at Myra's. I'll answer any questions you have when you get here."

"Be there in five." He hung up.

I tucked my phone away and glanced toward Birdie again. "Everyone's on their way."

"Good. Thank you."

Sin came around the corner of the castle, on the

opposite side from where he'd started. "This thing is rock solid. And there's no way in or out that I can see."

"Because they scale the wall. See the scratches?" I pointed the marks out. "Yetis have talons like bears."

He stared at the lines in the ice. "Those are claw marks?"

"Yes." The deep grooves cut through the ice all over the fortress, making the walls seem patterned.

"Yikes. I hope they don't have teeth like bears too."

I shook my head. "I don't think bears' teeth are that sharp or pointed, but I could be wrong."

His brows shot up. "These things sound awful."

"Because they are. Take a deep whiff. What do you smell?"

He inhaled. His nose wrinkled as he grimaced. "Hot garbage and wet dog with a hint of left-in-the-sun seafood. With maybe a hint of overloaded diaper."

"That's an accurate description."

"Of what?" He looked slightly green. Still hot, but definitely green.

"Of a yeti's natural musk."

He shoved a hand through his hair. "That is unfortunate. For all of us."

"You can say that again."

The sheriff's car and the fire chief's truck skidded to a stop on the opposite street we'd come in on. Bridget got out of Titus's truck just as Jack pulled up in his. The four of them made their way over to us. None of them looked happy.

Birdie waved down like she was welcoming them to a garden party. "Hello, my darlings."

"Aunt Birdie, what the heck is going on?" Bridget asked. "What are you doing up there? Where did this thing come from?"

Birdie nodded at me. "The princess will explain."

And so I did, giving them a crash course in yetis, how they'd come through the portal at Myra's and how I was waiting on news from my dad on how to close up that magical yeti delivery system.

The sheriff crossed his arms. "How do we get rid of the yetis after it's closed?"

"I'm hoping my dad has some thoughts on that, too, but one way or another, we'll figure out how to round them up."

"More importantly," Jack said. "How do we get Birdie out of there *now*?"

Titus stepped forward, his gaze on the ice wall. The fire chief looked a lot like his older brother, but without the super seriousness that made the sheriff so intimidating. "I can handle that."

He shook his arms out at his sides, like he was preparing for something. Then he rolled his shoulders and his eyes lit with a wolfy glow, and I knew exactly what that something was.

"Um, Chief? Titus?" I'd never had much

interaction with the man, so calling him by his first name felt a little odd. But considering what I was pretty sure he was about to do, it was the best way to get his attention. "I don't think that's such a good—"

He crouched, then leaped into the air, shifting into his wolf form as he went. He made it to the top of the wall, landed, and launched forward. It was a very impressive move.

"Titus!" Birdie's exclamation was followed by the sounds of snarling, biting, some yowling, scratching, and hissing. And more yelling from Birdie. "Get off him, get *off* him, you horrible little monsters! No! Stop that. No! No! No!"

Seconds later, a hunk of wolf-shaped ice came hurtling over the wall. It crashed at our feet and broke open to reveal a very angry Titus, still in wolf-form. He shifted back to his human self. His uniform was shredded and he had scratches and bite marks all over him. He got to his feet, glowering like a lit fuse.

He jabbed a finger at the fortress. "Those things are evil."

Bridget went to him. "Are you okay, Bro? You look like you got used for a chew toy."

Hank snorted, causing Titus to shoot him an angry look before slanting his eyes at his sister. "Thanks for your concern. I'm fine."

"Sorry," I said. "I tried to warn you, but you

jumped before I could say anything. Yetis are not like anything you guys would have run into here."

"Apparently." He wiped a little yeti saliva off his arm, then glanced up. "What are we going to do about Aunt Birdie?"

"We'll figure something out." I yelled up to her. "Birdie, you sure you don't need anything?"

"Other than to get out of here? Maybe some air fresheners." She leaned over. "I really am okay. The yetis have brought me all kinds of food, drinks, and odds-n-ends. Including the Millers's mailbox, a single tennis shoe, a red plastic kid's shovel and a large assortment of garden gnomes. They've also made me a bed out of a random assortment of quilts, pillows and blankets. I assume pilfered from the neighboring houses."

I thought about that a moment. "So they're not threatening you at all?"

"As long as I'm not trying to escape, they've been very nice. Almost reverent. It's weird."

"Weird, but good. Stay safe up there. And warm. We'll get you down just as soon as we can." I really needed to talk to my dad.

The sheriff approached. "This escalates things. We need to get rid of these yetis immediately." He looked at his brother and shook his head. "Why don't we just get Van in here to fire-breathe these things out of existence?"

Bridget planted her hands on her hips. "With

Aunt Birdie in there? Are you nuts?"

Sheriff Merrow's expression didn't change. "We'll have Nick swoop in and pick her up, then Van can come in behind him and melt this fortress into vapor. Taking the yetis with it."

Bridget frowned. "It's not like you to be so blood-thirsty."

His eyes narrowed. "Look what they did to Titus. And they're holding Birdie hostage. Who knows what they plan on doing to her? They might be getting ready to make her into their dinner, for all we know."

I shook my head. "Yetis don't eat people."

He snorted. "As far as you know."

"I do know. And if they so much as see the shadow of Nick or Van come close to them, I can guarantee they'll retreat with Birdie so deep into that fortress that no one will be able to get to them. At least this way, we can communicate with Birdie."

The sheriff crossed his arms. "How are you so sure?"

I stood my ground. "They're from the North Pole, same as I am. And I have a pretty good idea of why they took Birdie."

"Oh?" He rocked back on his heels slightly. "Would you care to share that with the rest of us?"

I took a breath. "They're going to make her their queen."

Bridget's mouth fell open. "For real?"

"For real," I said.

"Their queen?" Sin asked. "What makes you think that?"

"There's a story all winter elf children know, about how a little girl ran away from home because she didn't want to obey her parents, and the yetis found her and made her their queen and her parents never saw her again." I shrugged. "We were always taught that it was a real thing that happened. I suppose it was to keep kids from running away from home."

Bridget frowned. "It doesn't sound like that big of a deterrent to me. Being queen? That might make some little girls want to run away."

"Well, the yetis smell awful, make you eat raw fish, and were generally considered scary creatures. It wasn't a fate any child wanted."

"Oh," Bridget said.

Jack glanced at the fortress. "You sure they're going to treat her all right?"

I shrugged. "If they plan on making her their queen, I can't imagine they wouldn't. From what Birdie's told me, they're feeding her, bringing her gifts, and have even made a bed for her."

"But why Aunt Birdie?" Titus asked. "She's not a winter elf."

"I know that, but she's still rocking that blue hair and..." I chewed on my lip. "She's also wearing a necklace of winter elf crystal. A snowflake pendant that's actually the house seal of the Winter Court."

"Where did she get that?" the sheriff barked.

I tried not to cringe when I answered. "I, uh, gave it to her. As a thank-you gift for watching my cat. I guess the yetis are taking it to mean she's their chosen one."

He sighed. "You need to talk to your father and get a solution to this immediately."

"Agreed. I'm going to my apartment now to do just that." I looked at Sin. "You'll take me back, right?"

"Of course. Just say the word."

"I'm ready." I looked at Birdie's family, and Jack, and wished I had more to offer them. "Sorry to leave you all with this situation."

"Are y'all making the princess feel bad?" Birdie shouted down. "You'd better not be."

I waved at her and smiled. "It's all good."

Bridget leaned back to talk to her. "Now Aunt Birdie—"

She scowled at her niece and nephews. "I'm stuck in an ice fortress, I'm not deaf. Be nice."

Jack snorted while Hank, Titus and Bridget shifted around awkwardly.

I pretended not to notice while I finished my conversation with her. I hitched my thumb toward Sin's SUV. "All right, I'm off to talk to my dad and figure this whole thing out. I'll be back as soon as I can."

"Take your time, Princess. I'm fine up here. Just found a large box of chocolates these wretched fiends were hoarding in one of their piles of food. Seems they love sweets as much as I do."

"They do." I gave her a wave and a smile, then nudged Sinclair. "Let's go."

We turned, and he put his arm around me as we trudged through the snow to his SUV. "You okay?"

"I'm fine."

"No, you're not. You feel responsible for this, don't you?"

I shrugged. "Yes, but how could I not?"

"Babe, this isn't your fault."

"That's kind of you to say, but I'm the one who gave her that pendant. And if you really want to dig down, none of this would have happened if winter elves weren't a thing."

"Whoa." He stopped me in front of the car, putting his hands on my shoulders and turning me toward him. "Hang on a second. I'm not going to listen to that kind of talk."

"I'm not wishing I'd never been born or anything like that, but you heard the tone in the sheriff's voice. Saw the look in his eyes. He's unhappy with me. With my kind. They all are. And who can blame any of them?"

"I get that. But the sheriff is unhappy because his aunt is being held hostage and his brother just got the snot knocked out of him by a bunch of yetis. Not to mention that the town he's in charge of protecting and serving is currently experiencing a new ice age. However, none of this is your fault."

I appreciated his efforts to make me feel better, but the best I could do was shrug, unconvinced.

He shook his head, his hands firm on my shoulders. "Not an acceptable response, missy."

A little half-smile crept onto my face and I was powerless to stop it. "What do you want me to say?"

"That this isn't your fault."

"I don't think I can do that."

"How about it's not *all* your fault?"

I stared at him for a moment, seeing his belief in me shining bright in his eyes. He was such a good man. "It's not all my fault," I mumbled.

"That's my girl." He pulled me into a hug, then

with his arm back around my shoulders, started us walking toward the passenger's side. "Now let's get you to your apartment so you can talk to your dad."

"What about your shop?" We were steps from the SUV. "You still haven't checked on it."

He opened my door. "I'll drop you off, then do that, then come right back. The snowplows are running. I saw one go by earlier. So it shouldn't take me as long. Plan?"

"Plan." More than ever, I wanted Sinclair around. Because, despite what he'd made me say, I did feel like most of this was my fault. Not just mine, but all of the winter elves. And that bothered me. A lot. I didn't want any of this to reflect poorly on my family or my people.

I didn't think that was my royal side talking either. I thought it was just that I loved being a winter elf. I was proud of who I was and where I came from. Proud of my family and my hometown and all the hardworking people who lived there. We were basically responsible for Christmas! How could I not be proud of that? And how could I not be bothered by anyone or anything that casted the North Pole in a bad light?

My dad and I *had* to figure this out.

Soon.

I decided on the ride to the warehouse to call him from my office, which I did the second I went inside. Fortunately, he answered the snow globe almost instantly. "How's it going there?"

"Not great. Things have escalated." I brought him up to speed on Birdie, the ice castle, and my theory on the yetis making her their queen.

He went a little ashen. "That sounds like exactly what they're doing."

"So why do you look like you just found out Christmas has been canceled?"

"Jay, the yetis chose a queen for one reason only. They believe the queen brings them protection from the wendigo."

"Makes sense. The wendigo is their one natural enemy." I still didn't see what my dad was getting at. "What's wrong with wanting protection?"

He scrubbed a hand across his mouth. "Because they get that protection by *sacrificing* the queen."

I stared at him. "When you say sacrificing…" I stared at him a little harder. "Say it in plain English."

"They're going to trade Birdie's life for the protection of the tribe."

That sent a brand-new kind of cold through me. "That cannot happen. We have to get her out of there more than ever."

He nodded.

Then I got a little mad. "Why was the whole sacrificing thing never part of the children's story? Seems to me that's a pretty important part."

He sighed. "It was deemed too frightening by polite society, and most people stopped telling that part. Eventually, a lot of people forgot it was the queen's fate."

"You know about it."

"I'm the king."

"And I'm next in line. Why am I just finding this out now?"

"I don't know. Look, we're going to get Birdie out of there. We're going to close that portal, round up those yetis and make all of this unnatural winter go away."

"Great. How?"

His mouth thinned to a hard line. "I don't know yet. But I'm calling an emergency meeting of my council immediately. We will work on this until we have an answer. In the meantime, don't attempt anything until I get back to you. Yetis are unpredictable."

"That much I do know."

"Good, because you don't want to do something that could make things worse."

"That's for sure." I tapped my fingers on my desk, thinking. "I guess I'll start carrying this snow globe with me so you can get ahold of me as soon as you have an answer."

"I'm all for that." Then his brows pulled together. "Do you plan on being out much?"

I shrugged. "I can't predict anything at this

point. But I'd hate for you to come up with something and me not be around to get the call."

"Right."

"Hey, what do you think about putting out sweets and such for the yetis? You know how they love sugar. I'm thinking we could keep them in a happy mood that way."

He thought a moment. "I guess that would be all right. I'll check with the council about that first thing and let you know if it's not a good idea for some reason."

"Thank you. I'll talk to you soon. Tell everyone I said hi."

"Will do. Love you, Jay."

"Love you, too, Dad."

We hung up, and I sat there for a moment, listening to the drone of the big generator. I was used to the sounds that filtered in from the shop. The subtle hum of background music, the highs and lows of conversations, the occasional laugh or squeal of a happy child, the bells of the door and register. It was odd not to hear all that. And it made me melancholy.

I got up and walked into the store.

Light filtered in through the windows, making it bright enough to see without using electricity, but it was a bleak, watery light that perfectly mirrored how I felt inside. I needed to snap out of it, I knew that, but my mood was getting worse, not better.

I took a few breaths and tried to shift my spirits in an upward direction. It wasn't often that I saw the shop like this. It almost felt like I was seeing it through new eyes. But the toys and games looked trivial. Who needed any of that when a woman I cared deeply for was in such peril?

I wrapped my arms around myself and stared out the windows. The snow was still coming down. The streets were empty, and rightly so. No one would be out in this weather unless they had to be, but that would change if the weather didn't break.

People would get cabin fever cooped up in their houses. They'd get bored. Tired of their kids being underfoot. The streets and sidewalks would get busy again.

Then what? People would figure out what had happened to Birdie, and word would spread that some horrible little monsters from the North Pole had taken her hostage. If that news wasn't already traveling through town.

People would look at me to solve the problem that I must have caused.

But I still hoped my father worked fast. For Birdie's sake. I could handle the fallout if people wanted to blame me, but I could not handle something happening to a woman I considered a dear friend.

16

The sound of the warehouse door opening was
followed by Sinclair's voice calling my name.
"Jayne?"

"In here," I answered. "In the shop."

He came in through the door I'd left open. "Hey."

"Hey. That was fast."

"I've been gone half an hour."

I guessed I hadn't realized how long I'd been
standing in the shop moping. "Oh."

"You okay? You still look...not yourself."

"Does being a necromancer give you the ability
to pick up on moods? You always seem to know
how I'm feeling."

"Nah. You're just easy to read. For me,
anyway." He pulled me close and kissed my head.
"I know it's easier said than done, but you have to
stop letting this get to you." Then he put some
room between us so he could see my face. "Or did

151

your dad tell you something new that's got you bummed?"

I needed a breath before I could answer. "The yetis' plan is to sacrifice their chosen queen to bring them protection from the wendigo. Which is another really awful, but thankfully rare, North Pole creature."

His brows lifted. "Sacrifice?"

"Yes."

"As in—"

"Yes."

He grimaced. "That can't happen."

"That's what I said."

"So what's the plan?"

"I don't know yet. My dad's calling his council together and they're going to figure this out, then he's going to let me know as soon as possible. Which reminds me that I'm supposed to be keeping a snow globe with me in case he's trying to reach me. Since I won't be in my office much, I might as well make that one my backup." I started for my office.

Sin walked with me.

"How's the doughnut shop? Everything okay?"

"It's fine. I picked up enough supplies to make a couple batches of doughnuts at your place, but then I realized you probably don't have a fryer. Or do you?"

"I don't think so. But there might be one in the company apartment on the third floor. It's a pretty well-stocked unit." I opened my office door. "We'll go up and look, because that reminds me that I do have a sort of temporary plan to keep the yetis occupied."

"And that is?"

"Stock them up with sweets. They love sugar. More than I do."

He looked skeptical. "I find that hard to believe."

"Shocking, I know. Once I get the go-ahead from my dad, I'm going to tell the sheriff we need to get power turned on fully to all the businesses in town capable of producing sweets. Your place, Delaney's, Mummy's, Howler's—any place that can turn out some large quantities of goodies."

"Why not just dump a big pile of sugar next to the fortress?"

"Believe it or not, those little blue buggers are pickier than that. I mean, they'd eat it, but they'd get bored fast. A variety of sweets and pastries and chocolates will keep them entertained and interested. We could even get some jars of jam from the Shop-n-Save, since they liked the ones from Myra's basement so much."

"I can make all the doughnuts you want." He cracked his knuckles. "I'd be happy to. I miss baking."

I gave him a look. "It's been one day."

He laughed. "I love my job—hey! I just thought of something. Why don't we serve them a batch of drugged goodies? Something to make them sleep? Then we can get Birdie out."

"That's a *really* good idea." I should have thought of that, but tainting sugary treats was a little against my general way of thinking. In this case, however, it was perfect. "But I need to run it past my dad first. I don't know what would work on a yeti. And we don't want to accidentally give them something that's going to make them mad or speed them up, you know?"

"Right. That would not be good."

"I'm going to send out a group message about the plan so that we can get things ready to go for when my dad says it's okay." I sat at my desk and pulled out my cell phone.

Sin took a spot on the love seat and waited. "Anything I can do?"

The snow in the globe on my desk started falling. My dad was on the line. "Yes, you can send that group text for me. My dad is calling."

"Done." He got up and headed out to the warehouse to give me some privacy.

I answered. "Dad, what did you find out?"

He looked tired. And mad. "We can't close the portal. Not while Birdie is in danger. Closing the portal will most likely make the yetis panic. They could think they're being attacked or threatened. It could cause them to escalate their plan for their queen."

"Yikes. That's a big no, then." I tugged on a loose strand of hair. "Does that mean yetis will continue to come in through Myra's house, then?"

"Unfortunately, yes. NP security has been notified, and they're currently searching for the portal's opening on this side. If—*when* we find it, we're going to barricade that area off so that no more yetis get through. Until then, we won't be able to stop them."

"Did you talk about my plan to overload the yetis already here with sweets to keep them happy?"

"I did and the consensus is that's a good idea. Go ahead with it."

"We will. Hang on a sec." I stood up and leaned so I could see through my office door. "Sinclair, the sweets are a go."

"Got it," he yelled back.

I sat down and went back to my dad. "Okay, Sinclair is texting the Ellinghams about getting some dessert production underway. One more thing about that plan—what about loading a batch of sweets with a knock-out drug? Something to tranquilize them so we can get Birdie out."

His eyes narrowed. "Maybe. But I don't know what you'd use yet. The yeti physiology is a strange thing. I'll have to get some more research on that. Oh, and if you run out of sweets, you can always dump some fish out for them."

"I don't know how the Ellinghams would feel about piles of dead fish in one of the town's parks. Sure, the cold will keep it from smelling too much, but you've seen the way yetis eat."

He wrinkled his nose. "Hmm, yes, scratch that. I'm sure the Ellinghams have enough to deal with. No need to add an explosion of fish scales, heads and guts to their list. Speaking of explosions, how are things on a personal level?"

I put on a happy face. "All good."

"Jay, I'm your father. I know you better than that. I know you take things personally. And in a situation like this, how could you not? But really, honey, don't internalize this. It would have happened whether you were in town or not. You're not the reason Myra had a snow globe."

"I know. And about that, did you find out anything more about her?"

"ER is still digging. They have some suspicions, but nothing concrete yet. I'll keep you posted."

"Thanks, Dad. I'll have a globe with me from now on, so call when you know anything new."

"You too."

We hung up. I walked out to see how Sin was getting on with his task. Due to the power situation, only every other overhead light in the warehouse was on, which provided plenty of light, but made for some slightly eerie shadows. I was glad he was here.

He was on his phone, nodding. "Yes. Perfect. I'll tell her. Thanks so much."

He took the phone from his ear, tapped the screen, then stored it in his back pocket. "It's done. The Ellinghams are going to have extra power diverted to the shops that need it, and dessert production will be underway shortly."

"That's great."

"It is." He smiled at me. "Do you have anything you need to do here?"

"Not with the shop being closed. I mean, there's always work to do, right? But I'm not going to make stuff up just to keep my employees busy. After Christmas, we can all use the time off."

"Good. Because I could use some help. And I just happen to have an apron in your size."

"You want me to help make doughnuts? I'm totally willing, but you know I'm not exactly an Iron Chef."

He laughed. "I'll make sure you get a foolproof job. Like frosting. Or flipping."

"You flip doughnuts?"

"Some of them, yes. You'll see. You want to run up and check on the kids before we go?"

The kids. He slayed me when he called our cats that. "Yes. Spider's probably out of food by now."

We jogged up the steps and down the hall to the apartment. As I jostled for my keys, Juniper opened her door. Her apartment was across from mine.

"Hey, Juni. How are you doing over there?"

"Bored silly. Hi, Sinclair."

He nodded at her. "If you're bored, you could always come with us and make doughnuts."

She straightened. "What? What's going on?"

I gave her the short version. "Yetis have invaded town and kidnapped Birdie. We're making doughnuts to keep them occupied so they don't turn her into a sacrificial offering. A bunch of other businesses are making sweets and desserts too."

She looked shocked for a second, then shook her head. "Whatever, I'm in. I bet you Kip and Buttercup would come too."

Buttercup stuck her head out of her apartment, which was next to Juniper's. "I heard my name. Not that I was listening at the door."

I gave her the same quick explanation I'd given Juni.

She nodded. "I'm in." Then she squinted. "What about Holly? And Rowley and his wife?"

Juniper glanced toward the third floor. "Holly's got a cold. And I'm sure Dorothea would love to help, but Rowley told me this morning that this cold is affecting her arthritis more than she wants to let on. That's part of why they came to Nocturne Falls. Warmer weather."

Poor woman. Her years of baking in the North Pole kitchens had earned her a break. "Rowley probably won't want to leave her alone with all that's going on."

"I agree. He's very protective of her."

"Which is sweet. And it'll be nice to have them here keeping an eye on the building and such. Especially with Holly under the weather." I tipped my head. "Juni, would you mind running up and telling them we're all going over to Sinclair's? I don't want them to find us all gone and worry."

"Sure! I'll be down and ready to go as soon as I can."

"Thanks. We're going to feed the cats, then we'll be ready as well."

Sure enough, Sugar's and Spider's bowls were empty. We filled them, then headed back down to the SUV. The rest of the crew were along within minutes.

"It's so nice of you guys to come help make doughnuts."

"Make?" Kip said. "I thought you needed help eating doughnuts."

Sin laughed. "You'll have all you can eat, I promise."

"Yes." Buttercup rocked her fist in the air.

I clucked my tongue at Sin. "You have no idea what you just did."

He playfully slapped his hand to his forehead. "Unleashing winter elves in my shop is probably a horrible idea. I hope you all take pity on me."

We laughed and bantered the whole way to Zombie Donuts, except for when I was explaining what had happened to Birdie. That took the humor out of the air pretty quick, but they were winter elves, same as me. They deserved to know what was going on.

The desire to save Birdie and make things right in town again energized them. When we got to the shop, Sinclair gave us a crash course in doughnut making. He was a good teacher. We learned all about hoppers and extruders and proofing boxes. But it wasn't too hard, especially with him doing the hard part of mixing the dough, and we fell right into our jobs. It was fun with all of us there. Plus, we had a purpose.

Three hours later, we'd turned out more glazed doughnuts than any of us could count. We'd eaten more than our share, too, but we decided to call that lunch. We packed the back of Sin's SUV with boxes of doughnuts until it wouldn't hold any more.

He shut the vehicle's doors. "Great job, you guys. Too bad I like Jayne so much or I'd try to hire you all away from her."

Kip, Buttercup, and Juniper beamed.

"Hey," I said. "Don't get any ideas."

"It was really fun," Juniper said. "Your doughnuts are so good. It's really cool to know how they're made."

"Yeah." Kip patted his stomach. "Today was a good day. Are you going to drop those off at the park?"

"Why?" I asked. "You want to see the yetis?"

The three of them nodded. I got it. Yeti sightings were rare, and being that they were such a big part of our childhood, the curiosity about them was ingrained in us.

"All right. Let me just text the sheriff that we're on our way with the first batch." Sinclair pulled out his phone and started tapping away at the screen. "After we drop them off, we can head back to the apartments."

We loaded into his SUV and went to Balfour Park. The whole block was partitioned off with yellow sawhorses marked Nocturne Falls Sheriff Department, except for one entrance on the south side, which was where Sin parked.

Deputy Blythe stood at that entrance, keeping lookie-loos out. The valkyrie was a good choice for a gate guard. She did imposing well.

Sin loaded us each up with boxes. "Good thing you guys came or I would have been making a lot of trips."

We trudged through the snow with our sweet cargo. Deputy Blythe gave us a nod as we came past.

"Anything new?" I asked.

"Nothing yet."

"I guess that's good."

She shrugged. "I suppose. You need help? I can call Cruz."

"We've got it," Sin answered. He stopped and lifted the lid on the top box. "Want one?"

She smiled and took a doughnut. "Thanks."

Despite the snow coming down, the rest of the walk was easier due to the path that had been worn from the street to the ice fortress. I guessed that Birdie's family, and Jack, had kept her company for quite a while.

"Wow," Juniper whispered as we got closer. "That thing is crazy."

"I'll say." Kip whistled low and shook his head.

One by one, Sin took the boxes from us and dumped the contents into a big pile on the ground. It was a little sad, seeing all those yummy doughnuts being sacrificed like that. But better the doughnuts than Birdie.

Buttercup sidled up to me, smiling. "That fortress is really something, huh?"

"I'll say." She looked oddly excited. Like she was on the verge of sharing a secret. "What is it?"

She hemmed and hawed a second more before she answered. "I really want to go inside."

My eyes widened. I knew Buttercup was pretty adventurous, but this seemed like a stretch even for her. "I don't think you mean that."

Her smile turned into a smirk. "Come on, it's a very impressive structure. Aren't you curious what the inside looks like?"

I hadn't thought about it much. "Yeah, I guess."

She nudged me. "Think how much fun the kids in town would have playing in there. After the yetis are cleared out. Obviously."

"Obviously. Except there's no way in. I don't think the parents would look kindly on their children having to scale the walls with ice hammers and snow cleats."

Buttercup stared at the edifice and shrugged. "So we'll put a door in. We've got the skills. This thing is epic. We can't just let it go to waste."

I stared at it with her and thought about that. She had a point. If I looked past the stench and the yetis and Birdie being kidnapped, the fortress the little monsters had built for their queen was very impressive.

Turning it into something fun for the kids in town might be a way to get some decent PR out of this whole mess. A way to balance the bad the yetis had brought. "I'll think about it."

A car pulled up. I turned to see Sheriff Merrow getting out of his patrol car. He walked over to us. "I see Operation Sweet Tooth has begun."

"Is that the official name for what we're doing?"

He nodded, but his attention was focused upward. He cupped his hands around his mouth. "Aunt Birdie, check in."

Sin finished emptying the doughnuts out and joined us. We all craned our heads back to look for her.

No sign.

The sheriff tried again. "Aunt Birdie, it's Hank. Are you okay?"

Finally, a glimpse of blue that wasn't a yeti. She peeked over the parapets. "I'm here."

I sucked in a breath. Her voice was weak and her skin was pale.

Everyone else noticed it, too. I could tell by the looks on their faces. Concern. Worry. And from Sheriff Merrow, anger.

"Aunt Birdie, what's going on? You don't look so hot."

She laughed, a thin wobble of a sound. "Hot I'm not."

Of course she wasn't. I understood exactly what was going on. "It's the cold," I said. "She's not built for it the way a winter elf is. And that fortress is like the ultimate deep freeze. We have to get her out of there."

The sheriff's gaze stayed fixed on his aunt, but the muscles in his jaw twitched. "I'm about to take a pick ax to this thing myself."

"Maybe…" An idea came to me. A crazy, risky, brilliant idea. "Maybe I could offer myself as a substitute."

That got his attention. "You mean like a hostage swap?"

"Exactly."

He grunted. "As much as I appreciate that, we need you here to communicate with your father."

"I could do it from inside."

"And what reaction do you think the yetis will have when they see your snow globe?"

I frowned.

He continued. "And what if the yetis don't accept you? You might make them angry. And if they take that anger out on Birdie—"

"I'll do it," Buttercup chimed in.

We both looked at her.

165

"What? I'm as much a winter elf as you are."

"It's not that, it's just that this is a pretty dangerous thing to do." I bit my lip. "On one hand, I want Birdie out of there yesterday. But on the other, I can't ask anyone to take her place."

Buttercup smiled. "You're not asking me. I'm volunteering. Willingly."

The sheriff cleared his throat. "That's mighty kind of you, miss."

She gave him a nod. "Buttercup Evergreen. At your service."

I stared at her, my thoughts going a mile a minute. "You're serious about this."

"As all get out."

The sheriff shifted closer to us, but his question was for me. "You think this would work?"

I thought a second longer. "We could tip the scales."

"What do you mean?" the sheriff asked.

I glanced at him. "I'll have my parents send my court gown and my court jewels. We'll dress Buttercup like the most over-the-top winter elf that ever lived. We'll make it impossible for the yetis not to think she's their chosen one."

I shifted my attention to Buttercup. "So long as you're game."

She nodded. "I'm not much for fancy stuff, but in this case, have at it. Make me Winter Elf Barbie. Anything to make this go as smoothly as possible."

The idea of swapping Buttercup for Birdie didn't thrill me as much as it scared me. "I'm going back to the car. I need to call my dad."

The inside of Sinclair's SUV was as quiet as a tomb. I pulled out the snow globe and gave it a shake.

My dad answered right away. "Hi, Jayne."

I could tell from what was around him that he was in his council chambers. No doubt also with his council members, so this wasn't going to be a private call.

"Hi, Dad."

As if reading my mind, he turned the globe. "You can see I'm in a meeting about the yeti issue right now. Have been for a couple hours."

I waved to all the familiar faces. "Hello."

They all said hello in response as my dad brought the globe back to him. "What's going on? Anything new?"

"What's new is Birdie's not doing well. The cold is getting to her. Werewolves are strong people, but they're not cut out to handle the kind of intense cold she's experiencing. But we have an idea."

"The cold a winter elf could handle would debilitate most others. Even supernaturals. No wonder she's suffering. What's the idea?"

"Buttercup has offered to take Birdie's place. She's completely willing and on board and knows the risks."

"Very kind of her. And brave." He let the idea settle for a moment longer before speaking. "You think the yetis will go for that?"

"I want to make it impossible for them not to."

"How?"

"I want everything of mine that signifies the Winter Court. My court gown, my court jewels, anything that might help the yetis see Buttercup as a better choice for queen than Birdie."

"Okay, we can do that. I'll get your mom and your aunt on it."

"Perfect. As soon as possible, too, all right?"

"Absolutely. I know time is of the essence. We have the forest rangers and the local veterinarians testing a couple of tranquilizers."

My brows lifted. "Testing?"

"The rangers captured a few yetis this morning near the Newton glacier. Those yetis have become volunteers, as it were. They'll be released when we're done."

"I hope you can find something that works."

"We will. I'm sure. Need anything else?"

"No. Go ahead and get Mom and Aunt Martha on the princess stuff."

"Will do. Talk soon."

"Bye." We hung up. I stuffed the snow globe back in my purse as I got out and went back to meet the sheriff.

He, Sinclair, Buttercup, Kip and Juniper had

moved to the entrance of the park where Deputy Blythe was standing. A glance at the fortress told me why too. The yetis were investigating the doughnut pile.

Clumps of blue fuzz peered over the edge of the ice wall. They were chattering, like cats watching birds, and full of excitement. If I could smell the sugar, which was thick in the air, then they certainly knew what those doughnuts were.

The chattering got louder, more frantic, until one sharp squeal cut through it and they all fell silent.

Sin leaned over. "Any second, they're going to send one over to investigate."

"How do you know?" I whispered back.

"Hunch," he said.

Sure enough, one single yeti flipped himself over the wall, stuck his claws in and screeched all the way down. By the way, the sound of talons on ice isn't much different than nails on a chalkboard. Slightly more bearable, but not by much.

He hit the ground and stopped. I could practically see his nose working as he sniffed the air. He inched forward, cautiously. He stopped, sniffed the air some more, then continued. He might almost be cute if not for all his other qualities, like the stench and the bitey-ness.

The stop-and-start pattern went on for a minute or two until he finally reached the doughnuts.

Above him, the growing crowd of watching yetis had doubled. How many was that? Fifty? Seventy-five? More? I couldn't believe there were that many of them in Nocturne Falls. We could not afford to anger them. If they decided to run loose through the town, we were in trouble.

More trouble, I should say.

The watching yetis seemed to go up on their tiptoes as they peered over the wall.

The lone soldier picked up a doughnut and sniffed. A low, rumbly purr came out of him. I understood. Sugar did that to me too.

He glanced back at his fellows in the fortress, then his attention belonged to the doughnut. Tentatively, he licked it. He smacked his lips a few times, and apparently, it passed whatever test it needed to pass, because the next thing he did was shove the entire doughnut into his mouth.

He chewed maybe twice, then swallowed. He patted his stomach and smiled. I grimaced at the sight of so many teeth.

He squatted by the pile, grabbed another doughnut and shoved it into his mouth as well. A third followed. Then a fourth.

The yetis on the wall were restless, milling about and chattering up a storm. They quickly realized the yeti on the ground was too busy eating the sugary treats to give them any more reports, and over the wall they came.

They swarmed the pile of doughnuts like a wave of blue locusts and as quickly as they'd arrived, the doughnuts were gone.

"You have to be kidding me." Sheriff Merrow's arms dropped to his sides. "They didn't even chew."

"They chewed, but not much."

He looked at me. "We're going to need a lot more sugar."

Sin stuck his hands in his jacket pockets. "I have a lot. I can make more doughnuts than you can imagine. I just need the crew, but I can call my employees and see if they'll come in."

Kip spoke up. "I'm happy to help again if Jayne doesn't need me."

"Me too," Juniper said. "And I can call my boyfriend, Pete, to help. The pharmacy's closed and I know he's bored."

I loved these elves for their willingness to help. "You have my blessing. But Buttercup and I are going to have to be back at the warehouse for a while." At least until the things I'd requested showed up in the Santa's Bag.

Footsteps crunched through the snow behind us. We turned to see Deputy Blythe greeting Hugh and Sebastian Ellingham.

Hugh nodded at us as they walked closer. "I thought you were bringing doughnuts, Mr. Crowe?"

"I did. Nearly thirty dozen," Sinclair said. "They lasted about three seconds."

Both Hugh and Sebastian looked surprised. Sebastian glanced at his brother. "You'd better tell Delaney to double whatever she's doing."

Hugh pulled out his phone.

Sin tipped his head toward the car. "We should go." He addressed the vampire pair. "I'll be back when I have more doughnuts made."

"Excellent," Hugh said with the phone still at his ear. Then Delaney must have answered, because he said, "Hi, honey," and walked off to talk to her.

"Listen," Sebastian said. "Whatever costs you incur for time and materials, including whatever hours you and your employees put in making these doughnuts, keep track of all of it. The town will reimburse you."

Sin nodded appreciatively. "Thank you, that is very kind and unexpected."

Sebastian tucked his hands into the pockets of his long, camel overcoat. "We don't want anyone to suffer for this more than they already have. Now if you'll excuse me, I need to have a word with the sheriff."

"And I need to get back to my shop." Sin hooked his arm through mine, and we all went back to the SUV. "That's very nice of the Ellinghams to do."

"It is." But the comment about not wanting anyone to suffer more than they already had stuck in my chest like a dagger.

Nothing could change how badly I felt about all of this.

Nothing except getting Birdie to safety and the yetis back to the North Pole as soon as possible.

Sin dropped me and Buttercup off at the warehouse, then (after a kiss) he left for his shop with Kip and Juniper to get busy making more doughnuts. I think he was going to pick up his employees, too, so they wouldn't have to trudge through the snow.

Buttercup and I had our own mission. We went straight to the Santa's Bag. It was empty.

I sighed. "Hopefully it won't be too much longer."

"I'm sure it won't be." She smiled, a little tentatively, but with good reason. She was about to willingly head into the lion's den, so to speak. She fiddled with the bracelets stacked on her wrist. "I'm going to check on Holly, then I'll be in my apartment. Unless you want me to stay with you?"

"No, go ahead. Make sure Holly's okay." I had a

feeling she wanted a few moments alone to think and settle into the reality of what she was about to do. Maybe even consider the very unlikely possibility that she might not be coming back. I forced that thought right out of my head. We would figure out a way that gave everyone, including the yetis, a happy ending. I was sure of it. "I'll be up as soon as everything comes in."

"Okay, see you in a bit." She headed for the stairs.

I pulled over a crate and sat, staring at the Santa's Bag. After a few minutes, I tipped my head back against one of the shelving units. A couple weeks ago, they'd been overflowing. Now there were empty spots. They'd stay that way for a bit longer. No sense in having a ton of backup merchandise now. The hum of the generator lulled me into a zone where I lost track of time for a few minutes. It was almost like the drone of car tires on the road. I probably could have drifted off.

Almost did, except I checked the Santa's Bag again. It was full.

I hopped up and untied the drawstring. One package. I got it out. It was a large plastic container of my aunt Martha's eggnog fudge. Not at all what I'd been expecting, but there was a note taped to the top.

I opened it up and read.

Dear Jayne,

Your mom and I thought if Buttercup carried a plate of this fudge with her, it might help the yetis choose her. You can have one piece first if you want. The rest of the princess gear will be along shortly.

Love,

Aunt Martha

I smiled. It would definitely help. It was a good idea. I put the box on the crate where I'd been sitting, then went into my office and scribbled a quick note.

The fudge is a great idea. Thank you!

Love,

J

I stuffed the note into an envelope and put it in the Santa's Bag. I closed the drawstring and watched as the bag went from bulging fullness to flat and empty. The note had been sent. I sat back down on the crate, putting the container of fudge on my lap. It smelled incredible, but for Birdie's and Buttercup's sakes, and the sake of this swap going as well as possible, I wasn't taking a single piece of the delicious confection. The bigger the stack of fudge, the more enticing it would look to those yetis.

I stared and waited and thought and ran scenarios in my head and made myself crazy for the next ten minutes, which was how long it took for the Santa's Bag to puff up again. No matter what was inside—a single envelope or a year's supply of stuffed animals, the Santa's Bag always looked completely filled.

I undid the drawstring and this time found three packages. Two were velvet cases that I knew held my snowflake tiara and the rest of the snowflake accessories that made up my official court jewelry. The second was a large satin garment bag that would contain my court gown and probably the slippers that went with it.

I scooped it all into my arms, grabbed the container of fudge and headed upstairs. Time to turn Buttercup into a princess.

When I got to her place, she answered my knock quickly. "Come in the bedroom and we can lay stuff out on the bed."

"Okay." I followed her back. "You look... different." She'd scrubbed off her dark eye makeup, leaving only a hint of mascara behind. She'd also taken off all her silver jewelry, including the multitude of earrings and bracelets she normally wore.

She laughed. "I look weird, I know."

She looked shockingly innocent. Maybe in part because the ever-present glint of cynicism that normally shown in her eyes had been replaced by the spark of fear.

I grabbed her hand. "You don't have to do this, you know."

She shrugged, and the fear I'd seen disappeared. "I know. But I want to."

"You're sure?"

She snorted. "Totally. This is going to be a real adventure."

"That's for sure." I set everything on her bed.

The rest of the transformation took less time than I'd expected. We were about the same size, although she was a smidge taller than I was. With my court gown on, she could have easily passed for royalty. This was going to work.

She stared at herself in the bedroom mirror. "I look like a total poser."

"No, you don't. You look amazing."

"Thanks. Still kinda weird, though. I'm not a dress person."

"You are today." I opened up the case that held my tiara. The diamonds glittered in the light.

Buttercup turned, her hands on her stomach and nervousness in her gaze. "Are you really going to put that on me?"

"Yes. You need to look so much like a queen the yetis have no choice but to accept you as Birdie's replacement."

She sucked in her cheeks. "But it's, like, really expensive, right?"

"Right. But Birdie's life is at stake. And yours. Compared to that, diamonds are worthless." I dangled the tiara off one finger. "I would trade this in a heartbeat if it meant putting everything back to normal."

She nodded. I took that to mean she was agreeing with me. And ready for me to put the tiara on her. With a little smile, I lifted the tiara and snugged the little combs into her hair.

She swallowed, putting a hand up to adjust the crown. "This is surreal."

I laughed softly. "So is having yetis overrun Nocturne Falls."

"True enough. Has anyone besides you ever worn this crown?"

"Nope." I opened the second case and put the bracelet, earrings and necklace on her as well.

She took a deep breath and glanced in the mirror again. "I'm just not going to think about how much all of this costs."

"Good idea." The garment bag was slipping off the bed, so I picked it up and realized there was still something in the bag. I fished around and came up with a flat envelope of navy-blue suede tied with matching ribbon. Another piece of jewelry? I untied the ribbon and opened the envelope. My mouth gaped as the object came into view. "How about that."

"What?" Buttercup turned to see what I was talking about. Her eyes lit up when they landed on the blade in my hands. "Cool. Is that a dagger?"

I nodded. "And there's a strap to attach it to

your thigh. Apparently, my mom and aunt want you protected when you go in."

Buttercup's grin broadened. "They're all right. You tell them I said thanks, okay?"

"I will." I gave her the dagger. The handle was set with a piece of winter elf crystal and had a pattern of snowflakes worked into the blade. It was gorgeous. But I also hoped Buttercup had no reason to use it.

She took the blade, planted her foot on the bed so she could hike up the gown, and strapped the dagger into place. "There."

"You know what? Take your cell phone too."

"You think that's a good idea?"

"Yes. Just for emergencies. The yetis ate Birdie's when she tried to use it."

"Got it." She dug it out of her purse, tucked it in next to the dagger, then put her foot back on the floor and smoothed the gown out. "I feel like a warrior princess now."

I smiled. "Is that one of the options in your video games?"

She laughed. "It is, actually, but not one I've ever picked. I might now, though."

"So…are you ready to do this?"

"I am."

I slipped my phone out of my pocket. "I'll text the sheriff and let him know we're on our way."

"How are we going to get there?"

"Huh. Good question. I hadn't thought about that. You know what? I'm sure he can send someone to pick us up." I started texting.

We're ready to make the swap, but we need a ride to the park.

I looked up at Buttercup. "We could go wait in my office."

"All right." She picked up the container of eggnog fudge. "I feel too antsy just to stay up here."

About halfway down the stairs, Sheriff Merrow texted me back. *Car on the way.*

"Our ride is on the way," I announced.

"Good."

I sent Sin a quick text. *Headed to the park to make the swap if you can break away.* Maybe it was selfish of me to pull him from his doughnut making, but having him there would mean a lot to me.

His response came as we headed out to wait at the warehouse door. *Be there in ten.*

The snow was still coming down when we walked outside. We stood there for a moment, and then I looked at her, all decked out in my royal finery and was struck by her willingness to put herself in harm's way. "Thank you."

She glanced at me. "You're welcome."

"I can't believe you're doing this. I mean, I kind of can. You're pretty fearless. I really admire that about you, Buttercup."

She squinted at me. "Thanks. But don't get all

mushy on me. That's not my gig, you know?"

I laughed. "I know. But you need to hear how much I appreciate your part in this."

"We're both winter elves. It's as much my responsibility to help end this as it is yours."

"Thank you." Those words weren't enough. "I promise you won't be in there long. My dad and his council are going to come up with a solution very soon."

"I know they are." She tipped her head toward the end of the street. "Our ride has arrived."

I turned to see a black SUV with the Nocturne Falls pumpkin logo on the side. Inside the pumpkin was the town name. I guess this was an official vehicle.

Chet, the bouncer from the Insomnia nightclub, hopped out and came around to open the door for us.

"Hey," I said. "Do you work for the town too?" I hadn't been to Insomnia in a while. Greyson liked to hang out there, seeing as how he worked part time for the owner, a reclusive retired reaper by the name of Lucien. Because of that, I stayed away. Running into him would be awkward. Especially if Sin was with me.

Chet smiled. "Hi, Miss Frost. Yes, I do a little driving for the town when needed, which isn't often. Happy to take you and your friend to the park."

"Well, we appreciate it." We got in and he shut the door. I waited until he was back at the wheel to ask my next questions. "So you know about Birdie? And what's going on?"

"I know she's being held hostage by yetis who came in through a magical portal that's linked to the North Pole."

"You pretty much know the whole thing, then." I sat back.

He shrugged and glanced at me through the rearview mirror. "Word travels fast in this town."

"I'll say." I stared out the window, wondering how many of the people who knew what was happening were also blaming me. At least for the moment, everything that was going on could be fixed. I checked the snow globe in my purse, but the snow was still.

I closed my eyes and wished as hard as I could that the exchange went well, that neither Birdie or Buttercup were harmed, and that my dad would find a solution to all of this before something happened that couldn't be fixed.

Balfour Park looked the same as when I'd last seen it, which hadn't been that long ago, but I'd sort of expected there'd be a crowd at some point. Chet let us off and we walked up to the entrance where Deputy Blythe was still on gate duty.

Sheriff Merrow, his brother Titus, their sister Bridget, Hugh and Sebastian Ellingham, and Pandora Williams, witch and real estate agent, met us as the deputy waved us in.

Sin's black SUV arrived as we walked toward those waiting.

Hugh's uneasy smile greeted us. "Royalty becomes you, Miss Evergreen."

Buttercup had the box of fudge tucked under one arm. She did a little curtsey. "Thank you."

I held up one finger. "Quick question. How are you keeping the crowds away? I thought this place would be mobbed by now."

"We cast a spell," Pandora said. "Me, Marigold, and our mom, Corette. We set up a disillusion spell over the park. Any human who looks at the park won't see anything but snow, and they'll get a feeling that there's a better place to be. Can't do anything about what supernaturals see and feel, but the humans are who we need to protect."

"That's good. Thank you."

"Sure thing." She smiled. "Gotta protect the property values."

Sin joined the group. "Hey."

"Hey." His presence went a long way toward calming my nerves. I gave him a little smile, then shifted my focus to Sheriff Merrow. "So. Any thought on how you want to do this?"

"We've been working on a plan," he said.

Hugh Ellingham patted the messenger bag hanging off his shoulder. I hadn't noticed it because the black bag blended with his black overcoat. "Delaney sent me with a large quantity of chocolates. We're going to make a trail of them that leads from the fortress to Miss Evergreen."

Pandora stepped in closer. "That's when I'll work my magic. Literally. I'm going to cast a spell of enchantment over her. The yetis will be drawn to her like woodland creatures to a Disney princess."

I nodded. "And with the container of fudge she's carrying, they should be unable to resist."

Titus crossed his arms, his gaze tapering. "While

the yetis are occupied with their new queen, Hank and I are going to storm the castle and get Birdie out."

I hoped Titus didn't end up another giant wolf-cicle like he had the first time. "I can help. I can make a snow ramp up to the top. That way you won't have to jump to the top. Or jump down when you have Birdie."

Titus nodded. "Much appreciated. It would be easier if we knew where Birdie was inside the fortress, but hopefully she'll hear us and meet us halfway."

An idea popped into my head. I held up my hand. "Give me just a second to talk to Sinclair. Sin?" I tipped my head to one side, urging him to join me in a private conversation.

We walked a little ways off.

"What's up?"

"I was wondering…could you send Ada in to do some recon?" Ada was his ghost helper. He'd explained to me after her part in his daring rescue of me (at the hands of jewel thieves, no less), that she was an entity who'd attached herself to him after he'd moved to Nocturne Falls. It happened sometimes, he said. Necromancers were an easy target for lonely ghosts because the ghosts could sense that the necromancers were capable of seeing them.

Fortunately for Sin, Ada was the helpful type.

He nodded. "Great idea. She'd love that. Let me call her." He closed his eyes for a second. When he opened them again, they were silver-white with no visible pupils. I'd never seen that before. "Ada, I need your help."

The older woman appeared between us, wearing the same long flannel nightgown and sleeping cap that she'd worn the first time I'd seen her. And just like that time, she was still transparent. The white of the snow made it worse, actually. I had to really focus to see her. "What can I do for you?"

He pointed at the ice castle. "I need you to go in there and find the woman the creatures who built it are holding hostage. We need to know where she is so our rescue party can find her when they breach the walls."

She nodded. "You got it." Then she disappeared.

She returned a second later.

"That was fast," I said.

She smiled. "Efficiency is life."

"I'll remember that."

She looked at Sin again. "She's on the second floor in a room in the middle. Those little blue creatures are all around it. Like they're guarding her."

"Snowballs. But that's about what I suspected. Thank you, Ada."

"Yes," Sin said. "Thank you so much."

She smiled, her face crinkling up in a way that reminded me of my aunt Martha. "Happy to help."

Ada vanished and we rejoined the group. Sin shared what we learned.

Sheriff Merrow nodded. "That helps a lot, thank you." He looked at Buttercup. "Are you ready?"

"Oh yes." Buttercup rubbed her hands together nervously. "Not saying I'm losing my nerve, but sooner would be better than later."

Sheriff Merrow tugged at the brim of his ball cap. "All right. Pandora, Hugh, Sebastian. You're out front with Miss Evergreen. Sinclair, Titus, and Miss Frost will join me to head around the side and get into position for the recovery. We're going in as soon as the bulk of the yetis are on the ground. Anything goes sideways, send up the signal."

"The signal?" Buttercup asked. "What's that?"

Sebastian Ellingham pulled a flare gun from the pocket of his overcoat. "We thought this would be easiest to see."

My eyes widened. "I think you made a good choice." I turned to Buttercup. "I know you're not big into hugging, but I'm going to hug you."

She smiled, but the tremble of her bottom lip gave away her nerves. "It's okay."

I hugged her, hard. "Thanks again," I whispered. Then I let her go before I teared up myself. "See you on the other side."

I walked around the long way with Sin, Titus and the sheriff. "I feel eyes on us."

"Mm-hmm," Titus said.

Sin just sighed. And while none of us looked at the fortress, the feeling of being watched was unmistakable. The yetis knew something was up.

"They can probably smell the wolf in us," the sheriff offered. "Or they recognize the scent from Birdie and are curious."

"Maybe." I hadn't thought about that. "Doesn't matter, though. That chocolate will become their main focus soon enough."

"Sure about that?" Titus asked.

"I was right about the doughnuts."

"Yes, you were," Sin said.

I smiled a little, really happy he'd come along.

We stopped behind a stand of pine trees and turned to watch. From this angle, we could only see about a few feet out from the front of the castle but not the wall itself. Hugh and Sebastian were almost done with the path of chocolates. How close to the ice wall it started, I had no idea, but it stopped just in front of Buttercup.

Her hands were at her sides. Her right hand seemed to be pressed to where the dagger was strapped to her thigh. Couldn't blame her for wanting that reassurance. But otherwise, she stood with the same regal bearing any true royal would have had, chin up, facing the inevitable onslaught like she'd been born for that moment. And maybe she had been. I was proud of her for all kinds of reasons.

The Ellinghams retreated until they were a couple yards away from Buttercup. Pandora was off to the side, behind a big drift of snow.

Small, furry blue shapes had begun to gather at the top of the ice wall.

"Look," I whispered.

The Merrow brothers nodded.

"It's working," Titus said.

"And they already know we brought them doughnuts with no strings attached. Probably won't take as long for them to investi—"

Three yetis slid down the ice wall and out of sight.

"That's my cue." With one eye on Buttercup and one eye on the section of the wall in front of me, I lifted my hands and started forming the snow ramp. It was tough going. This magical snow was slow to respond and stubborn, just like the ice in my apartment had been. I grunted a little at the effort.

"You okay, babe?"

I nodded at Sin. I could do this. I *would* do this.

"Anything we can do to help?" Hank asked.

"No," I whispered, trying not to break my concentration while still keeping tabs on Buttercup.

Sin seemed to sense what I was struggling with. He took up the lookout spot. "There's about fifteen yetis approaching Buttercup. Wait. Fifteen in front and I'd say another...twenty behind them. The chocolates are almost gone from what I can see."

The ramp grew, slowly inching up the wall. Stupid stubborn magical snow.

"There must be forty of them now. They're clustering around her in a semicircle. They don't seem to be going any closer than about three or four feet." He leaned to the side a little. "Pandora must be doing her thing. Her hands are up like yours. The air around Buttercup is sort of shimmery. Must be the magic."

The ramp was about halfway up. Sweat trickled down my back, and my hands were starting to shake.

Titus and the sheriff crouched near the front of our spot, anticipating the moment they could leap into action.

"A second row of yetis is forming. Maybe another twenty in that group. They're staring at her. And I think sniffing the air."

The eggnog fudge was working. I smiled for a second, then gave up on any facial expression that took effort. The snowy slope was nearing the top. Maybe two feet away. Close enough. I stopped building it and started working on compacting it enough to hold the weight of three people.

Sinclair made a soft, throaty noise. "The yetis are bowing down. That has to mean something."

Hank punched his brother in the arm. "Means it's time to get Birdie out of there."

"Ramp's ready," I managed. "Go."

The two of them leaped forward, shifting into their wolf forms and racing up the incline to the top of the fortress. Despite the work I'd put into it, I didn't trust the snow to hold on its own, so I maintained my focus and my magic to keep it strong until they were back down.

That didn't take as much effort as building the ramp, so I was able to shift a quarter of my attention to Buttercup. Just in time, too, as she let out a little squeal.

I sucked in a breath. "Sin."

"I know," he answered.

The yetis had swarmed her and were now carrying her crowd-surfing-style back to the fortress. I looked at the top of the ramp, but there was no sign of Titus, Hank or Birdie.

I knew they had to get to the center of that fortress, but I still willed them to hurry. I willed Birdie to be okay. I willed the yetis to just go home already.

A tuft of blue danced at the wall's edge. A yeti? No. Birdie. I sighed in relief. One of the wolves leaned over the wall, letting her hold on to him as she climbed over. She dropped onto the slope.

Her feet went out from under her, and she plopped down onto her backside. She started scooting down the ramp, which was fine with me. Down was down.

Hank and Titus came sailing over the wall right

behind her, although in their wolf forms, I wasn't sure which was which.

They hit the snow and caught up to Birdie, woofing at her. She grabbed hold of the fur at their necks and they took off, pulling her down the ramp like sled dogs without a sled. When they reached the bottom, I dropped my hands and released my magic.

The slope crumbled like bad cake.

I went to my knees along with it, exhausted from the effort I'd put in and a little heartsick that Buttercup was now the yetis' prisoner. Don't get me wrong, it was great that Birdie was out of danger. I was *thrilled* about that. But I was torn between my happiness over getting her out and the sadness and anxiety of Buttercup taking her place.

Sin went to his knees beside me, his arm around me for support.

I took a deep breath and leaned into him. At least Buttercup would do better against the cold. And she had the dagger and her cell phone. I took as much comfort in that as I could and lifted my head to watch Birdie and her nephews run toward me. They radiated happiness, and that put a smile on my face as well.

"Princess! You did it!"

Titus offered me a hand. I waved it off. I wasn't ready to be on my feet just yet. "Wasn't me. It was Buttercup and your nephews and Pandora."

She kneeled down and Sin moved out of the way so she could hug me. "You were a big part of it."

The hug felt nice. "Thanks. But I think I might pass out now."

I must have done exactly that, because I woke up in the back of the sheriff's car. The heater was on and it felt like it was a thousand degrees. Birdie was in the front seat. "Oof. Am I being cooked?"

She cranked the heat off. "Sorry. Didn't want you to get a chill."

I rubbed my head. "How long was I out?"

"Only about ten minutes," Birdie said.

"How are you?" She was wrapped in a blanket and still looked kind of pale to me.

"I'm okay. Better now." She smiled at me. "You ready to go home?"

"Yeah. I'm more than ready for this whole thing to be over." I sat up. "Hey, where's my purse? I need to see if my dad's found out anything new."

"Should be on the seat next to you." She pointed.

I glanced down. Yep, there it was. I dug into it and pulled the globe out. The snow was still until I gave it a good shake.

My dad's face showed up a couple seconds later. "How did the swap go?"

"As planned. Birdie's out, she's also here with me, and Buttercup is in." I looked through the windshield at the fortress. There was no movement or sign of yetis. Sin was standing with the Ellinghams. "I guess she's okay."

"Good. Have you found anything else out about Myra Grimshaw?"

"No, but Birdie was the one doing the investigating. And she's only just been freed, so…"

"Right." He nodded.

Birdie leaned over the seat. "I'll get back on it as soon as I'm home and on my laptop."

He looked toward her voice. "Thank you."

She glanced at me. "Did you tell him about her being adopted?"

"What was that?" my dad asked.

I answered him. "Birdie found out Myra Grimshaw might have been adopted. Which we think could mean she was actually a winter elf and not fae like she claimed. Does that help you at all?"

His eyes narrowed. "It might. Can you get me her date of birth?"

I looked at Birdie.

She nodded. "I'll have it to you as soon as I get home."

"Did you hear that?"

"Yes, thank you. With that info, I should be able to track her down. Winter elf adoptions are a rare thing." He paused for a moment. "I have some news too."

"Which is?"

He shook his head. "Not good. The tinker who was in charge of the snow globes in question is Eustace Brightly. And apparently Eustace put a little of himself into the magic that operated them. We don't know if he did it intentionally or not, but because of it, our tinkers now have been unable to successfully close any portal created by one of his snow globes."

"What do you mean a little of himself?"

"You've heard the saying blood, sweat and tears?"

"I have."

"We think he used blood. Just a drop."

"Okay, gross." I grimaced. "Does that happen a lot?"

"No, thankfully. It's very old school and it's been discouraged for years, but sometimes, when a tinker can't get something to work, they resort to that level of magic."

"Wow." Then I thought about what he'd said. "Wait. Back up. You've had the tinkers open portals using the retired snow globes?"

"Yes. They've broken four of them so far and successfully opened portals each time. Fortunately, the portals have only been to other parts of the NP, but creating a portal seems a natural occurrence because of the magic within them."

That was interesting. "So what does that mean that they haven't been able to close one?"

"We think it means that only Eustace, or someone from Eustace's family, has the right magic to close the portal. Someone with his blood in their veins."

"And that's bad news because?"

"Because Eustace passed away eight months ago. And from everything that our records indicate, he was the last of the Brightlys."

I felt like I'd been punched in the gut. And Birdie looked like she was about to cry. "There has to be another way to close the portal."

My dad's chest rose and fell with a deep breath. "We're working on it. I promise."

"I know you are."

"I'll be in touch as soon as I have something."

"Thanks, Dad." I hung up. And just sat there, staring through the windshield, a little numb and a lot unsure what to do next. "You heard all that, right, Birdie?"

"I did, Princess." She smiled at me. It was a very mothering smile. "You okay? You don't look okay."

"I'm...I don't know how I am. I feel lost. It's not often my dad doesn't have an answer, you know?" I blew out a breath. "And I can't help but feel responsible for all of this."

She reached back and patted my knee. "You know what I do when I feel like the weight of the world is on my shoulders?"

She was being sweet and trying to comfort me, but I'm not sure Birdie had ever felt the weight of a thing like this. Even so, I gave her my full attention because I had no doubt she had some wisdom to share. And I needed some wisdom desperately. "What's that?"

"I do what I can do," she said matter-of-factly. "And I lean on my friends."

I looked at her. "I'm not sure I know what you mean about the doing what I can do part."

"What are you good at?"

Right now, it didn't feel like anything. "I don't know."

She clucked her tongue at me. "Come on, now. You're very good at managing. People especially. And you have a lot of friends. One who's sitting in this car with you right now."

"What are you saying?"

With a slightly wicked grin, Birdie leaned in. "Let's go dig up every bit of dirt on Myra Grimshaw we can. Her birth date, her school records, her favorite brand of ice cream. Everything and anything."

"You want to go to the station?"

She gave me a look. "I was thinking something a little closer to home."

"Your house?"

"Closer to a different home."

Then I realized she didn't mean on the computer. "You want to go to Myra's."

She tapped the side of her nose. "Now you've got it."

"Do you have a key?"

She tipped her head like I was being silly. "Jayne. I know you can get in."

Yes, she did. She'd seen me perform the Santa Slide. She'd stood guard while I'd done it. "You're right. It's time to see what else Myra's been hiding."

Birdie scooted over to the driver's side.

"Wait, are we going right now? In this car? Isn't this the sheriff's car?"

"Yes, and I'm his aunt." She threw it in reverse.

The sound turned a few heads. And got the sheriff walking.

"Um, your nephew is on his way over here."

She sighed. "I see him. Play along."

Like I had a choice.

She rolled down the window as he approached. "Just going to borrow your car to—"

"No."

"Hank, don't sass me. I need the car."

"Not my patrol car you don't. Where do you want to go?"

"My house."

I guess we'd be going to Myra's from there. On foot. Good thing I'd put my boots on.

He pointed at the passenger side. "Move over. I'll drive you."

She obliged, and we were on the way to her place in minutes. The sheriff radioed Deputy Blythe to tell her what was going on and asked her to inform his brother as well. When he clicked off, he spoke to Birdie again. "I would have thought you'd rather go to the station. Catch up on what you missed while you were tied up."

"I wasn't tied up. I was free to walk around. Mostly."

I was sitting behind Birdie now so I could see the side eye he gave her. "You know what I mean."

"After being detained, such as I was, I want to be in my own house for a bit. See that all's well there. Then I'll worry about whatever catching up I need to do. Who's taking care of the front desk, by the way?"

"Jansen. Desk duty is all he deserves right now."

His punishment, I supposed, for breaking the snow globe.

Sheriff Merrow glanced at me through the rearview mirror. "Warehouse?"

"No, I'm going over to Birdie's too."

An understanding light came into his eyes. "I see."

I'm sure he did. But thankfully, he didn't seem to mind whatever he thought we were about to get up to. He didn't press the issue, either. Whatever he was thinking, he had to know our mission was to solve this thing. At least that was what I guessed, as he was quiet the rest of the way. We all were. A lot on our minds, no doubt.

He dropped us off at Birdie's, we said goodbye, and in we went. Birdie did a quick check of her place. "Everything looks fine. And now that I'm here, I'd really like a hot shower and a change of clothes. You all right with that?"

"Absolutely. After what you've been through? You've earned it."

"You want to see if you can rustle us up something to eat too? I'd made a lasagna for Jack right before the yetis snatched me, but obviously that never got to him. Why don't you heat us up a few pieces?"

"I'm on it."

"Thanks." She started for the bedroom, then stopped, her gaze landing on me in a way that made me feel like she was sizing me up. "You know how to heat up lasagna, right?"

"I'm not *that* helpless in the kitchen." I put my hands on my hips. Then dropped them. "Microwave?"

"Half power, covered with a damp paper towel so the noodles don't dry out."

"Got it." I headed for the kitchen. A few minutes later, I heard the shower running.

I managed to heat up two big pieces of lasagna without setting anything on fire, and by the time Birdie had rejoined me, I'd also set the table and added two glasses of lemonade from the pitcher I'd found in the fridge. It was a slightly odd drink on this deep freeze of a day, but it was that or water.

"That looks great. I never thought I'd feel this way, but I'm sick of sweets. It's all the yetis brought me." She'd changed into jeans and a sweat shirt. I couldn't say I'd ever seen her in that combo before, but if she wanted to be comfortable, it was perfect.

"Are you glad we didn't ply them with raw fish?"

She made a face as she took her place at the table. "Oh, I texted Jack."

I sat across from her and we dug in. "To tell him you're okay? I'm sure he's thrilled."

"He is, but that's not the only reason I texted him. He's got a truck. He's coming to get us and take us to Myra's."

I went still, my fork in mid-air. "Um...about that. I...I don't really like people knowing about my breaking and entering skill. You're pretty much the only one in town who's seen it."

She finished the bite of lasagna she'd forked up. "Not even Sinclair?"

"Nope. Not yet. It's just one of those things that

could implicate me in a lot of shady business if word got out. Know what I mean?"

She nodded and sipped her lemonade. "Sure, I understand. Tell you what, I'll distract him in the truck while you go around back and go in that way. Then you can unlock the front door. Does that work?"

"It does. But how are you going to explain me getting in?"

"Key under the back mat." She leaned in. "And listen, Jack is going to be so grateful that I'm all right, he's not going to care how you got in."

"Okay." I hoped she was right, but it was a small thing to worry about when the town was in need of a serious de-frosting.

Jack showed up half an hour later and we were ready. The downed tree that had blocked my and Sin's path earlier had been removed, so it didn't take us long to get to Myra's. As planned, I went around back and slipped through the door that went into the kitchen.

I took my time, sitting on the tile floor for at least five minutes until my head was as clear as a summer sky. I didn't need to fall down those basement steps because I was still dizzy. When I got to the front door, only Birdie was there.

I looked past her. "Why is Jack still in the truck?"

She pushed past me into the house and closed

the door. "This is a stealth mission. He's on lookout. If anyone, like my nephew, comes by, he's going to call me and warn us to get out."

"I see. So he knows we're not really supposed to be in here?"

"Sure."

"And he's okay with that?"

"Jack's cool."

I smirked. "Apparently. All right, let's get to work so we don't have to be in here any longer than necessary."

"Right. I'll check this part of the house, you take that cabinet in the basement since that's all winter elf stuff."

"Sounds good." I looked around. I doubted Birdie would find anything. The place was still a wreck from the yetis storming through. "Holler if you find anything."

"You too."

We split up and I headed back to the kitchen and down the steps, flipping the light on as I went.

I sighed when I saw the ice puddle had grown. Again. The last thing this town needed was more yetis in it. If one came through while I was here, I wasn't sure what I would do. Whack it on the nose? Or did that only work with sharks?

I stood at the bottom of the steps, staring at the portal and racking my brain for any genius idea on how to close it. Nothing came to me. Which was probably good, because my dad had told me closing it could make the yetis panic. I sure didn't need them feeling threatened while Buttercup was their hostage.

Stepping carefully around the portal, I made my way to the cabinet. I'd glanced at the newspaper clippings when I'd been here before. This time, I wanted to dig into some of the boxes on the shelves.

I started with a small one about the size of a recipe box, only to find it actually held recipes. They were all North Pole favorites. Reindeer chow. Fish stew. Wintermint popovers. Syrup pudding. Stuff like that.

I closed the box and shook my head. Why would Myra have been interested in North Pole recipes unless she was a winter elf? My belief that her true heritage was the same as mine was only strengthened by the things in this cabinet. All those pictures of my family…was it possible Myra was a distant relative? Or was she just fascinated by the royal side of things?

Further digging turned up two more pieces of winter elf crystal, including a small heart pendant and a penguin figurine. A larger box on the bottom shelf looked well-worn. I picked it up next.

It was full of letters, each one in a creamy ivory envelope that I recognized instantly. It was standard NP stationery. None of the letters had an address, just a beautifully drawn M on the front of the envelopes. Myra.

These letters hadn't come by standard post. I glanced at the ice puddle. Had they come through the snow globe? That would mean she'd been communicating regularly with someone in the North Pole.

It felt a little snoopy to read through someone else's mail, but I had no choice. I opened the first envelope and pulled the letter out. The paper was the same creamy ivory. I skimmed down to the bottom, but the short note was only signed with S.

I went back to the top to read and see if that would help me figure out who S was.

"Princess! I found something. I think." Birdie jogged down the stairs holding a man's handkerchief. "It was under her pillow."

I didn't want to think about Birdie riffling through a dead woman's bed linens. "It's a guy's hankie?"

"Yes, but that's not the interesting part. Look." She held out the square of bright white fabric so I could see the corner.

It was embroidered with an S.

I held up the letter I'd been about to peruse. "I found the same thing. This letter is signed S too."

Birdie looked at the linen square in her hand. "Hmm. Men's handkerchiefs are usually monogramed with the initial of their last name, but it seems unlikely a man would sign a note to a woman that way."

"Agreed. But then again, maybe that initial isn't for his first or last name at all. Maybe it's for a nickname. A pet name they only shared between themselves."

"Great, that makes it easy." Birdie rolled her eyes. "I guess we should just focus on figuring out who S is? I really hope it's not Santa."

I swallowed. I really hoped that too. "I'm sure it's not my uncle, but that's exactly why we need to dig into this. And we should also figure out who he was to her." I pulled out about half of the letters.

"Here. You read through these, and I'll read through the other half, and we'll compare notes."

She took them. "On it."

We sat side-by-side on the steps and went through each envelope, scanning the letters for clues.

Birdie paused in the middle of her third or fourth one. "Do you get the feeling they saved the juiciest bits for their talks through the globe?"

"Yes." I gave the letter I was holding a little shake. "It's like these letters were just teases. Lots of gooey sentiment and poetic turns of phrases, but nothing of value. Not yet anyway."

"Same. Maybe that'll change."

We went back to reading, but by the last letter, we were no closer to figuring out who S was. We did, however, know that Myra must have been seriously in love with him. And he with her.

I tucked the letters back into the box.

Birdie leaned back on the steps. "That was kind of a waste of time."

"Not entirely. We know that Myra was in love with someone in the North Pole. And he with her. We know that whoever that man was, he made trips here."

Birdie's face lit up a little. "That's true. In two of my letters, he said something about how he couldn't wait until he arrived."

"That might make it easier to figure out who the man was. There are travel records, after all."

"But how does that help us solve this yeti problem?"

I stared at the box in my hands. "I'm not sure. But it can't hurt. And it's better than doing nothing while we wait for my dad and his council to find us a solution."

"I suppose so."

"Look, I get it. I want there to be an answer spelled out in black and white, but this isn't going to be that simple. Unfortunately." I got up and walked the box back to the cabinet, putting it in the same spot I'd taken it from. I straightened and my gaze landed on one of the many newspaper clippings. Did any of those articles have a connection with the man named S? Besides Santa. It couldn't be him, though. Everyone who was close to him called him Kris. I stared at a clipping, trying to see whatever I hadn't seen yet.

And then I stared closer. My eyes skimmed the article. I went to the next one and skimmed it, studying the picture. Then to the next, and the next. "Birdie. I think I found something."

"You know who S is?"

"Not a clue, but look at this." I started pulling the clippings down. "In all of these articles and pictures, there's one common thread."

She came closer to look. "They're all your family?"

"Mostly, but not exclusively."

"Oh, right." She tapped the one on top of the pile in my hand. "That one's about the tinkers' annual ball. But your uncle was the guest of honor, so technically, it's still your family. Are we sure that S isn't for Santa?"

"*Yes.*"

"Okay then, I give, what is the common thread I'm missing?"

I fanned the clippings out. "Eustace Brightly is in every single one. Either named or just in the background of the picture, but he's there in some way. See?" I pointed him out in the background of one of the snaps that highlighted my dad giving an award to the kindergartener who'd read the most books in her class.

She leaned in. "Well, butter my biscuit. You're right." She tipped her head back to see the ones I'd left in the cabinet. "Look at that. Every. Single. One."

All of a sudden, she gasped. "I know exactly what happened."

"What?" I was glad one of us had figured it out.

She stabbed a finger at one of the clippings. "We're pretty sure that Myra is adopted, right?"

"Right."

"She must have researched her birth parents and found out that she was a winter elf. At some point, that discovery led her to another one. She had a brother. That brother was Eustace Brightly."

I thought about it and ended up nodding. "Seems plausible."

"These clippings aren't about your family. They're about hers."

"Wow, that makes real sense." I was also super relieved that Myra hadn't been stalking us. "But where does the mysterious S come in?"

"I bet she went to the North Pole to meet her brother, and while she was there, she met a man."

"Mr. S."

"Exactly."

I pondered that a moment. "You know, that might be enough for us to track him down. I mean, if we assume that he's a winter elf and that he was a friend of Eustace's, and more importantly, that he traveled to Nocturne Falls on several occasions, which we know from the letters, then that really narrows the field. Hey, I wonder if he was a tinker too? He could have been if he was a friend of Eustace's. That would definitely explain how he got access to the snow globes."

"It would indeed," Birdie said. "Too bad we don't know if that S is for his first name or last name."

I groaned. "I hadn't thought about that."

"Don't worry, we'll figure it out. It's probably his first." Then she let out a big sigh. "I just wish it got us closer to losing the yetis."

"I know."

Birdie shrugged. "Maybe there's no point in trying to figure out who Mr. S is."

"Except, if Mr. S is still alive, he might be able to help us."

"How do you figure?"

"Well, he *must* have been a friend of Eustace's if he had a snow globe too. Maybe he was enough of a friend that Eustace let him in on the secret of how he created the magic that made them work. Maybe there's another way to close the portal without Eustace's blood."

She made a face. "That would be great."

I nodded. "For sure. I need to get my dad to send me all the travel records for the last forty-two years. Since the experimental snow globes were first created."

"That's going to be a lot to sort through."

"Yep. But what else have I got to do?"

"Call me when you get them. I'll come over and help."

"It's a date. Especially if you want to bring the rest of that lasagna."

She laughed. "In that case, maybe I'll bring Jack too. Hey, get Sinclair to come over and we'll make a night of it."

"Ooo, digging through musty old files. How romantic." I giggled. "I'll ask Sin. It would be a great way for him and Jack to get to know each other."

"And then when this deep freeze is over, we can all go out to dinner like old pals."

I had to work to keep my smile in place. I loved her enthusiasm, I just didn't have any idea when this magical winter was going to come to an end. And that made putting on a brave face pretty hard. "Why don't you let Jack know we're done here? I'll call my dad and be right out."

"Sure thing, Princess." She gave my arm a little squeeze before she left.

I had no doubt she understood what I was feeling, at least to some degree. I pulled the snow globe from my purse and called my dad.

"Hey, Jayne. How's it going?"

"It's…going. I actually think we've made a little progress. We think Eustace Brightly and Myra Grimshaw might have been brother and sister. Maybe not fully. We don't know if they shared one parent or two, but it makes sense from our side."

"How so?"

I explained to him about the clippings and the letters and our theory about Mr. S.

He nodded. "You're right, it all works. So what can I do to help further?"

"I need all the travel records of any winter elf that might have traveled to Nocturne Falls going back forty-two years. Also, for that same time frame, I want the tinkers' register."

His brows lifted. "You're asking for a ton of paperwork."

"I know, but I've got a team of people ready to help me go through it."

"I'll have it to you in an hour."

"Perfect. Thanks, Dad."

"Now, I have a little news to share."

Every nerve in my body paid attention. "Does it have anything to do with my yeti problem?"

"It does." He held a hand up. "We've managed to temporarily close one of the portals we opened."

"Temporarily?"

He nodded. "I wish it was better news, but I feel like it's progress."

"How did you do it?"

"Salt water."

"Of course." Why hadn't I thought of that? "Salt water wreaks havoc on winter elf magic, so why wouldn't it do the same to the yetis' magic? But only temporarily, huh?"

"So far."

"Well, it's progress. Any idea on how to get the yetis back through the portal?"

"Still working on that one."

I nodded, sort of out of words.

"I know you're disappointed."

I sighed. "I just want to bring Buttercup home and get things back to normal."

"I know, sweetheart. We all want that too." His

smile was tight-lipped and stress lines bracketed his eyes. "I'll get that paperwork sent ASAP."

"Thanks. Love you."

"Love you too." He hung up.

I tucked the globe back into my purse and headed up to the truck. Something had to give, and it had to give soon.

True to his word, my dad sent the boxes through the Santa's Bag an hour later. Fifty-three minutes later, to be exact. I had no doubt that everyone in the North Pole was working on this problem.

With the help of Kip, Juniper, Sinclair, Birdie and Jack, we hauled the boxes, all twenty-seven of them, up to my apartment. Then Kip and Juniper went to meet Juni's boyfriend, Pete, who was driving them in his Jeep to Balfour Park to check on Buttercup. I asked them to report in if there was anything to report.

The boxes were sturdy cardboard with handles on the sides and lids that fit snugly. They were a little dusty and a lot heavy. And because my dad had pulled them so quickly, they hadn't been pre-sorted in any way. We were looking at years of general travel records for NP citizens that could have been going anywhere in the world. And all those decades of the tinker's registers. All of it was done by year, no alphabetizing.

A daunting job lay ahead of us.

And stacked in my apartment, those boxes looked more like a hundred and seven than twenty-seven. Be that as it may, Jack, Birdie, Sinclair and I settled in to sort through every sheet of paper inside them. Spider and Sugar helped by sitting on and *in* some of the boxes.

Both cats seemed especially interested in Jack. Perhaps it was the shifter side of his familiar kind. He could transform himself into a raven, after all. In fact, I could have sworn Spider licked him.

Birdie gave Spider a pat on the head as she went into the kitchen to set the oven to warm up. When she finished that, she took a spot at the dining table with Jack.

Sinclair and I set up on the sofa, using the coffee table as our workspace. He'd thoughtfully brought eclairs for our dessert. He glanced at me. "How do you want to do this? Should we just call out when we find a name that starts with S?"

"I think so."

Jack raised his head from the file he'd already begun reading. "First name, last name, or both?"

"Both," Birdie answered. "We don't know which it is for sure. Probably first, but who knows?"

He glanced at me over his glasses. "This is quite a manhunt you have us on."

"Tell me about it." I pulled the first file from the box before me and sat back to read.

"You know," Jack added. "You should talk to your father about computerizing this stuff."

I smiled. "We can't. Electronics are spotty at best in the NP. Too much magnetic interference."

He nodded. "I should have known that."

We fell into silence for a while. Sugar curled up on a box while Spider chose a spot on the dining room table next to Jack. Both of the cats fell asleep, letting out little snores once in a while. After a bit, the oven dinged that it had heated to the right temperature. Birdie got up, put the lasagna in, set a timer, then went back to work.

The cats, awoken by the bell, trotted off to the bedroom. Probably looking for a quieter place to nap.

I got up to grab a Dr Pepper from the fridge (and the stash that never ran out thanks to the same set of wishes that had turned Spider's voice box on). I held the bottle up. "Anyone else?"

"I'll take one." Birdie held her hand out.

Jack glanced up. "Have any coffee?"

"No, but I could make some."

With a soft laugh, Sinclair got to his feet. "I'll make the coffee. Jayne's talents don't lie in that direction."

I pursed my lips. "I'd say something to the

contrary, but he's telling the truth." I handed Birdie her Dr Pepper on my way back to the couch.

Sinclair returned to his spot shortly after and we all went silent again, the only sounds coming from the coffeemaker and the shuffling of papers.

About halfway through my file, Birdie spoke up. "I found a Simon Hart."

"Age?"

"Hmm." She rifled through the file. "Never mind. He was seventy at the time this registry was recorded. Which was thirty years ago."

"Yeah, probably a long shot."

We kept going.

"Here's one," Jack said. "Francis Saint. Age seems right."

I looked up. "Let's start a stack for all possibilities."

"Will do." Jack put that file in the middle of the table.

When the oven timer dinged, we'd added three more to the pile of possible mystery men. Birdie dished up the lasagna while Jack moved the files from the dining table to the breakfast counter. We ate pretty quickly with a little small talk, but each one of us felt the press of time. We were back at the files in short order.

Birdie cleaned up while we worked, something I really appreciated. Just like I appreciated the group effort to help with this.

When she sat down to work again, she leaned back in her chair to look at me. "Princess, do you think there's any chance the mysterious Mr. S is Tempus Sanders?"

"The Sandman?" He had been a special guest at the store a while back because he'd written a children's book guaranteed to make kids fall asleep. "I don't think so. Pretty sure the book signing was his first and only visit to Nocturne Falls. I like that you're thinking outside the box, though."

"He popped into my head, so I figured I'd ask."

"Nothing ventured, nothing gained." My phone chimed. I checked the screen to see a text from Juniper.

Buttercup is doing fine. You want help with the files?

Glad to hear that, I texted back. *Thanks for the offer, but we're doing great.* I knew she wanted to spend time with Pete, something she wouldn't do if I took her up on the offer of help.

I let the group know. "Juniper says Buttercup is doing fine."

"I'm so glad to hear that," Birdie said.

"Me too." Jack put his hand over top of Birdie's. "She's a brave woman to take Birdie's place."

"That's for sure," Sin added.

I tucked my phone away and we all returned to work.

The soft sounds of shuffling paper filled the space once more. One by one, another dozen files were added to the keeper stack. It was slow going. And tedious.

An hour had passed when Sinclair closed the file he was reading and stretched. "Éclair, anyone?"

I put my file down too. "I'm in. My eyes are starting to cross."

Jack nodded. "Same here. But we're making good progress."

I glanced at the stack of keepers. "S is such a common letter. That's still a lot to go through and we're not half done with the boxes." I scrubbed my hands over my face. "I really hope this isn't a waste of time. But it sort of feels that way right now."

Jack got up to refill his coffee cup. "I'm sure it does, Princess, but if we can find this guy and he's the link we need to close that portal, then it will all be worth it. And even if we don't find the guy, or we do and he turns out not to be any help, we've still had a nice evening together."

I laughed. "I'm glad you think sorting through decades of paperwork is a nice evening."

He smiled. "I think making new friends and being able to help them is a nice evening anytime."

"Thank you. That's very kind." He was a sweet guy, and I was really glad he and Birdie had connected. I loved that she had a man like Jack Van Zant in her life.

"He's right," Sinclair said. "Even if all of this turns up nothing, we get the benefit of feeling like we're doing something. Like we're helping. There's a lot of people out there who are probably sitting on their hands and going stir-crazy because they don't know how to help. Or can't, because there isn't anything for them to do."

Birdie nodded. "Nocturne Falls is that kind of town. People want to be involved. They want to look out for each other and pitch in. So don't even think that this is wasted time. It's not." She smiled. "Especially when we also get to eat eclairs."

I laughed. "I thought you were sick of sweets?"

"That passed."

"Speaking of..." Sinclair got up and walked over to the box on the kitchen counter. He opened it, then got some paper plates out of the cabinet. "There are traditional eclairs filled with *crème patisserie* and some non-traditional raspberry-chocolate mousse filled. I brought six of each so there's plenty if you want more than one."

"Hah. This is a high-metabolism crowd here. More than one? How about more than two?" I picked a raspberry-chocolate mousse one first, then looked at Jack. "I'm assuming familiars have the benefit of the standard supernatural metabolism, but I don't know that much about familiars either."

He took two traditional eclairs, carrying one to Birdie. "We do. Maybe not as much as my shifter sweetheart here, but we can get away with extra helpings." He took his seat again. "And if you want to know anything about being a familiar, just ask."

"Thanks. Likewise if you want to know anything about being a winter elf." In my peripheral vision, I could see Sin cringing. I knew he didn't want to answer questions about being a necromancer. He was pretty private about that part of his life. I changed the subject quickly. "I think we should call it a night after these eclairs. We're going to lose focus if we push ourselves to do more."

Birdie swallowed a mouthful of éclair. "I don't mind getting through a few more boxes."

"Birdie, you need to get some rest." I had a strong feeling Jack would back me on this one. "You just got out of the yetis' lair today. You need a good night's sleep in your own warm bed."

"She's right," Jack said. "Tonight isn't the night to overdo it."

She gave him a look, but consented. "Fine. But I'm willing to help tomorrow if you want."

I smiled at her. "I know you are, but if you're really up to working tomorrow, I'm sure your nephew would like to have you back at your desk at the station. I have no doubt he's missed you."

She grunted. "I suppose."

Sin came up beside me, his hand on the small of my back. "How's the éclair?"

"Half gone. And delicious."

"Good. I'm glad you like them."

Me liking his eclairs wasn't in question. But I

had a feeling that was his way of thanking me for changing the subject.

Half an hour later, Birdie and Jack had said good night, leaving Sin and me to organize the rest of the files for tomorrow. I yawned while I was moving a box.

"Go to bed," he said.

"I will in a minute. I still need to feed the cats."

"We're both beat. The rest of this can wait until morning, and I can fill their food dishes."

I put the box down. I was too tired to argue with a man who only had my best interests at heart. "You're right. Okay, I'm off to bed. Thanks for taking care of the cats." I gave him a quick kiss. "See you tomorrow."

But as tired as I was, I ended up lying in bed, staring into the dark. My thoughts were churning too fast for me to drift off. Maybe I should get up and start going through the stack of possible men who might be Mr. S, but that would mean going out into the living room and I didn't want to disturb Sinclair.

Judging by his soft, rhythmic breathing, he *was* asleep. Sugar was probably curled up with him on the sofa bed, the way Spider was nestled in by my feet. I sighed and tucked my arm behind my head. If I couldn't sleep, and couldn't risk waking Sinclair up by working some more, I might as well organize my thoughts.

If I could. It was worth a shot.

Mr. S was a big part of those thoughts. I snorted softly at Birdie's idea that Tempus Sanders, the legendary Sandman, might have been Myra's secret beau. I loved that she thought outside of the box, but that was *really* outside of the box.

If only Tempus was here. I'd get him to send me to dreamland so I could—I sat bolt upright in bed. Tempus was the Sandman. His whole job revolved around putting people to sleep. And if he could put people to sleep, why not yetis?

My dad's sleepy face blinked at me through the snow globe. "Hi, honey. What's happened?"

"I had an idea. Listen—"

"Are you in the closet?" He squinted like he was trying to see past me.

"Yes." I hadn't wanted to wake Sinclair, so I'd also closed my bedroom door to help block out the closet light. "Did I wake you?"

"Don't worry about that."

"But how? How did snow falling in a globe wake you?"

He scrubbed a hand over his face. "I had mine retinkered to chime as well."

"Ooo, smart. Listen, I have an idea about how to get rid of the yetis."

That seemed to wake my dad up a little more. "All right, what is it?"

"Tempus Sanders."

"I don't think he knows anything more about yetis than we do."

Okay, so my dad wasn't that awake. "Dad, he doesn't have to know anything about them. He just has to put them asleep. Deeply. Then we can pop them back through the portal, close that thing up, and call it a day."

That got his attention. "That might actually work. Nicely done, Jayne. I'll reach out to him and see if he can actually put yetis to sleep. And if he can, how soon he can be in Nocturne Falls."

"We can't wait on his schedule. He has to do it now. This is an emergency. Send Uncle Kris in the sleigh for him as soon as he says yes on the yeti naps."

My dad nodded. "I hear you, and this is great, but putting the yetis through the portal is only effective if we can keep them from coming back through. That portal has to be shut down as soon as they're all through."

That part I hadn't worked out. "Are you any closer to figuring out how to do that?"

He frowned, giving me my answer. "No. But it feels like we're on the verge."

I smiled encouragingly. I knew he and his team were trying. "You'll get there."

"Let's hope it's sooner rather than later. Have you dug into those files?"

"Yes, but we're not quite halfway through."

"Okay, let me know what you turn up. And if I can help in anyway."

"I will."

"In the meantime, get some sleep, honey. I know this whole mess is probably making that hard for you to do, but you've got to take care of yourself."

"I know. And I'm trying. I promise."

"Good. I love you."

"Love you too. Give my love to Mom and Aunt Martha and Uncle Kris as well."

"I will. Night, Jay."

"Night, Dad." I hung up, then lay back on the floor of the closet and let my thoughts take over again. If Tempus could knock the yetis out, and we could send them back to the North Pole via the portal, how could we then secure the portal so they couldn't return? Even if it was just a temporary fix. There had to be something we were missing.

Soft scratching at the closet door interrupted my train of thought. I pushed to my feet and opened the door a sliver.

Spider squeezed through the crack to rub against my legs. "Mama not sleeping."

"No, I'm not. But neither are you."

He sat in front of me. "Spider likes Birdie."

"I'm glad to hear it."

"Spider likes bird man too."

My brows lifted. "You mean Uncle Jack?"

"Uncle Jack has good flavor."

229

"Spider, it's not polite to taste our visitors, even if they do have a secondary form you find appealing."

"What's appealing?"

"Appetizing." Then I realized he might not know that word either. "Tasty. Like Chicken Party."

He stood up, his tail going straight into the air. "Spider loves Chicken Party."

"Yes, I know."

"Dinner?"

"No. Not dinner."

"Breakfast?"

"Nope, not breakfast either. Or lunch, before you ask. Bed. Let's go." I opened the door all the way and shooed him out as I turned off the light and went to open my bedroom door again. He might not want to sleep, but I needed to or tomorrow was going to be a very long, very unproductive day and no one—not myself, not Buttercup, not the town of Nocturne Falls—could afford that.

Somehow, sheer exhaustion maybe, I did manage to sleep. Not long, but I'd take what I could get. When I was awake enough to move, I climbed out of bed, pulled on my robe and went to the window.

It was still snowing.

I'd never said or thought this in my life, but the sight of that snow drifting down made my heart sink. I realized that was the kind of statement that might get my winter elf card revoked, but more snow was the last thing this town needed. Okay, maybe more yetis was the *real* last thing this town needed, but you get my drift. No pun intended.

With a sigh and a need for caffeine, I trudged out to the living room.

Sin was sitting on the couch with a stack of files in front of him and a cup of coffee at his side. "Morning, beautiful."

"Hey." I smiled at him. It was impossible not to. "Morning yourself, handsome. How'd you sleep?"

He shrugged a little. "Okay."

"That sleeper sofa isn't that comfortable, is it?"

"It has nothing to do with the mattress. Just too much going on in my head."

"We're sharing a brain on that one."

"You didn't sleep that well either?"

"Not the best, no."

"Well, there's coffee."

I headed for the fridge. "I need something stronger than coffee this morning." I pulled out a bottle of Dr Pepper, unscrewed the top and downed about half of it. Which was going to result in a very un-princessy burp, but certain things couldn't be helped. Maybe I could hold it until I was in the shower.

Spider had followed me into the living room, but instead of begging for breakfast like I expected, he hopped up onto the back of the couch and settled in next to Sugar, who was sleeping on the cushion behind Sin. Most likely, Sin had already fed them.

I tipped my bottle at the pair. "I think Sugar calms him down, believe it or not."

"That's because they wear each other out running around." His eyes sparkled with a deeper meaning. "Playmates are very important."

I took another sip before I answered. "They are."

He laughed softly. "You ready for breakfast?"

"What is it?"

"Cranberry white chocolate pancakes and sausage links."

"That sounds amazing." Man, I could get used to this. "I want to shower first, though. Cool?"

"Cool."

I headed for the bathroom with my Dr Pepper, but paused on my way by the couch. "Find anything interesting in those files so far?"

"Couple more S's to add to the pile, that's about it."

"I'll take over when I'm showered so you can make breakfast."

"Deal."

The shower was long and hot and just what I needed to wake me up and clear my head for the day to come. I dried my hair, put on a touch of makeup, then threw on jeans and a sweater. Cute, but casual.

I walked back into the living room and took over for Sin as planned. He made breakfast, which was delicious, then we both got busy. I wasn't sure how much longer it would take us to get through the rest of the boxes, but we had nothing else going on for the day.

Although I did want to go by Balfour Park and check in on Buttercup. Despite Juniper and Kip's visit last night, I wanted to see her for myself. I stared at the air in front of me and sighed. She hadn't texted, which was good since she was supposed to use the secret phone only for emergencies, but that wasn't enough to stop me from worrying about her.

"What's got you distracted?"

I glanced up at Sin. "Thinking about Buttercup."

He nodded. "You want to take a break and drive over to the park? See if you can talk to her?"

"I'd love to, actually."

He closed the file in front of him. "Let's do it."

Someone knocked on my door. I jumped up. "Right after I get that."

I opened the door to find Rowley and his wife, Dorothea, standing there. She had a platter of cookies in her hands. He nodded at me. "Morning, Miss Frost."

"Morning, Rowley, Dorothea. Please, call me Jayne." But they were old school, and I knew that kind of informality didn't come naturally to them.

I pulled the door wide. "Come on in."

Dorothea held the plate out as they entered. "I made you some sugar cookies."

"How awesome. Two of the things I love most: sugar and cookies." I took the plate and used my elbow to gesture to Sinclair. "This is my friend, Sinclair Crowe. He owns the doughnut shop in town." I looked at him. "This is Rowley and Dorothea Gladstone. Rowley works in the shop."

He smiled at them. "Nice to meet you both."

Dorothea clasped her hands in front of her heart. "You own Zombie Donuts?"

"That's the one," Sin answered.

"Oh my, those are very good. And it is very nice to meet you." She linked her arm through her husband's. "You're dating our Jayne, aren't you?"

He chuckled. "I am."

Rowley cleared his throat. "We just came to see how you were getting on with the storm and all. And if there was anything we could do to help."

I shot a look at Sin. "Actually, there is." I put the plate of cookies on the dining table and gave them the rundown of what we were doing with the files. "We're trying to sort out the men who might have visited Nocturne Falls in addition to any tinkers who have a first or last name starting with the letter S."

"That should be easy enough," Rowley said. "I bet I know a good number of them."

Of course he would. "I don't know how I forgot you were a tinker, Rowley."

"I loved that job." He beamed with pride. "Those were very good years. Not that I'm not enjoying my semi-retirement here. I am."

"No worries. I know this is a much different gig than working for my uncle. So listen, if you don't mind helping, you'd probably be better at this than the rest of us." I shook my head. "I don't know why I didn't ask you to help sooner. Too much on my mind."

"That's completely understandable, Miss—I mean, Jayne. I'm assuming this has something to do with the yetis in town?"

"It does. Specifically about the snow globe that Eustace Brightly designed."

Rowley nodded. "I know the one. Never could get the kinks worked out. Stacey was so disappointed in that."

I went still. "Stacey?"

"Eustace, sorry. All of his friends called him Stacey. At least those of us who knew him well."

I sat down on the coffee table, and not just because my knees had gone weak. "So you were a good friend of his?"

Rowley nodded. "I'd say so, yes."

"We had him over for dinner quite a few times," Dorothea added. "Very sad to hear about his passing."

"Did he ever mention a sister? Or a half-sister, maybe?"

"Sure, Sarabelle," Dorothea said. "Sweet woman. Not well, though. Passed on about ten years or so ago."

I tapped my fingers on my chin as I got back to my feet. "Myra didn't have any mentions of her, which is odd. Because having a sister might even be better than having a brother. But then, she didn't have either, did she?"

"I'm not sure I follow," Rowley said.

"Just talking to myself." I looked at Sin. "We can stop going through those files."

He nodded. "Eustace was Mr. S."

We moved to the dining table with coffee and Dorothea's cookies and the remaining eclairs. I told Rowley and Dorothea everything that had happened, everything I suspected, and how desperate we all were for a way to close the portal. Why not? I had nothing to lose and everything to gain. Besides, they were winter elves. They would understand better than anyone what was at stake here.

Rowley hesitated for a long moment. I let him be. If it took some time to think back to his days as a tinker, so be it. Finally, he tipped his head and spoke. "You think Myra and Stacey were having a relationship, then?"

"I do."

"He never said a thing." Dorothea turned her coffee cup so that the handle was at a right angle to the edge of the table, but didn't drink. She seemed lost in thought.

Rowley glanced at me. "Why wouldn't Myra just move to the North Pole, then? I could see why he wouldn't move. He was one of the top tinkers. But if they loved each other, I would have thought they'd have done anything to be together. So what kept them apart?"

"That's a good question. One I don't have an answer to. Why would a woman in love with a man not move to be with him when he had a job like Eustace had? I don't think she had any kind of job that was too amazing to leave."

"Birdie could find that out," Sin offered.

"You're right. I need to ask her about that." I looked back at the Gladstones. "What could have been so important as to keep Myra here in Nocturne Falls? Her great-nephew, Nate? I could see that being true until he went away to college and started his own life, but after that?"

Dorothea put her hand on Rowley's arm, but kept her gaze on us. "There's not much that could keep me from Rowley."

He smiled at her and patted her hand. They were so adorable together. He looked at me again. "Maybe it wasn't a matter of staying here. Maybe it was a matter of not being allowed into the North Pole."

I frowned. "She would have to have done something pretty rare and extreme for that to happen."

Rowley shrugged. "But it *does* happen. You know that better than most."

"True." Lark, my old frenemy, had been the most recent banishment, but due to my being one of the victims of her crimes, my father and uncle decided I was too close to the events and should abstain from her hearing. Which I did. Gladly.

However, I had been in on two royal hearings where the outcome had been possible banishment. One had been a case of espionage. A baker had been accused of selling the seven-mint blend of our candy canes to a human-owned confection company. The second had been an elf who'd attempted to bring a human into the North Pole without special dispensation.

The baker had been found guilty and banished. The elf who'd failed to bring an unauthorized human into the NP had not.

After both cases, my father had discussed at length his decisions and when banishment was appropriate and when it wasn't, using each case as a teaching tool. When I took his place, those decisions would be mine to make.

With a serious sigh, I flattened my hands on the table. "I guess I need to talk to my father about who's been banished in the last century."

"Unpleasant business to be sure," Rowley said. "But it may give you a clue as to who Myra was."

"That's not going to be easy with her using an assumed name," Dorothea said.

"Not an assumed name," I said. "I realize I said that when I was telling you her story. I meant an adopted one. My mistake. We believe Myra was adopted into a fae family."

Dorothea made a slightly mortified face. "A winter elf child? Adopted to a family outside the North Pole?"

"I know. It's an uncommon thing."

"If it's true, I feel sorry for her."

I did, too, the more I thought about it. Missing out on a childhood in the North Pole seemed like a cruel and unusual punishment. Not that a childhood elsewhere wouldn't be lovely, but the North Pole was essentially a kid's dream. Tons of candy and sweets, every day's a snow day, Santa Claus in residence, new toys constantly in need of testing…it was the most magically suited place for children I could think of. To be a winter elf and not grow up there seemed tragic to me.

What had happened in Myra's life to cause her to lose her parents? And her place in the North Pole? I had to find out. But there was one more question I had to ask Rowley. "Maybe this is private tinker information, but I need to ask you one more thing, Rowley."

He didn't seem bothered. "Go ahead."

"Do you know anything about Eustace using his

own blood in the magic of the snow globe he crafted?"

Rowley's mouth dropped open. "That would be highly frowned upon. I assure you."

And yet, he'd done it. But if Rowley wasn't aware of it, he couldn't know how to close the portal without it. "Thank you. I appreciate you both spending some time with me today. And thank you so much for the cookies, Dorothea. They're delicious. A real testament to your time in the North Pole kitchens."

She preened a little, clearly pleased with my compliment. "Thank you, Princess."

"You're welcome." I pushed my chair back and got to my feet. "Now, if you'll excuse me, I have so much to do and I really should get to it."

"Of course." Rowley stood and helped his wife up. "You just let us know if you need anything."

"I will."

Dorothea smiled at Sinclair as he stood. "It was so lovely to meet you, Mr. Crowe."

"It was nice to meet you both. And Sinclair, please. We're friends now."

Her smile broadened at that statement. "Very well, then, Sinclair."

"Thanks again." I walked them to the door and said goodbye before turning back to Sinclair. "I need Birdie on her computer and digging. And I need to get all these records back to my dad."

"And have new ones sent." Sinclair leaned against the table. "But if that doesn't work, it's time for us to pay Myra a visit."

"But she's in the morgue—oh! Sin, no. We talked about that. I don't want you using your gifts when it costs you so much."

"I can spare a few minutes to help you, and for the sake of Buttercup, my town and the people in it. This needs to come to an end."

"I agree, but let's see what Birdie finds. I'm sure she'll dig up something." But all of our leads so far had been dead ends.

No pun intended.

Sin called Birdie while I called my dad, then we hefted the first load of boxes down to the Santa's Bag and sent them back to the NP.

After that, we hopped in Sin's SUV and made our way to Balfour Park. Deputy Cruz was on gate patrol this time. He waved us in. "How are you?"

"Okay." My gaze was fixed on the ice castle. "Anything new? Any sign of Buttercup?"

"Nothing new, and we've seen her a few times walking on the top there. Although I haven't seen her yet today."

"How did she seem when she was spotted?"

"Good. The yetis follow her everywhere."

"Have you talked to her?"

"Not really, no. Your winter elf friends were here, but the rest of us have given the fort a wide berth since getting Birdie out of there. The sheriff thought it might be best to let things settle a bit."

"Probably. Has there been any more food delivered?"

He pushed the brim of his hat back a little. "Bridget came by with eight pans of peach cobbler."

"And?"

"Yetis devoured them, but they were cautious coming out."

I made a face. "Because last time we offered them chocolates, we breached their fortress."

He nodded. "They're not so dumb, are they?"

"Unfortunately, no." I sighed. "I'm going up to the fortress. I need to check on Buttercup. Make sure she's all right and not in need of anything."

His eyes narrowed. "You have the sheriff's permission?"

"Do I need it?"

"I think I should at least call it in." He reached for the radio on his shoulder.

Sin cleared his throat. "Jayne is the Winter Princess, heir to the Winter Throne, and while I realize this is still Nocturne Falls, for all intents and purposes, this park has become the North Pole. The yetis are from the North Pole, the woman they're holding hostage is from the North Pole, and frankly, Jayne's the only one who's ever had any dealings with these creatures before. Her asking for the sheriff's permission to check on one of *her* citizens seems a little unnecessary to me."

Deputy Cruz frowned, but dropped his hand. "Be quick."

"I will be." I smiled at Sin, hopefully expressing my gratitude with my eyes. "I'll just be a minute."

He crossed his arms and leaned on one of the saw horses marking off the perimeter. "I'll be right here."

I dashed through the snow, which had gotten thick again since no one had been on the path much lately. I stopped a few yards from the ice wall. I could just see over the top of it. "Buttercup," I hissed.

There was no immediate response, but I did my best to be patient. Standing there, yelling for her might not go over so well with the yetis.

I waited about thirty seconds, then did my loud whisper again. "Buttercup!"

More seconds ticked by with no sign of her. I didn't like that at all. I was about to use my normal speaking voice when she appeared at the top of the wall.

She looked...different. The tiara I'd put on her head was gone, replaced by a towering crown of ice shards far more regal—and intimidating—than my delicate diamond snowflakes. She had a scepter of ice in her hand. It reminded me a little of my father's scepter. Of course, his could wield winter magic. This one I wasn't so sure about.

Lastly, my court gown was hidden under a robe of white fur. Real or not, I couldn't tell, but I was a little afraid to spend too much time thinking about where the yetis had come up with that.

I waved. She didn't wave back, just stared impassively at me. That didn't seem like a good sign. "Buttercup, are you okay?"

"I am Queen of the Yeti. The Chosen One." Buttercup tended to be rather monotone at times, but her speaking voice now made her sound programmed.

"That's great, I guess, but how are you—"

"Ruler of the Ice Palace. Defender of the Defenseless."

I rolled my eyes. "The yetis aren't exactly what I'd call defenseless—"

She tapped her scepter on the ice to interrupt me. "She Who Will Be Sacrificed."

My heart went still. "Buttercup, don't say that."

Without another word, she turned and walked out of sight.

"Buttercup? Come back. Buttercup!"

And just like that, it stopped snowing.

I ran back to Sin and Deputy Cruz, slipping and sliding but refusing to slow down until I reached them.

Cruz greeted me with a smile. "Hey, nice job, whatever you did. It stopped snowing."

"That's *not* good news." I grabbed Sin's arm. "We're running out of time. Buttercup's been assimilated."

"Assimilated? You mean like the Borg?"

His Star Trek reference wasn't completely lost on me, even though I wasn't a Trekkie or anything. "Close enough. At least I'm starting to think so. They've brainwashed her into believing that she *is* their queen. Worse than that, she seems to have accepted that she's supposed to be sacrificed."

Sin recoiled. "What? That's terrible. But why is the snow stopping not good news?"

"I think it means they're done building their

fortress or turning Nocturne Falls into the North Pole or something like that. What it means exactly, I'm not sure, but it feels to me like they stopped the snow because they're ready for the next phase of things."

"Which is sacrificing Buttercup."

"Right."

Cruz grabbed the radio on his shoulder. "Sheriff, you'd better get over here."

I shook my head at him. "I don't have time to stay here and explain. You heard what I said, just repeat that to him."

"Will do."

"Sin." I squeezed his arm as I pulled him toward the car. "I didn't want to do this. But I think we need to talk to Myra."

He nodded. "I agree. Is she at the morgue?"

"I'm not sure. Birdie would know." I dug out my phone and called her. She answered right away.

"I don't have anything new to tell you yet, Princess, sorry."

"That's okay. We're going to take a different route. Where is, uh, Myra's body?"

Birdie sucked in a sharp breath. "Sin's going to do his thing, isn't he?"

I swallowed. "Yes."

"She's still in the morgue. Because of the weather, the funeral plans were put on hold. And it seemed silly to move her to the undertakers with the roads the way they are. Plus, her great-nephew hasn't been able to get into town because of the storm either."

"Makes sense to keep her at the morgue, then. Where is that?" I felt like I should have known, but the morgue wasn't a place I'd even thought about visiting.

"The morgue is in the hospital basement. I'll meet you there in twenty minutes or so. Not sure actually, because of the roads, but I'll leave immediately."

I should have counted on her wanting to come. "Birdie, I appreciate that, but I don't think Sin wants an audience for this."

"And I appreciate that, but how else do you think you're going to get into the morgue? I have clearance."

"Oh. Right. Good point. Hang on." I put the phone on my shoulder. "Birdie needs to be with us to get us into the morgue. Are you okay with her being there?"

"Sure." He shrugged. "Might be good to have another set of ears, too, you know?"

"Okay." I went back to Birdie. "Twenty minutes. Or however long it takes."

It took twenty-seven. The snow might have stopped coming down, but the plows were behind. It wasn't until we got closer to the hospital that the streets were better cleared. Made sense. The hospital was a priority.

It was bright, too, so they obviously had plenty of electricity. Everything seemed to be in working order, including the elevators. I made a mental note to tell my dad to look into the hospital's brand of generators.

Birdie was already in the lobby when we got there. "Ready?"

I looked at Sin. This was his deal. He nodded, the look in his eyes a mix of determination and resignation.

I slipped my hand in his. "I owe you."

He smiled, but it was tight and restrained. "No, you don't. I'm doing this for everyone."

"Then the town owes you."

"She's right," Birdie said. "This is a great thing you're doing."

"If we get the right answers," he said.

Birdie fished something from her purse. A slim black wallet. She flipped it open, revealing a town ID. "We will. Because we're going to ask the right questions. Come on, let's get down there."

She showed her ID at the front desk. We all signed in, then followed Birdie to the elevators. Except the one we took was down a separate hall by itself. The interior was enormous. Big enough, I realized, to hold a gurney with a body on it. After that lightbulb moment, I stood slightly away from the wall so I didn't touch anything. Birdie slid her ID through a card reader, then tapped the button for the basement.

We stepped off into a small lobby that split into two directions. One had a sign saying Pathology, the other Employees Only.

We headed down the Employees Only side.

I looked back at the signs. "Um, shouldn't we be going toward Pathology?"

"Nope," Birdie said. "That's the human morgue. We need the supernatural one."

"Oh. You learn something new every day." Two morgues in one basement? A little involuntary shiver went through me.

Have I mentioned how I don't like basements? This one was well lit, and painted in a soothing green with white tile floors that made your shoes squeak. But the antiseptic smell did nothing to hide what I imagined was the aroma of dead people, and the farther down the hall we walked, the more that soothing green seemed the same color as swamp water. Or mold. As basements went, it wasn't my favorite.

Or maybe the destination was influencing my thoughts.

Thankfully, there were no more hospital personnel to see. Until we got to a door labeled Unit Nine. Apparently, that's what they called the supernatural morgue to keep from labeling it anything more obvious.

Birdie pushed open the door and approached

the desk just inside. Sin and I followed dutifully. The air here had an undercurrent of something sickly sweet that no antiseptic could overcome.

A young woman looked up from a laptop and greeted us. If my guess was right, she was a vampire, which made morgue attendant seem like a pretty on-the-nose job for her, but then, this was the supernatural side of things. She wore a lab coat over a black-and-white polka dot dress and had a daisy barrette holding back her brunette waves on one side. With her cat-eye makeup and crimson lips, she reminded me of the pinup girl tattooed on Arty's arm. She smiled. "Hi, Birdie."

"Hi, Druzy. We need to see Myra Grimshaw." Birdie straighten as if she'd suddenly remembered why she was there. "Official business."

"Sure." Druzy got up. She was a curvy girl and exceptionally beautiful, which wasn't that surprising for a vampire. Her smile widened, giving us a peek at her fangs. "Right this way."

Her shiny red heels click-clacked on the tile as she led us into a large room with lockers on either side. I knew what they were. Body storage.

She opened number three, which made me wonder if one and two were already occupied. I erased that thought. I didn't want to know.

Druzy pulled the shelf out.

And there was Myra. In a body bag, but the label clearly had her name written on it.

My light-headedness was coming back.

Druzy nodded at Birdie. "I'll leave you to it. Holler if you need anything."

"Thank you."

When Druzy had left, Birdie unzipped the bag, proving it was Myra, and then turned to us. "Do we know what questions—Princess, you okay?"

I yanked my gaze off the body bag. "What? I'm fine. This is just weird. Super super weird."

Sin put his arm around me. "Pretend she's sleeping."

Hard to do when Myra was the color of paste. I nodded. "Right."

"So," Birdie started again. "Do we know what questions we're going to ask?"

I refocused on what we were there to do. It helped not to look at Myra. "What her real name is. What her relationship with Eustace Brightly was about. If she ever used the snow globe as a portal, and if she did, how did she close it?"

"Sounds good," Birdie said. "Sinclair, do you need to prepare in any way?"

"No. I just have to put my hands on her and call up her spirit. She'll wake up, then you can ask her anything you want. She might be a little out of it at first. People often get disoriented after being pulled out of the afterlife."

"Okay," I said. "Let's do this."

"Wait." Birdie fished in her purse for something,

taking out her phone a couple seconds later. "I want to record this. So we don't miss anything. Just audio. I'm not posting it to YouTube or anything."

"Good to know," Sinclair said.

She got her phone set up, then nodded. "All ready."

Sin stretched out his hands.

I tightened up, the way you do right before a big firework explodes and you know the boom is coming.

He unzipped the bag and opened it so more of Myra was exposed. Then he reached in and took hold of her arm. Birdie let out a little gasp and I followed her line of sight.

She was looking at Sin. And with good reason. His eyes had gone the same silver-white as they had when he'd called up Ada. No pupils, just glowing silver-white light.

Myra gasped and sat up. "What's going on? Where am I? Is my oven on?"

Her eyes were wide, and she flushed suddenly, all the normal color coming back into her like someone had flipped a switch. Made it easier to look at her, I have to say.

Birdie jumped in. "Myra, listen, honey, your oven's not on and everything's fine. You're in the hospital, but don't worry about that. We just need to ask you some questions before we discharge you."

That seemed to calm her right down. Birdie was good. Really good. Myra nodded. "All right."

"We need to know your real name."

"Myra Grimshaw."

"What were you called before that?"

Her gaze took on a faraway look. "Daddy changed our name from…Coldwell. We were never supposed to talk about that, but I don't know why. Just that it was a big family secret." The faraway look disappeared. "You won't tell anyone, will you, Birdie?"

"Of course not. Now what can you tell me about Eustace Brightly?"

She smiled. And blushed. Which wasn't something I'd expected from a dead woman. "Oh, my, that Stacey is a sweet one. I love him so much."

"What's your relationship with him?"

"My relationship?" She laughed. "I'll tell you a secret. Stacey Brightly is my husband."

"You're married?"

Myra looked at me. "Yes. For nearly seventy-five years. It's been hard, not being able to be with him in the North Pole, but..." She got very sad. "I'm not allowed back there, you know."

It had to be a case of banishment. My father would know. "So you are a winter elf."

"Yes." She sighed. "I just wish I could have told Nate."

"Your great-nephew?"

She nodded, then hesitated. "He's not really my great-nephew."

"He's not?"

She smiled, still sad, but there was pride in her eyes. "He's my son. Our son. He doesn't know. I wish he did. I wish I could have told him. But he'll never get to know the truth about his father."

Every inch of me came to life. Eustace Brightly's

bloodline was not dead. I still had to confirm it. "Nate is your son. Eustace's son."

"Yes, but since I couldn't tell anyone about the marriage, I couldn't tell anyone about Nate. I even made up the lie about him being my great-nephew, and I don't have any brothers or sisters. That's why I had to say my family was all on the West Coast. Of course, Stacey knew, but he understood why we had to keep things secret."

Birdie leaned in. "Where is his birth certificate?"

"Safe-deposit box in First National. The key is in the false bottom of my jewelry box." She smiled. "Stacey made that box for me. He knew we had secrets to keep."

"Good on him." This was an interesting conversation, but these minutes were adding up and the invisible clock ticking in my head got louder with each passing second. Sin was losing time. So was Buttercup. "Speaking of secrets, did you ever use the snow globe as a portal?"

"A portal?" Confusion clouded her gaze.

That was enough answer for me. If she didn't know it was a portal, she didn't know how to close it. And we had Nate. I nodded at Birdie. "That's all we need."

Birdie nodded back at me. "I agree. We have our solution. Nate can close the portal."

"Portal?" Myra asked. "Has someone been using my snow globe?"

"Yes," I said. "But we're fixing to close it now that we know about Nate. Did Stacey tell you anything about how the globe works?"

She nodded. "He wrote up a whole paper on it for me. It's in the safe-deposit box too."

"Now we really have everything we need." I reached out to pat Myra's hand, remembered she was technically dead, and stopped halfway. "Thank you for all your help, Myra."

"Yes," Birdie said. "Thank you, Myra. You get some rest now." She picked up her phone and turned off the recorder.

I moved closer to Sin. "That's all, Sinclair. We're through."

He took his hands off of her.

Her eyes fluttered closed, and she lay back down. The color drained out of her like she was being photoshopped into black and white. And that was it. She was dead again. An unexpected wash of sadness went through me.

Sinclair's sigh shifted my attention back to him. His eyes were back to normal. But there was a new streak of silver at his temple. That made me a little bit sad. But it would forever serve as a reminder of the sacrifice he'd made for all of us. "Are you okay? I'm sorry that took longer than I'd hoped."

He smiled. "That's fine. You got what you needed, right?"

"Right. But are you sure you're okay?"

"I am. I could use a Coke. Some sugar."

"I think Mummy's is open," Birdie said. "We could get a milk shake. Or something. Do a little strategy session over some waffle fries."

Sin smiled. "That would work."

"Great. I'll take care of Myra. You guys go wait in the office with Druzy."

"Thank you." I was really grateful I didn't have to be the one to zip her up. I took Sin's arm and out we went.

Druzy looked up from her laptop as we walked out. "Get everything you need?"

That made me wonder how much she'd heard. "Yes, thank you." I decided to change the subject. "You look just like a pinup girl. But I guess you get that a lot."

She smiled. "Thank you. It's always nice to hear."

"In fact, do you know Arty over at Mummy's? You kind of look like his tattoo."

She laughed. "I know him. He's my dad."

"For real? But he's human, right? Not that that matters, I guess, but you must have been newly turned. Or he's older than he looks."

"He's an oracle. And he's older than he looks."

"An oracle?"

She nodded. "It's not a very common kind of supernatural. It's not all that exciting either. Especially if you're his kid. It basically means he's right about everything."

I thought back to all the breakfast suggestions he'd made to me. "Huh. I guess so. I've never gone wrong with any of the choices he's steered me toward."

She gave a little shrug. "Once in a while, he can predict the future, but generally, he's just right."

"Did you guys just move here?"

"He did. I've lived here awhile. When I told him how much I loved the town and how great a place it is for supes, he moved too. He loves working at Mummy's. He loves people, and it's a great way for him to put his skills to use."

Birdie walked out.

"We're actually headed over to Mummy's now."

Druzy turned to Birdie. "Everything zipped up?"

"Yep. I put her back in and closed the locker."

"Thanks. Tell my dad I said hi."

"Will do," Birdie said.

We walked back to the elevator, all of us quiet. Thinking, I guess. Unless Sin was being quiet because he was tired.

I studied him, trying to figure out how much the use of his magic had worn on him. "You want me to drive?"

He chuckled. "I'm just a little tired, but I can drive. Thanks."

"I can drive, you know." Not that well, but I could.

He winked at me. "I know."

For all his lightness, I could see the lines around his eyes were a little deeper. I knew the kind of toll magic could take. Fortunately, Mummy's wasn't that far.

It was, however, busier than I'd expected, but what I'd thought would happen, had. People were getting cabin fever from being in their houses for so long. Word had spread about Mummy's being open and people had flocked in. That meant people would be noticing the massive ice fort in Balfour Park. Supernaturals, anyway, if the witches' magic was holding.

I hoped it was.

Arty waved us through. "I've got a four-top clearing in the back corner." He leaned to see better. "Actually, they're getting up. Head back there now and snag it. I'll send Timmy to bus it ASAP."

We did as we were told, sitting down at the cluttered booth just as the busboy arrived with his gray tub. He stripped the table down with surprising efficiency, coming back seconds later to set us up with clean silverware, place mats and menus.

Arty was right behind him. "Hiya, peeps. What can I get you?"

Birdie tipped her head toward Sin. "He needs a Coke immediately."

I held up my hand. "And your daughter says hi." I figured I'd start with that and everything else could follow.

He smiled. "You met Druzy, huh? I guess I know where you've been. Better wash your hands, kids."

He walked away laughing, but I felt a little icky.

Birdie pulled a plastic bottle of hand sanitizer out of her purse. "Here."

I squeezed out a copious amount and gave it back. "Thanks."

Arty returned with the Coke and placed it in front of Sin. "There you go. Now, what else can I get you guys? And give me your drink orders, too."

Birdie took the lead. "Water for me. And cheese fries."

"Waffle or regular? You want waffle. Loaded? Of course you want loaded." He scribbled the order on his notepad, then looked at me.

"Is that what I should have too?"

"Definitely. With a Dr Pepper."

"I'm in."

He looked at Sinclair. "How about you?"

"Grilled ham and cheese. Regular fries."

"You got it." He took our menus. "Back before two shakes of a lamb's tail."

We all kind of leaned in as he left. I spoke first. "Do we need anything special to access Myra's safe-deposit box?"

Birdie nodded. "Yes. It's tricky. We'd need a court order, or another signer on the account, which probably only had one—Myra. However, in the case of her death, Nate should be able to get in without too much fuss."

Sin had already downed half of his Coke. "You need to bring him in anyway if he's going to help you close the portal."

Birdie pulled out her phone. "I need to call Hank. This is going to take a team."

While she did that, I checked the snow globe in my purse. I should have done it in the car, but I'd been too worried about Sinclair passing out behind the wheel. The snow in the globe was swirling like crazy.

I hugged my purse to my side and got up. "I'll be right back." I slipped away to the bathrooms. I figured it wouldn't be that weird to be talking to someone if I was in one of the stalls. People would just think I was some nutty woman using speakerphone in a public bathroom.

Thankfully, the bathroom was empty at the moment. I took the farthest stall from the door, then pulled out the globe and answered. "Hey, I'm here."

My dad's face appeared and I knew instantly what was going on. His hair was whipping around and I could see clouds behind him. "Honey, we're on our way."

"You're in the sleigh, aren't you?"

"Yes."

"Who's we?"

"Tempus, me, and your uncle."

Oh. Boy. "And you're coming here?"

"Where else would we be headed?"

"Right." Snowballs. "When do you think you'll arrive?"

"I'd say in about an hour and forty-five minutes."

Birdie had been more right than she'd realized. It was going to take a team. And they were about to show up. "Great!"

I went back to the table, happy to see the drinks and food had arrived. I slipped into my seat and stared at my cheese fries. They looked delicious, but I had more than food on my mind. I should have mentioned Myra's real name to my father, but that could all be handled when he arrived. I picked up a fry, not wanting them to go to waste.

"What's up?" Sin asked. The sugar had apparently done him good. He looked much more like himself again.

"Let me put it this way. Santa Claus is coming to town."

After scarfing our food down, we paid our bill and got moving. Birdie headed to the station to fill the sheriff in. They would take on the jobs of getting Nate into town, explaining things to him, and retrieving the contents of the safe-deposit box, namely the snow globe instructions Eustace had written up.

Sin and I would handle my family, setting Tempus up with whatever he needed to send the yetis to dreamland, and the logistics of getting all those yetis back to the portal.

Good thing Balfour Park wasn't far from Myra's.

Sin drove me back to the warehouse, and we went up to my apartment to wait for my incoming family. Which really just gave me time to stress out some more. Because while I knew he'd met my mom and aunt and been soundly approved by them, I was still a bundle of nerves about him meeting my dad.

My dad. And my uncle. The two harshest critics of the men in my life. I could have put off this introduction to another day and been very happy.

Further complicating things was Tempus Sanders, the Sandman, master of sleep, king of dreamland, and a guy who generally considered himself the universe's gift to all things supernatural.

I didn't care what he thought about Sinclair, but he still had to be kept happy so he didn't suddenly decide not to help us with the yetis.

He wouldn't do that, would he?

I wanted to eat sugar and go to bed. I wanted to eat sugar *in* bed. With the door locked, my phone turned off, and Spider on my pillow.

"Wow." Sin was sprawled out on the couch. "You're completely freaked out."

"What makes you say that?"

"You're wringing your hands, for one thing. You're also walking a path in the floor, for another."

I stopped pacing and dropped my hands to my sides. "You don't understand—"

"I think I do. Your dad and your uncle aren't going to be as accepting as your mom and your aunt. How was that?"

"Nail on the head." I sighed and leaned against the kitchen counter. Which put me next to the box of eclairs. I helped myself to one and took a big bite. I needed the sugar and it gave my hands something to do.

"You want me to get out of here altogether? Or pretend like I'm just here to drive you guys to the park?"

"No, and no," I mumbled around a very soothing mouthful of yumminess. "And for the record, I'm not ashamed of you or anything like that. I'm really very proud of you and everything you've done for me." He smiled. "I'm just nervous. This is the first time my dad and my uncle have been here since I took over the store."

I realized suddenly that had a lot to do with it. I wanted them to be happy with the job I was doing, which I *knew* they were, but having them here kind of put a finer point on things.

"I get it." He shrugged. "Parents."

"Especially ones you're in line to take over the throne from."

He laughed. "Right. That's more pressure than I've had experience with."

"But you know what? They're going to like you. How can they not? You're amazing. And because of you, we have a way to shut the portal down." He'd risked his life for me. On more than one occasion now. And yet, somehow, I was pacing again.

"If Nate cooperates."

That stopped me. "You think he might not?"

"It's going to take some thoughtful explaining. He's about to find out all sorts of new things about himself. Things that might rock his world a bit. Imagine if someone told you your great-aunt was actually your mother?"

I ran that through my head. "I'd be knocked off-center."

"For sure. Letting Nate settle into that might take a minute."

"True." This could be a real shock to him. "Good thing Birdie is getting Titus involved. She said he and Nate went to school together. Seeing a familiar face like that might inspire him to feel some compassion toward his hometown. Remind him that there's a reason to help."

"I hope so." He tipped his head to look around me and pointed at something behind me. "You're getting a call."

I turned around to see the snow globe I'd taken out of my purse had a raging storm going on inside it. I'd put it on the kitchen island to keep an eye on it. I answered. "Hello?"

My dad appeared. "We caught a tailwind. We'll be touching down in less than twenty minutes."

"Oh. Great!" That might have been a little forced, but I really was glad they were here. Better to move things along. "I'll see you up there."

We hung up. I grabbed my jacket off the dining chair where I'd thrown it. "Let's go."

"Where?" Sin asked.

"The roof. That's where they'll land."

He stood up, smiling. "Are they really coming in Santa's sleigh with eight tiny reindeer?"

"Yes and no. The reindeer aren't tiny and they'll probably only have two or three pulling the sleigh. Christmas Eve is the only trip my uncle uses all eight for. Otherwise, a smaller team is plenty when the sleigh isn't loaded with gifts."

His smile turned into a bright, shiny grin that would have looked perfectly at home on a child's face.

I laughed. "You feel about seven years old right now, don't you?"

He nodded as he came around the coffee table. "I can't believe I'm about to meet Santa Claus." He stopped short. "Is there really a naughty and nice list?"

"Oh, yes."

"Am I on it?"

"Everyone's on it. And I can see we're going to have to take a trip to the NP very soon."

His brows practically wiggled. "That would be amazing."

He pulled his jacket on, and together, we raced up the steps to the door to the roof. Which was frozen shut.

I slapped my forehead at how dumb I'd been. "Of course the door is frozen. There's probably a ton of snow piled up on the other side too. How on earth are they going to land if I can't get it cleared?"

"We'll get it open. How did you get the warehouse door open?"

"I absorbed the cold." I pulled my sleeves back a little. "And I can do it again here, but I have a feeling this is going to be tougher. There's more ice built up."

"What can I do to help?"

Well, that was an offer I couldn't refuse. "Keep me warm?"

"That I can do." He put his arms around me, fitting my back to his front. "How's that?"

"Good." I wiggled a little. "Nice bracing too."

"I'm multipurpose."

With a laugh, I stretched out my hands and planted them on the door. It was frigid to the touch. I took a breath and worked my magic.

Having Sinclair's arms around me really did help, but even I had a limit for how much cold I could handle. After another few seconds, I dropped my hands. "There. That's all I can do right now."

Sin gave me a hug. "I'm sure it's plenty." He eased me out of the way, then put his shoulder down. "Here goes."

He rammed forward, blasting the door open. Snow exploded out and up in a shower of white and he disappeared into it.

"You did it!" I ran out after him, still chilled, but pumped full of adrenaline from his success. Until I saw how much snow still covered the roof. "Ugh. Look at this. Hey, where are you?"

"I'm here." Sin was still digging himself out of the nearly shoulder-deep drift that had cushioned his entrance onto the roof.

I gave him a hand and pulled him out. "You might want to stand back for this."

"Are you sure I can't help?"

"I...well...maybe." I gave the problem a few seconds of thought. "I think you can help. Hang on."

"I'm hanging." Actually, he was brushing snow off himself.

I fired up my magic again, this time forming a plow blade from ice.

"I like it." He nodded. "Fighting fire with fire. Or ice with ice, as the case may be."

"Yep." With the stubbornness of the yeti-created snow, an old-fashioned plow was going to be faster and more efficient than my magic. The snow in my apartment had shown me that. "We'll each take one side and clear a path."

"You got it."

We got our grip and went at it, proving I was right. With our supernatural strength, we were able to clear half the roof in about ten minutes. It took us a little longer to decide where to put all that snow. Splitting it up seemed the best idea, so small amounts went over each wall, except for the one that faced Main. That way we wouldn't block the alley or side streets.

We were widening the landing area when Sin stopped sharply and whirled around.

"What's wrong?" I asked.

"Nothing," he said, smiling. "But I hear bells."

The grand red-and-gold sleigh appeared out of the clouds like a fairy tale, which in a way, I guess it was.

Wearing their everyday tack (which meant no bells—the ones Sin had heard were on the sleigh itself), *four* reindeer came dashing toward us, snorting steam from their glowing noses and tugging at their harnesses. Four made sense seeing Tempus Sanders in the backseat. The man was a mountain. A blobby, marshmallowy mountain, but still.

My dad was in the passenger seat up front. He smiled when he saw me. My uncle was beside him at the helm. He stood up and waved as the sleigh descended. "Hullo, Jaynie!"

I waved back. "Hi, Uncle Kris!"

Sinclair nudged me. "I thought only Rudolph's nose glowed."

"Human myth. The truth is tinker Rudolph Pringle developed a balm for the reindeers' noses to protect them from the cold when they're flying. He added a little magic to make the balm glow and give the reindeer a little extra light to see by."

Sin shook his head. "You learn something new every day."

They were closing in now. Uncle Kris wound the reins tighter in his hands and called out, "Halt, you beasts."

The reindeer landed, digging their hooves into the snow. The sleigh set down behind them, skidding a little as the gleaming gold runners found purchase.

"Prancer!" I ran forward to hug the closest reindeer. He grunted hot breath onto my neck and nuzzled me as I spoke to the three men in the sleigh. "I'm so glad you're here."

"Us too," my dad said.

I kissed Prancer's downy cheek and stepped back to make introductions. "Dad, Uncle Kris, Mr. Sanders, this is my boyfriend, Sinclair Crowe."

My uncle was the first one out of the sleigh and the closest to Sin. He extended his hand. "Pleasure to meet you, son."

For all his mastery of death, Mr. Crowe looked mighty star struck. He shook my uncle's hand. "Pleasure to meet you, too, Sant—um—sir."

My uncle put his hands on his prodigious

stomach and laughed the loud, booming laugh he was famous for. "Call me Kris."

My father was next, his boots crunching through the snow as he approached Sinclair. "And you can call me Jack."

I tried to see my father through Sin's eyes, with his wild spiked mop of dark blue hair, his thick arched brows and tall, willowy form. Swirls of frost and tiny snowflakes danced around him as he moved forward. He was showing off his magic. A little demonstration for Sinclair's sake, I was sure.

They shook hands, then my dad stepped to one side as Tempus came around.

The Sandman was dressed pretty much as he was every time I saw him, in a loose tunic and matching loose pants. It was his uniform, and the best description I could give the outfit was fancy daytime pajamas. Given who he was, the uniform made sense. Today's pj's were a deep, dusty blue. His hourglass, his most prized and protected possession, dangled from the silk cord at his waist.

I didn't know what sort of mood he was in, but I figured a little flattery couldn't hurt. "It's so nice to see you again, Tempus. And it's so gracious of you to help the town of Nocturne Falls this way."

He stared down at me, hands on the waist of his tunic where the silk cord sat, and smiled.

Relief went through me.

"I'm happy to help, Princess. You were kind to

host me when I was promoting my book." His voice, which was already deep and melodious, lowered even further as he leaned toward me. "And you took good care of me during the unpleasantness that followed."

You bet your sweet dreams, I did. But those words never left my lips. Instead, I smiled graciously (royal upbringing at its best) and touched my hand to my heart. "It was my honor."

And my job, but I digress.

I held my arm out toward the door. "Let's head in and figure out how we're going to do this."

My father led the way with Tempus behind him, then my uncle. Sinclair waited until I was beside him, then fell into step with me.

"Aren't you forgetting something?"

I stopped, causing him to stop too. "What?"

He bobbed his head toward the sleigh. "There are four reindeer on the roof of the building."

I nodded. "They'll be fine. They're used to waiting at all those houses on Christmas Eve. I promise, they'll be okay up here." I blew Cupid a kiss. "Won't you, boy?"

He snuffled in response and nodded, pushing his nose into the air.

"See?" I smiled at Sin. "Plus, I can have Rowley check on them if things run long. I'm sure Uncle Kris brought them some feed."

"All right then. Let's get to it."

A couple minutes later, we were all seated in the living room of the third-floor company apartment. Sin and I were on one couch, Tempus on the one across from us, my dad and uncle on the cattycorner chairs. Made for a cozy group, and one that was conducive to conversation.

My dad had let the show of power go once we'd stepped inside, something I was taking as a good sign. With that and my uncle's warm greeting of Sin, my nerves had basically disappeared. I was grateful, because this was my show and I needed to run it with confidence. I got the meeting underway. "Tempus, how long will it take you to put the yetis to sleep?"

He twisted his fingers through the cord that held his hourglass. "I can't say. I've never done it before."

I looked at my dad. "No experiment? I thought you had *volunteers*?"

He shrugged. "There wasn't time. Our focus was getting here as quickly as possible."

"I appreciate that, but not knowing what the process is going to be like gives us an unknown to deal with."

"Shouldn't be too big of a deal," my dad said.

"Unless it takes longer than we think and the yetis get wise to what we're doing. If they take off and run wild through the town—"

Uncle Kris groaned. "We can't have that. Those little terrors will destroy the place."

"Right," I said. "More than they already have."

Silence fell over us, the sound of thinking.

Then Sin spoke up. "We can ask the witches to help. They're doing it already by hiding the fortress from human eyes. Maybe they can add some type of containment spell to keep the yetis from leaving the park."

"Good thinking," my dad said.

I nodded in agreement. "That's perfect. I want Juniper and Kip there, too, since they know what's going on."

Sin took out his phone. "I'll reach out to Pandora. See what she thinks of that idea. You text Juniper."

"Great." I slipped my phone from my purse and shot Juni a quick text filling her in. Then I looked at my dad. "Are you prepared to help me combat their magic if the yetis attack?"

"Absolutely." His gaze went to Uncle Kris. "We both are. And with your employees there, we'll have plenty of winter elf power on hand to fight ice with ice if need-be."

"True. I better let Juniper know about that." I added a second text to her and got one back almost instantly saying she, Kip, and Pete were on board and that Kip would drive them to the park. I sat back, feeling relief. "They're in. Now we just need to know that Birdie's got everything lined up on her end and we're good to go."

"What's this Birdie doing?" my uncle asked.

"Her nephew is the sheriff, and her other nephew is the fire chief and he went to school with Nate Grimshaw, who, as it turns out, is actually Eustace Brightly's son."

"That reminds me," my dad said. "I looked up the name you gave me. There was an Owen Coldwell registered as a tinker. I dug deeper and found that he'd been found guilty of selling a toy design to a human manufacturer. He and his wife and child were banished as a result."

I braced myself. "And that child was Myra."

He nodded. "Myra Coldwell."

"Who became Myra Grimshaw after her father changed their family name. So she wasn't adopted after all, but banished."

"Terrible thing," my uncle muttered. "But rules are rules."

I nodded, thinking about what that had to have been like. About what would have driven Owen Coldwell to do something so risky. Something with such awful consequences. "Then she was a winter elf. And Nate is full-blooded."

I looked at my father. "If he helps us by closing the portal, you should give him a special dispensation. Let him back into the North Pole."

"I...guess I could think about that." He glanced at my uncle, who shrugged.

"You're the Winter King, Jack, not me."

My father sighed. "It's not a good precedent to set."

"What?" I said. "That helping the crown resolve a problem doesn't buy you some mercy?"

"Jayne, it's not that. It's like Kris said, rules are rules. A banishment is for life."

"But Nate had nothing to do with it. He doesn't even know the truth of who he is."

Sin cleared his throat softly and looked up from his phone. "He does now. And Birdie said he's happy to help."

I shot my father a stern look. "He deserves a special dispensation. And I will be very cross with you if one is not forthcoming."

Before my father could say another word, I stood up. "We should meet with Birdie and her crew and get our timelines right. This needs to go smoothly."

Sin got to his feet. "She's ready for us at the park, actually. I'll go bring the car around."

I had a feeling he was happy for the excuse to leave. "See you downstairs."

My uncle got up. "Come on, Tempus, let's give these two a moment."

The Sandman pushed to his feet and followed my uncle to the door without comment.

When they'd left, my father sighed. "Jayne, I understand your side. I do. But our laws are there to protect us. The fact is, if Eustace was still alive, he'd be in trouble for being married to a banished winter elf. He knew that too. Why do you think he kept it a secret for his entire life?"

"Dad, I understand the need for laws. But this is a special case. Nate is going to help us undo the magic his father created. That's got to be worth something. He's going to be saving Buttercup's life. Doesn't that balance the scales?"

My father sighed again, and the muscles in his jaw tightened.

I pushed harder. "And what about the fact that he's an orphan now? Both of his parents are dead. And he's just now found out that he's a winter elf. What do you think the first thing he's going to want to do is?"

My father made a face. "Visit the North Pole."

"Are you prepared to tell an orphan he can't go home?"

One side of his mouth quirked up in what might have been a smile. "You have your mother's flair for embellishment, you know that?"

I slouched a little, like it was no big deal that he was about to give in. Because he was. I could feel it. "Are you letting Nate in or not?"

He blew out a long breath, sending spirals of icy vapor curling through the room. "Just like your mother," he muttered.

"That's not an answer."

"Yes, I'll let him in. But only if he gets that portal closed."

I sprang to my feet. "He will."

My father stood with less enthusiasm. "You'd better hope so. Because if he doesn't, you're going to be the one to tell him why the North Pole is off-limits."

The scene at the park was about the same as it had been, except for two big changes.

One was the gathered crowd inside the barriers was the largest it had been so far. Most of the extra people were witches, there to help with the containment spell. Besides them, there was a large group of firemen, who were standing by a school bus at the far end of the park, and on our end, two paramedics with an ambulance and my crew of Kip, Juniper, and Pete.

But there was another guy standing with Birdie, someone I didn't recognize at first. Then I realized he was the man of the hour. Nate.

The other big change was the emergence of an odd-looking addition to the center of the ice castle. It was almost a platform, but made of thick ice spikes. Like a bed of nails. But a lot scarier.

My uncle whistled when he saw it. "The sacrificial plank."

I stared at him, horrified at all the new images those words created in my head. I couldn't stand the idea that the yetis had erected that for the sole purpose of putting Buttercup on it. "Please don't say any more."

He put his arm around me. "It's not going to come to that, I promise."

"No, of course it won't." I accepted his assurance with a smile, but my stomach was in knots.

He gave me a squeeze. "Now I better go check in with Tempus. You know how he can be."

"I do. Thanks, Uncle Kris."

He winked at me, then walked over to where my father and Tempus were talking to Sheriff Merrow, Birdie and the man I assumed was Nate Grimshaw. Or Brightly, considering the circumstances.

Birdie caught my eye and brought Nate over to meet me. He was a nice-looking man with hair so blue it read black, but there was a sadness in his eyes that made him seem a little lost.

I guessed I'd look like that too if I'd been handed the same information he had today.

I shook his hand and smiled at him, wishing I could bring his parents back and give him the childhood he'd missed out on. I couldn't, of course, but that didn't stop me from wanting to make it happen. "It's so good of you to help us like this. The city owes you its gratitude."

"Seeing as how it's kind of Aunt Myra's fault that—" He cut himself off and the lost look intensified. "I guess I should say my mother." He stared at the ground. "That's going to take some getting used to."

"I can imagine. Are you doing okay?"

"It's a lot to take in."

"It is. But being a winter elf is a wonderful thing. I promise."

He lifted his head. "You would know, wouldn't you? Since you're the princess and all." Naturally, that's how Birdie had introduced me to him. "Should I bow or something? I don't know anything about being a winter elf yet. I've always thought I was fae. I guess I have a lot to learn."

"No bowing," I said. "And you have lots of time to learn."

"Lots of time," Birdie repeated.

"Right now," I said, "we just need to figure out how to close that portal. Were you able to get everything from the safe-deposit box?"

Birdie nodded, but let Nate answer. "I've been reading through the notes my, uh, father left, and it seems pretty straightforward. A drop of my blood and the portal disappears."

I sighed with relief. "I'm so glad it's that easy.

Your father was a smart man." He was also kind of a ninny for using his blood in designing that faulty snow globe, and in giving it to Myra, but Nate didn't need to hear that.

"Thanks," Nate said.

"Looks like everyone's preparing to start." The witches had spread out along the inside of the perimeter, which allowed them to surround the fortress but keep a safe distance from it too. "Come on, let's make sure we know where we're supposed to be."

"Lead the way, Princess," Birdie said.

The three of us crunched through the snow to join the men. The small circle opened to make room for us.

Sheriff Merrow addressed Nate. "I'm going to take you to your mother's house now. Not only do we need you out of harm's way in case things go south here, but I thought you'd want some time there before we start carting these yetis in and you have to close the portal."

He nodded. "I would like that. It's been a few years since I've been back."

The sheriff looked at his aunt. "Birdie, why don't you come with us?"

It wasn't really a question. I thought she'd want to stay here where the action was, but she didn't fuss.

"I'd love to," she said.

285

Maybe being around Nate had kicked in her nurturing instincts. He certainly could use some taking care of.

Made me proud of her. "We'll be seeing you over there soon enough."

The sheriff grunted in reply, and the three of them headed for his patrol car.

"Are we sure a school bus is the best thing to transport the yetis to Myra's in this weather?" I asked the group. I had a vision of the bus skidding on all the snow and spilling yetis everywhere.

Titus nodded. "Positive. That bus weighs about 28,000 pounds, and that's without anyone on it. Plus, the treads on those tires are very deep. It'll be just fine on the snow."

He seemed pretty sure. I looked at the bus again. "Okay."

"And the bus can hold seventy-two kids, so we figure we can easily cram a hundred or so sleeping yetis in there."

"Still, it's a good thing we don't have far to go."

My uncle settled his hands on his waist. "Tempus and I will go with the firemen. If any of the yetis awake, we'll be able to get them back to sleep or turn them into ice cubes."

"That sounds really good. That's a solid plan." I liked that a lot. I didn't want to mention how incredibly cramped (and smelly) the bus would be with the addition of my uncle and the Sandman, but it was a short trip. I looked at Tempus. "What do you need from us while you're doing your thing?"

"Just quiet while I put them under. Restful thoughts couldn't hurt either."

"You got it." I went back to addressing the whole group. "So Tempus sends the yetis off to dreamland, then what? Who's getting Buttercup out? Who's taking charge of getting the yetis on the bus?"

Titus spoke again. "I've got my firemen ready and waiting to assist with the yetis."

My dad put his hand on my arm. "Jay, I think you and I should get Buttercup out. Then we'll have the paramedics give her the okay before she goes anywhere else. Juniper and Kip can take over from there. That will free you and me to go to Myra's with Uncle Kris and make sure everything goes smoothly with the portal. Sound good?"

"Sounds good." I smiled as I turned to Tempus. Out of the corner of my eye, I saw a flash of blue on the fortress. "I don't want to rush you, but the yetis are moving."

We turned as a group to see what was going on.

Buttercup was on the top of the fortress, and the yetis were gathering around her.

My blood chilled. "Tempus, whatever you're going to do, do it now."

His hand went to his hourglass, but that's all the movement he made. "Patience, Princess. All in good time. I must prepare for—"

"No," I snarled at him. "Your job is putting people to sleep. So do it. Now."

"These aren't people," he snapped back. "I have to prepare."

My uncle cleared his throat and looked over the rim of his glasses. "Tempus, put the yetis to sleep now, or I'm putting you on the naughty list."

Tempus swallowed.

I almost laughed. I knew the naughty list was a powerful thing, I just never thought it would work on the Sandman himself. I guessed no one wanted coal in their stocking.

Tempus faced the fortress and raised one hand. He began whispering in a soft, sing-songy voice. I couldn't make out the words, but it sounded very much like a lullaby.

One by one, the yetis gathering around Buttercup shifted their attention toward us. Toward Tempus, really.

But they didn't seem the least bit sleepy. Instead, they trotted over to the top of the ice wall and peered down. Curious, for sure, but bright-eyed all the same.

My gaze flicked from Tempus to the yetis to my dad. He shrugged. I glanced at my uncle. He was focused on Tempus in that way of his that said he was still undecided which list the Sandman would end up on.

I appreciated that.

Back at the ice fortress, the yetis had lost interest in the Sandman's tune. They were facing Buttercup again, their little hands in the air around her like they were getting ready to worship their queen. A low keening drifted out of them, and the ice started vibrating in frequency. That caused a new, high-pitched hum to fill the air.

I grimaced at the sound. It was like we were surrounded by wasps. The noise made my skin crawl and all the little hairs on the back of my neck prickled with magical energy.

The spikes of ice stretched higher, creaking as they grew. Buttercup walked toward the spikes.

I held my breath and clenched my hands into fists so hard my nails bit into my palms. Things were not going well.

Fortunately, Tempus understood that his lullaby wasn't working. He unhooked the hourglass from his belt and held it out. The glittering diamond sand inside it began to pulse with waves of light.

The waves washed over the snow in bands of pure, calming brilliance. They were impossible to look away from.

The itchy droning of the yetis stopped. They were all at the edge of the wall again, staring at the hourglass. But now the back of my head felt thick. I wasn't sure how long it had been since I'd blinked.

A new song slipped from Tempus's throat, still in words I couldn't understand. Was he speaking yeti? They were mesmerized by it. The crowd of them at the wall had tripled, and Buttercup seemed to be forgotten. And she'd stopped walking toward the spikes, which was a very good thing.

I made myself blink to clear the fog in my head, but that didn't give me much relief. I had the slow, sinking thought that Tempus was putting us all to sleep. I slogged through the snow with great effort, trying to reach him. Getting my feet to move was hard. So hard I wanted to sit down and nap a little.

No.

I pinched myself. The pain helped a little. I made it to Sanders and tugged on his robe. "You're making us all fall asleep."

He nodded, but didn't stop with the singing.

My lids were drooping, and when I blinked again, I was kneeling in the snow. I wanted to sleep so bad I wasn't sure why I was even fighting it. I couldn't see Buttercup on top of the fortress anymore. Maybe the yetis had moved her. That could be bad. They might have hidden her away inside that monstrosity of ice and snow.

Tempus's song grew softer. Or I was drifting. I wasn't sure. I didn't care.

I lay down in the snow and closed my eyes.

"Princess."

"Go 'way." The bed was trembling. I waved a hand, trying to shoo Spider. When had his voice gotten so low? And why was it so cold in my room?

"Princess."

I knew that voice and it wasn't Spider's. My eyes blinked open. This wasn't my bed or my room. I was sprawled in the snow at Balfour Park. And Tempus Sanders was shaking me awake.

"You need to get up. The yetis are asleep. We have to wake everyone else."

That did it. I was up instantly. I jumped to my feet, sending clumps of snow flying. All around me, people snoozed on the frozen earth. All but Sin, who was walking toward me.

"Why aren't you asleep?" I asked.

"I was, but the minute he stopped chanting, I

woke up." He looked at Sanders. "How long will the yetis be out?"

His hourglass was back on his belt. "I don't know."

"Then we need to move." Sin hooked his thumb over his shoulder. "I'll get the firemen up. The sooner we have those yetis on the bus, the better."

"Agreed. I'll work on the sheriff and my family." I looked over at Tempus. "You wake the witches."

He nodded and headed for the first sleeping spellcaster.

It didn't take long to get everyone up, because as we woke people, they started waking others. In minutes, the firemen had ladders up against the ice fortress and had begun handing the yetis down the line of volunteers and passing them right into the bus. It was like an old-fashioned bucket brigade. My uncle and Sin helped arrange the yetis on the bus.

While that was going on, my dad and I cautiously approached the castle from the opposite side of where they were working. We needed to get Buttercup out, but we certainly didn't want to cause the yetis to wake up.

We reached the wall. I stared up at it, towering over us like blue glass. "How do you want to do this?"

He put one hand on the wall. The ice glowed softly under his fingertips. "The easy way."

"Works for me." But I wasn't sure what that meant. Especially because nothing about this had been easy so far.

He took a step back, so I did too. Then he lifted his hand, pointed his finger and sent a spark of magic into the ice. He used it to sketch out a doorway, cutting through the ice like it was whipped cream.

When the door was finished, he directed his magic to ease the slab out of the way and float it to the ground.

He dropped his hand, and a blade of ice filled it, gleaming sharp and crystalline. He looked at me as if he hadn't just made something really hard look incredibly easy.

I was proud of him, and a little jealous, but I knew with time, my magic would mature to that level too. "That was great, Dad."

"Thanks. Let's go get Buttercup."

I formed a blade of my own. Shorter than his, but just as effective. "Let's get her."

"Follow me." He went through the doorway he'd made.

I was right behind him.

The temperature inside the ice castle was so shockingly low it made it hard to breathe. That helped with the stench, but the air crackled in my lungs and caused my chest to ache. How had Buttercup survived this? Or had the yetis only recently dropped the temperature in preparation for the sacrifice? Whatever the case, the frigid temps just drove me to want to get her out that much more.

I sent up a big wish that she was okay, and that whatever brainwashing the yetis had done to her was completely reversible.

A maze of halls and rooms and stairs made up the interior. We stopped just a few feet in at a set of stairs. Passageways led away on both sides, and they looked well used by the amount of scuffs and scratches on the floor. My father pointed to me, then toward the left, then at himself and to the right.

I nodded, understanding we were going to sweep the first floor.

He gave me a smile, put his finger to his lips, and disappeared down his side of the hall.

I went the other way, keeping my blade in front of me and my ears and eyes open. I searched room after room, amazed at how intricate the fortress was. Tumbleweeds of blue fur drifted by now and then. One room had stacks of mail in it. That would have to be redelivered. Another had strands of Christmas lights that would never be untangled. In a third, a large collection of welcome mats covered the floor. More blue fur was stuck to them, making me think the yetis had been sleeping on them.

But not a single one held Buttercup. I hoped my

dad had better luck. I completed my side and met up with him back at the stairs.

He was alone.

He pointed up.

I followed and we repeated the same sweep as we had on the first floor. I was in the middle of a room stuffed with quilts and blankets, digging through them in case Buttercup was somewhere underneath, when I heard my dad's voice quietly but firmly speak my name.

"Jayne."

I straightened, perking up my ears. "Here," I said softly.

"Leave," he said in the same resolute voice.

That single word made my chest ache more than the icy-cold air. I read a thousand different meanings into his tone. He was in trouble. The yetis had awoken and surrounded him. Or he'd found Buttercup and she was in trouble. Or worse.

Leaving was not an option either way. "No," I replied with the same even tone. "Coming to you."

"Downstairs," was his only reply.

I hustled for the stairs as quietly as I could. He didn't sound like that was where he was, but maybe he was ahead of me and headed in that direction. Sound reverberated through the fortress, making it impossible to tell where it was coming from.

I didn't see my dad until I hit the first floor and

came around the corner toward the door he'd carved.

He was about to step through it, but turned at the sound of my footfalls.

Buttercup was in his arms. So pale she was nearly as translucent as the ice fortress she'd been imprisoned in. Limp. Lifeless.

I sucked in a breath, my eyes heating with unshed tears.

He shook his head, then continued out the door. I ran after him, dropping my ice blade to grab her hand. I might have still been holding the blade for all the warmth in her.

"Is she..." I couldn't bring myself to say the word.

"I don't think so. But she's not well. She's very, very cold."

"Hypothermia."

He nodded.

"I'm going to prep the paramedics." I ran ahead to the ambulance, no longer caring about being quiet. "Get everything ready you possibly can to warm her up. She's in hypothermia."

"We're ready," the first paramedic said.

I skidded to a stop. "I hope so. Hypothermia in a winter elf is a lot harder to treat than in humans. Our bodies sometimes accept the drastically low temperature as the new normal and sink into a coma that can't be reversed." This was the winter elf equivalent of Cooper's mom having heatstroke. Just as deadly and just as serious.

The second paramedic nodded. "We've been prepped."

My dad arrived with Buttercup, and the paramedics threw open the ambulance doors. A push of heat washed over me. That gave me some assurance that they weren't kidding about being ready. They lifted her out of my dad's arms, put her on the gurney and started piling heated blankets on her.

Juniper and Kip came up to the vehicle as the paramedics were closing the doors. Juniper looked on the verge of tears. "How is she?"

"Not good, but I think she'll be all right." She had to be. She'd so willingly taken Birdie's place that she didn't deserve this end. "You guys will go with her to the hospital?"

Kip nodded. "We'll be there until she's ready to come home if need be."

"Thanks." I stared through the fogged-up windows on the back of the ambulance, wishing I could will her back to good health.

Sin jogged through the snow toward us. "The bus will be loaded in about two more minutes."

I nodded, still staring at those fogged-up windows and hoping that Buttercup wasn't slipping into a coma while we just stood here.

"Jay," my dad said. "We really need to go."

"I know." But I couldn't take my eyes off the vehicle.

"Go ahead, Jayne," Juni said. "Kip and I are going to make sure she's okay. We'll be right there the whole time. I promise."

"Thanks." I swallowed down the knot in my throat and managed to blink back the tears. I glanced at my dad and Sin. "I'm ready. Let's get these monsters out of town."

Thanks to Sin's driving, we got to Myra's house ahead of the school bus.

The sheriff met us on the front porch. "How did it go?"

"The bus is on its way," Sin said.

"Buttercup is in bad shape." I scrubbed a hand over my mouth, my eyes burning with the threat of tears. "She's headed to the hospital. Hopefully she'll survive."

The sheriff stepped away from the front door. "Miss Evergreen is a strong woman. I think she's going to be just fine."

"Thank you." I appreciated his words.

He nodded. "Birdie and Nate are in the kitchen. He's ready to go."

"Good." I went in, and Sin followed, leaving my dad and Sheriff Merrow to wait on the yetis.

Birdie and Nate were at the kitchen table,

having a cup of coffee. They both looked up, faces full of expectation.

Sin spoke first. "The yetis will be here shortly."

"How's Buttercup?" Birdie asked.

"Not great," I said. "On her way to the hospital."

Birdie got up. "Poor kid. I should go over there. Be with her."

That surprised me. "You don't want to stay and see how things go with the portal?"

She hoisted her purse over her shoulder. "Buttercup saved my life. And you'll tell me all about it." Then she came around the table and patted Nate on the shoulder. "Besides, Nate's got this."

He nodded, smiling a little. "I'll handle it."

"How are you going to get there?"

"I could drive her," Sin said.

Birdie waved his offer away. "You're needed here. No, I'm just going to walk back to my house. It's not far and my car's still there. And don't worry, I'll be careful." She gave me a quick hug. "I owe Buttercup."

"I'm glad you're going. Kip and Juniper are there too."

"I'll report in if there's anything to report. You do the same."

"I will." I hoped that report was nothing but good news. On both sides.

The front door opened, and my father and the sheriff came in. "The bus is here."

"You kids have fun," Birdie said. "I'm off to see Buttercup."

She left in such a hurry that I wondered if part of her reasoning for leaving was so she didn't have to come face-to-face with the yetis again. I didn't blame her. She'd had enough of them, that was certain.

"Nate," I said. "Let's go check out that portal."

"All right." He got up from the table and headed to the basement.

I went right behind him, and Sin followed. I wanted to reassure Nate about the situation. "Don't be scared of the yetis. Even if they wake up, my father and I will protect you."

He hit the landing and turned to look at me. "Birdie told me all about them. It's okay. I'm not scared. I mean, I am, but I'm not going to freak out."

"Good." I could see some of that fear in his gaze. I was okay with that. It was healthy. "And I promise that when this is over and you're ready to explore what it means to be a winter elf, I'll help."

He smiled and it reached his eyes. "Thank you. I'd like that."

The basement door swung open, and my father jogged down the steps to join us. "We're going to do this just like we did at the park. We're going to create a brigade of people, pass the yetis through, and pop them back through that portal."

"What about on the other side?" Sin asked.

He shook his head. "We were never able to find it."

I looked at Nate. "The polar forests are vast. That's where the yetis live and where we think the portal opened up."

I went back to my dad. "When are we starting?"

Titus appeared at the top of the steps, my uncle right behind him. Both of them were carrying yetis. The stench hit us a couple seconds later.

"Never mind," I said as they came down the stairs. A couple more firemen appeared behind them, forming the rest of the human chain.

Nate's nose wrinkled. "Why do they smell so bad?"

I shrugged. "It's their natural musk. I guess it's some kind of self-defense thing."

"That's exactly right," Uncle Kris said. He reached the portal and stood there, his hands filled with blue fur. "Should I just put him through?"

"Have at it," my dad said.

Uncle Kris held the yeti over the portal and dropped it.

The yeti hit the ice, bounced back, and awoke in a snarl of teeth and claws.

"Sweet and sour sugar plums!" My uncle

scrambled to catch him, but the yeti climbed the shelves in a blue blur.

My dad and uncle stretched their hands out at the same time, successfully using their magic to turn the rotten beast into an ice cube. He still managed to wriggle around a bit, but he was pretty effectively contained.

"How did that happen?" my dad asked the room. "The portal's been open this whole time."

I went to my knees beside it. "But we haven't tried sending anything back. We must not be doing something right."

"We don't have much time to figure this out," Titus said. He was holding his yeti at arm's length.

I would have done the same thing.

Nate looked horrified. "There was nothing in my father's directions about this. Not that I remember."

"Don't worry, we'll figure it out." I started to stick my hand through like I'd done before with Sin, then looked over my shoulder at him. "Hang on to me. Just in case."

"You got it." He knew what I was doing. He kneeled next to me and held on to my waist.

I took off my rainbow obsidian bracelet, tucked it in my pocket, then cautiously dipped my hand toward the ice. My fingers touched the cold, slick surface and a second later, my hand went through. "It's definitely open now. Try the yeti again."

My uncle picked up the frozen yeti and eased him into the portal.

He went through like a charm.

"That's it," I said. "We just have to keep the portal open."

My father frowned at the sight of me up to my wrist in the portal, but there was no other way to keep it open. "I'll take over."

"I'm already handling it. Just get those yetis off the bus and back to the NP." The cold was seeping into me, but how long could it take to get the yetis through?

Eighty-seven yeti and twenty-some minutes later and we were still going. I could no longer feel my arm from the elbow down.

"You're not okay, are you?" Sin whispered.

I made myself smile. "I'm fine."

"You look cold," Nate said.

"I'm fine," I gritted out through clenched teeth, still smiling. I needed to relax, but that was no small feat with my blood temperature dropping into arctic numbers. "I can handle cold." I flexed my fingers, hoping I wasn't causing any kind of shift in the space-time continuum by holding this portal open for so long.

Titus sent a message along the brigade line. "How many more yeti are there?"

The answer came back five yetis later. "Fifty-three, Chief."

One hundred and forty-five yetis. That was if the cold hadn't affected my ability to do math. I arched my back, stretching out the tension as best I could without removing my arm from the portal, and trying to give myself a little pep talk. I could do this. Cold was my jam.

But this cold was epic, and there was no pep talk in the world that was going to erase the fact that I was hurting.

Sin leaned in and kissed my temple. He whispered, "Babe, let your father take over."

I opened my mouth to answer that maybe it *was* time to switch out, when the fireman at the top of the stairs announced, "The yetis are waking up."

"Tell Sanders to put them back to sleep," my uncle shouted back.

The fireman shook his head as he passed a squirming yeti to the next person in line. "He says he can't without knocking all of us out again."

"Then everyone needs to move faster," my uncle answered.

There was no time to make a swap. I made quick eye contact with Sinclair. "I'm okay."

He sat back, frowning. "I'm worried about you." I could tell he didn't believe that I was okay at all. Why did he have to be so good at reading me?

"Jayne." My father's voice carried in the small space like a sonic boom. "Are you all right?"

"Yes." That was the shortest, easiest lie I could

manage. "Just hurry up." I did my best to look light-hearted. "I don't want to get bitten."

As if on cue, the yeti going through the portal snapped at me, missing my cheek by a few inches.

"Son of a nutcracker." I jerked back, somehow managing to keep my arm in place.

Nate went to his knees on the other side of the portal. The fear had returned to his gaze, but it was now mixed with determination. I gave him props for that.

Suddenly, he stuck his hand in. "Tell me what to do."

I hadn't expected him to do that, but I didn't have the energy to coach him through being a winter elf right now. I looked around the yeti going through. "This isn't the time."

"Let him," Sin urged.

I wanted to. I really did. Maybe it wouldn't hurt. He was a winter elf, after all. Sure, one with no idea how to work whatever magic was in his blood, but a winter elf all the same. And he was Eustace Brightly's son, so he had to have power within him. Maybe he also had some innate sense of how to use that power.

Pain from the cold reached into my shoulder and back now, making my teeth rattle with the unrelenting sting. My fingers might be black with frostbite for all I knew. That thought filled me with weakness and my resolve disappeared.

I sat back, tugging the dead weight of my frozen arm out of the portal.

"See?" Sin said.

Nate let out a terrified yelp, and we turned to look.

The portal had frozen over, trapping Nate's arm in it.

I jammed my other hand through, breaking the portal open again. "Get out," I hissed at Nate. "Get your hand out."

He jerked back, nodding and rubbing his arm. Then he crawled backward until he hit the shelves behind him. "Something bit me."

Blood dripped from his hand.

A new terror went through me. "Did you get blood on the portal? It'll close."

With my arm still in it. My heart was thumping in my chest, panicky at the thought that I might lose my hand. "Answer me."

"I don't know."

Ice formed around the edges of the portal. I glanced at my frozen hand for the first time since I'd gotten it out. My skin was gray from my fingertips to below my wrist. I tried to move my fingers.

Nothing.

I looked at Sin. "How many more yetis?"

"Thirteen."

"Hurry up," I shouted.

Two more went through.

The ice at the edges expanded. Time wasn't running out, it was gone.

I took a breath. "The portal is closing."

My father and my uncle turned to look at me. Realizing what was happening, my father leaped over the railing and shoved the yeti in his hands into the portal. He had to push to get it through what was left of the opening.

"Sinclair. Now." The command in his voice was clear.

Sin hauled me back, freeing me from the portal as it seized up. The hard surface shimmered with magic, then the ice disappeared, replaced by a puddle and some broken shards of glass. The broken snow globe was just that now, nothing more.

"It's done," Nate whispered.

"But there are still yetis left," I said. "Ten of them. That's more than enough to destroy the town."

"Nine," one of the firemen said. "We miscounted."

"Nine. Still nine too many." I slumped against Sin. I hurt so much I wasn't sure I'd be conscious much longer.

"Get her to the hospital." My father was talking to Sin like I wasn't even part of the conversation.

"Dad," I said. "The *yetis*."

"Your uncle and I will deal with them." His gaze went back to Sin. "The hospital."

Sin scooped me into his arms and ran up the stairs. The brigade flattened themselves against the wall to make room. I watched over Sin's shoulder as my father and uncle froze the rest of the yetis. They weren't going easily. One nipped my father, shredding his shirt and leaving behind three bloody scratches.

"Be careful," I called out, but no one was paying any attention to me anymore.

Sin didn't stop. He dodged the rest of the brigade with their arms full of snarling blue beasts and kept heading for the door. Tempus glanced at us for a second, but the yeti he was holding had the sleeve of his fancy daytime pajamas firmly between its teeth.

"Good luck," I told him, but he was too busy pulling the thing off him to answer.

Myra's house was in total chaos. I felt a little guilty for leaving, but what choice did I have?

"I can walk," I said as we left the house behind.

"No need," Sin answered. He stomped down the sidewalk and put me onto the first seat in the bus, then jumped behind the wheel. "I'm going to drive."

He did too. Probably faster and more recklessly than any school bus had ever been driven. If there had been kids on it, he would have headed for jail time.

As it was, I wasn't sure I was going to survive the ride. "Hey, slow down, this isn't exactly a luxury vehicle. These bumps are shaking my teeth loose."

He looked at me through the big rearview mirror. "Sorry. Just worried."

"I'm going to be fine." I looked at my hand. The skin didn't seem quite so gray now and I could twitch my fingers a bit. Plus, it hurt like someone was smashing it with a hammer over and over again, so the fact that I had feeling in it had to be a good sign.

Or maybe that's what a frostbitten, dying hand felt like. In that case, it wasn't so good.

Either way, I needed Sin to stop driving like my life depended on how fast I arrived at the hospital, because it didn't.

I smiled at him when he let off the gas a bit, despite the incredible pain. "Thank you."

He frowned. "You're not losing your hand because of me."

"I'm not losing it because of anyone. I can handle the cold."

"Have you ever been so cold you turned gray before?"

No. "I can't remember. Maybe as a kid." That wasn't exactly a lie, but I didn't want him freaking out. Or laying the speed on again. I reclined in the seat, resting my feet on the upholstery and my frozen arm across my stomach. "I'm beat."

"I'm sure you are."

I was. It felt like the enormity of what had just happened had suddenly hit me. All I wanted to do was close my eyes and sleep the pain away.

I couldn't, though. The pain was too intense. I did my best to rest until we arrived at the hospital, which thankfully wasn't too much longer.

The school bus wouldn't fit through the emergency portico where the ambulances dropped patients off, so Sin parked as close as he could and we went in.

I insisted on walking. It gave me something else to think about besides the throbbing.

Turns out, the sheriff had called ahead. Hospital staff were waiting for us. I was put in a wheelchair and whisked away for tests and meds and all sorts of fun stuff.

An hour later, I was in a bed, having been admitted, and doped up to the point that I wasn't sure if I still had an arm or not. And I didn't care.

Sin came in as the nurse was leaving. He had a big bouquet of roses, and Birdie.

I grinned. "Hiya."

"How are you, Princess?" Birdie rushed to the

side of the bed. "Sin filled me in. Has the doctor talked to you yet?"

Sin put the flowers on the window sill and came around to the other side of the bed. He looked like he wanted to take my hand, but didn't.

I smiled at him too. I was happy they were here. I was happy I was here. I was just happy. The drugs were pretty good. What had Birdie said about the doctor? Had he talked to me? I thought he had. What had he said? I thought hard. Which *was* hard. "I have hands," I announced, lifting them up.

I was a mummy from the elbows down. "Hey, what's all this?"

"Those bandages have to stay on," Birdie said. "At least for a little while." Then she snorted and looked at Sin. "I don't think we're going to have much of a conversation until she's got a little less happy juice in her system."

"Happy juice." I laughed. "I like that."

"Obviously," Sin said. "I like that you're going to be fine." His smile faltered. "I was so worried about you."

I felt bad for making him worry, but I loved the way he was looking at me. All lovey and sweet. "I'm indestructible."

Birdie rolled her eyes but Sin chuckled. "I don't know about all that."

"Sure, I am. Just like my dad."

"Speaking of your dad, you'll be happy to know that your father and your uncle got the rest of the yetis frozen, then Tempus managed a new sleep song that relaxed just the yetis and they were able to load them onto the sleigh. According to the sheriff's text, they took off for the North Pole about ten minutes ago."

Sadness replaced the happy I'd just been feeling. "They left without saying goodbye? But-but I'm in the hospital!"

"No, babe, sorry, just your uncle and Tempus left. Your father is on his way here. To the hospital."

"Oh. Okay. That's nice." Sleep had begun to creep in around the edges of my consciousness. "Are they going to execute my hands?"

"Execute?" Birdie's brows shot up. "You mean amputate? For lands sakes, no. I guess you don't remember what the doctor told you. You'll need some therapy on your right hand, but you're going to be fine. Just rest, recovery, and therapy."

My lids were heavy. They started to close. "That sounds good. How's…Butter…"

Sweet, soft darkness wrapped around me, and I drifted away on the raft of meds that was carrying me into sleep.

"She's fine. You rest now, Princess," was the last thing I heard before the lights went completely out.

The next morning, I was a new person. Still in pain, but much better. That was the good old supernatural healing at work. I told the nurses no more meds. I was a winter elf. I could handle a little ache. Plus, my memories of the day before went hazy not long after I'd gotten to the hospital. I chalked that up to the stuff they'd given me. With everything going on, I really needed to remember things.

My dad was my first visitor of the day. He brought me a peppermint milk shake, which was a huge improvement over the hospital breakfast I'd had. The food had been fine, but I was craving sweets.

I sipped on it while he talked.

"The doctors want to keep you for another day. Don't give them any grief about it, all right?"

I did my best to look shocked. "I wouldn't do that."

"You already told the nurses not to give you any more pain meds."

"Because my hands don't hurt much anymore." Well, my right one did, but I could deal.

He gave me a look. "Just do as the doctors ask."

"I will." Was that a promise? It didn't feel like a promise. I changed the subject. "How's Buttercup?"

"She's being released today. She probably still needs a day of rest at home, but she's going to be fine."

"I'm so glad to hear that. What about her head, though? The yetis seemed to have her under their spell pretty hard."

"Their magic disappeared when they went back through the portal. She's completely herself again."

I let go of the breath I'd been holding. "That is such a relief. We owe her."

"We do. I'll come up with an appropriate thank-you after I get back."

My dad was really good at thank-you's. I wondered what he'd cook up. I glanced toward the window. Everything was still white outside. "Speaking of you getting back...I'm kind of surprised to see you. Don't you and Uncle Kris have some yetis to deal with?"

"Your uncle already left with Tempus. He'll drop the yetis off in the nearest forest."

"Then how are you getting back?"

"I'm flying out tomorrow. First class, naturally." He grinned.

I rolled my eyes. "Naturally."

Then a little spark lit his eyes. "And you'll be happy to know I'm taking Nate with me."

"You are? That's awesome." I was thrilled that my father had relented.

"He proved his good character. He deserves a chance to see the North Pole, to learn about his heritage. He is Eustace's son. Nate should get to know what an amazing man his father was. Not to mention we could use his help closing the four portals we opened during our experiments."

I was so proud of my dad. "You're a pretty amazing man."

My dad smiled. "Thanks, honey." He leaned in and kissed my cheek, then pressed his forehead to my temple for a long moment. "I'm so glad you're okay."

"Thanks, Daddy. I wish you weren't going back tomorrow, but I understand."

He straightened, brushing his hand down my cheek. His gaze held a wistful look. "I wish I could stay longer too. Maybe you could come up for a visit again soon."

"I'd like that."

He sat on the edge of the bed. "You can bring Sinclair if you'd like."

"Funny you should mention that, but I just said something to him about visiting the North Pole. I'd love for him to see it."

My dad nodded. "He's a good man, Jay. He loves you very much."

I stared at the blanket covering me. "He's never said that. We haven't used that word yet."

"Whether it's been said or not, I can see it in his actions. He cares about you *very* much."

I lifted my gaze. "Why did that sound like a reprimand?"

"It wasn't. Just that...you seem to be a little...*fickle* when it comes to men."

"Dad! I'm not fickle. I was dumped. Sort of. Look, Cooper went home to help his mom recover from heatstroke and Greyson ditched me because I was dating Sinclair and he didn't like the idea of sharing me with a necromancer. It's just how things worked out."

My father tipped his head to one side. "So what are your intentions toward Sinclair?"

"Shouldn't you be asking him what his intentions are with me?"

"How do you know I haven't?"

Good point. "I like him. A lot."

"Do you love him?"

I sighed because the word pushed a wave of emotion through me. A longing that I'd never felt before. "More than is probably healthy. But I don't want to scare him away. I'm a lot to handle. I come with a lot of royal baggage. Not everyone understands what that means until they've been around my family."

"He's been around us."

"A little. And royalty looks fun until you dig into the nitty-gritty of it and figure out how much work it actually is. And how much responsibility."

"Is that why you want to bring him to the North Pole?"

I nodded. "He needs to see what my future holds. And he deserves a chance to back out if it's overwhelming." Although the thought of that made me sadder than anything else had in a very long time.

"He won't," my father said softly.

"How do you—"

The door to my room opened and Sinclair stuck his head in. "Am I interrupting?"

"No," my dad said. "Come in." He got off the bed. "I was just leaving."

Sin came over to the bed. "Don't go on my account."

"I'm not." My dad looked at his watch. "I have a meeting with Hugh and Sebastian Ellingham in half an hour." He patted my leg through the blanket. "I'll be back to see you this afternoon, sweetheart."

"Okay, Dad."

He gave Sin a nod and left, closing the door behind him.

Sin smiled. "How are you feeling today?"

"Really, really good." I held up my hands. "Ready to get these bandages off and go home."

"I'm sure you are. Spider's doing well, by the way. Did the doctor say when you can get rid of them?"

"Tomorrow, I think. I hope so. I want to put my bracelet back on. Which had better still be in my coat pocket."

"I'm sure it is, but I can check for you." As he went to the closet, his brows bent. "You seem a lot more like yourself today."

"No more pain meds. They were making me loopy."

His sweet laugh filled the room. "That's for sure." He held up the bracelet. "It's here. You want me to leave it in the pocket?"

"It should be safe there."

His expression turned serious on his walk back to the bed. "I wish I could hold your hand."

"You can. Just be gentle." As if he was anything else with me.

He took my hand in his like he was cradling a small bird. "I am so thankful you're going to be okay. You and Buttercup and Birdie. But especially you."

"Thanks." I couldn't help but see the new streak

320

of silver in his hair. The one he'd earned so that I could speak to Myra. How many minutes of his life had that cost him?

He looked into my eyes, and suddenly I wondered if something was wrong. He seemed…uncertain. A little chill went through me. My dad thought Sin loved me, but maybe this whole thing with the yetis had been too much.

Maybe he was breaking up with me.

His gaze shifted away from mine. "I need to tell you something."

I braced myself. Those words combined with him being unable to look at me could only mean one thing. I was getting dumped. Again.

Son of a nutcracker. "No," I blurted out.

He looked up. "What?"

"No. I don't want to hear it. Not while I'm in the hospital. It's not fair. I can't deal with this right now. I don't want to be all weepy and sad and miserable and stuck in the hospital."

"What are you talking about?"

I pulled my hand out of his, which wasn't hard to do since he was barely holding it. "I'm talking about I am not letting you dump me while I'm still trying to recover from frostbite. It's not nice and it's not fair."

He stared at me, openmouthed, but nothing came out. Apparently, I'd shocked him into silence.

Good. Because I was not having it. I sat back,

gingerly crossed my arms and looked out the window while I tried not to cry.

The single hot tear rolling down my cheek was outstanding proof that my efforts were useless, but still. I was putting in the work.

Loud, raucous laughter erupted out of him.

I whipped my head around to glare at him. "I'm glad you think this is funny."

"Oh, babe, honey, no. I'm laughing because of how completely wrong you are. I'm not breaking up with you."

"You're not?"

"No. Not even close." He took my hand in his again. "I love you."

I sniffed and broke into a big, shy smile. "I love you too."

"Good." He stuck his free hand in his pocket and pulled out a small velvet box. "Because I got you something."

"Oh?" I tried not to hyperventilate over the fact that the box looked the perfect size to hold a ring.

One-handed, he opened the box and revealed the most beautiful diamond solitaire ring set with royal blue sapphires on the sides.

I sucked in a breath. "That's gorgeous. But it kind of looks like an engagement ring."

His dark eyes held more emotions than I could name. "That's because it is."

Sugar plums. "Are you—" But I knew the

answer. He was. My heart thumped in my chest like it might break free.

Still holding my hand and the ring box, he got down on one knee. "Will you marry me, Jayne Frost?"

I wanted to say yes. I wanted to yell it so loud the nurses came running. But Sin needed to see the other half of my life. He needed to understand that at some point, I would be moving back to the North Pole to take my rightful place on the Winter Throne. He needed a chance to back out, no matter how much I hoped he wouldn't take it.

"It's the most beautiful ring I've ever seen." I smiled, hoping that would make the rest of what I had to say a little easier to take. "I just can't answer you yet."

He got to his feet. "If you need some time, I understand. I know we've only been involved since right before Halloween, so maybe this feels sudden to you, but I know how I feel. Those feelings aren't going to change. But if you want some time, I'm good with that."

I shook my head slowly. "It's not that. It's…my life in the North Pole. My responsibilities there. I need you to see all that and really understand it and to be okay with it."

"I'm sure I would—"

"No, Sin. It's not something you can guess at. You need to experience it for yourself."

He nodded. "So we need to go to the North Pole. As soon as possible."

"As soon as possible. I promise." I might even ask Uncle Kris to come get us on the sleigh, because I finally had a resolution for the New Year.

Get that ring on my finger as fast as I could.

Want to be up to date on new books, audiobooks & other fun stuff from Kristen Painter? Sign-up for my newsletter on my website, www.kristenpainter.com. No spam, just news (sales, freebies, releases, you know, all that jazz).

If you loved the book and want to help the series grow, tell a friend about the book and take time to leave a review!

Other Books by Kristen Painter

COZY MYSTERY

Jayne Frost series
Miss Frost Solves a Cold Case: A Nocturne Falls Mystery
Miss Frost Ices the Imp: A Nocturne Falls Mystery
Miss Frost Saves the Sandman: A Nocturne Falls Mystery
Miss Frost Cracks a Caper: A Nocturne Falls Mystery
When Birdie Babysat Spider: A Jayne Frost Short
Miss Frost Braves the Blizzard: A Nocturne Falls Mystery

Happily Everlasting series
Witchful Thinking

PARANORMAL ROMANCE

Nocturne Falls series
The Vampire's Mail Order Bride
The Werewolf Meets His Match
The Gargoyle Gets His Girl
The Professor Woos The Witch
The Witch's Halloween Hero – short story
The Werewolf's Christmas Wish – short story
The Vampire's Fake Fiancée
The Vampire's Valentine Surprise – short story
The Shifter Romances the Writer
The Vampire's True Love Trials – short story
The Vampire's Accidental Wife

Nothing is completed without an amazing team.

Many thanks to:

Cover design: Keri Knudson
Interior formatting: Author E.M.S.
Editor: Joyce Lamb
Copyedits/proofs: Marlene Engel

About the Author

USA Today Best Selling Author **Kristen Painter** is a little obsessed with cats, books, chocolate, and shoes. It's a healthy mix. She loves to entertain her readers with interesting twists and unforgettable characters. She currently writes the best-selling paranormal romance series, Nocturne Falls, and the spin off mystery series, Jayne Frost. The former college English teacher can often be found all over social media where she loves to interact with readers.

www.kristenpainter.com